JEKYLL/HYDE

Also by Amy Ross

Writing as M. Verano

Diary of a Haunting
Diary of a Haunting: Possession
Diary of a Haunting: Book of Shadows

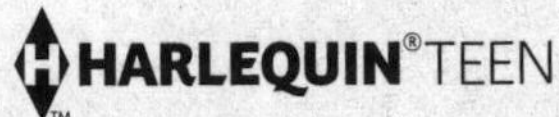

AMY ROSS

JEKYL / HYDE

Recycling programs
for this product may
not exist in your area.

ISBN-13: 978-1-335-00795-7

Jek/Hyde

This edition published by arrangement with Harlequin Books S.A.

For questions and comments about the quality of this book, please contact us at CustomerService@Harlequin.com.

Printed in U.S.A.

For Edna Medora

"If I could rightly be said to be either,
it was only because I was radically both."
—Robert Louis Stevenson,
The Strange Case of Dr. Jekyll and Mr. Hyde

CHAPTER

1

Now I remember why I hate costume parties.

I'm pushing my way through the mob stuffed into Jared Kilpatrick's living room, getting shoved an inch backward for every two inches of progress. The bodies surrounding me are wearing far less than usual, and I'm disgustingly aware of their alcoholic sweat pressing up against my own damp skin through nothing more than a layer of black mesh or bondage tape. The air is rank with an aromatic cocktail of adolescent hormones and cheap drugstore body spray, all heightened by the buzzing excitement of Friday night, Kilpatrick's legendary Halloween party and the promise of a whole weekend to sleep off its excesses.

I have a plastic cup of beer over my head, and I'm trying to keep it steady, but three boys dressed absurdly as some kind of steampunk submarine are crossing in front of me, forcing their way toward the kitchen while a peg-legged pirate tries to manhandle me from behind. One corner of the papier-mâché sub knocks my wrist and sends a foaming splash down on me, the pirate and his stuffed parrot. I curse under my breath, but my annoyance gives me an extra boost to shove my way forward and finally break through to the sliding doors opening onto the back porch.

The shock of cold autumn air raises goose bumps on my skin, thanks to my beer-damp clothes. This polyester lab coat wasn't exactly designed for Midwestern fall weather—especially with nothing underneath but leggings and a black bra. Maybe Sexy Mad Scientist wasn't the greatest idea for a costume, but at least I could throw it together with stuff I had lying around the house—protective goggles, latex gloves, a lab coat borrowed from a neighbor, plus about three cans of hair spray to make me look like I've been electrocuted.

I relax against the railing and watch the crowd through the glass doors. There's something about a party where you know everyone but they all look *different*. Someone will speak to you in a familiar voice and you turn to find yourself face-to-face with Cleopatra or an evil clown or a giant cereal box. It's disorienting and leaves me slightly seasick. Everyone is disguised, and everyone wants to be noticed. Not that I'm any different.

I turn away from them and lean out over the backyard as I pull my phone from my pocket. It's too late in the year for fireflies, but the lawn is dotted with glowing tips of cigarettes and joints clustered in twos and threes, and the effect is not so different. The manicured backyard extends into low bushes and then the gently sloping fields beyond. The nearest neighbors on this cul-de-sac aren't visible from this angle, but off to the left there's a twinkling of lights from town, the view partially blocked by the twinned hulking forms of Donnelly and Lonsanto corporate headquarters. On sunny days, their curved, mirrored surfaces catch the sunlight and reflect the clouds and green and gold corn fields, but tonight, picking up the orange glow from the town's streetlights, they look almost eerie.

"Lulu! You cannot abandon me like that."

My cousin Camila's voice nearly startles my phone out of my hand. She's the only reason I even came tonight—these red-cup ragers are really not my scene. When I first started at London High, I used to hit the local scene with Camila pretty regularly. For a while it was fun and exciting to drink our way through the town's liquor cabinets and hook up with different boys every weekend, but I lost interest in that stuff pretty quickly. People wonder these days what Camila and I see in each other, and if we weren't family, I'm not sure we'd see much. We don't move in the same circles or listen to the same music, and while she's practically famous in the party circuit around here, I prefer nights curled up in my pj's, marathoning old TV shows. But she'll be graduating this spring and starting work, and she acts like this means we'll never see each other again. I know she's just being dramatic, but I let her talk me into coming out again with her anyway, "for old time's sake."

Tonight she's dressed as a jockey, which is probably an excuse to wear tight pants and carry a riding crop.

"Sorry," I say. "Thought you were right behind me."

"I was, but I got distracted by the guy in the horse mask." She fondles her riding crop appreciatively. "Apparently he's been *very bad*."

Camila lifts her chin in my direction, as if daring me to make a comment about her shamelessness, but I just shrug. She's picked up this kind of talk from the rich kids who throw these keggers—they think it makes them sound sophisticated—but she'll have to try harder if she wants to shock me. I may spend more time at home with my books than hooking up with boys, but that doesn't mean I'm a prude.

"Sounds promising," I tell her instead.

"*I* thought so, but he wouldn't take off the mask and I got weirded out. What if he's ugly?"

"He's wearing a horse mask," I say, glancing back down at my phone. "Got to be hiding something."

Camila snaps the phone out of my hand.

"You're at a kegger with the entire junior and senior classes," she says over my objection. "Not to mention your favorite cousin. Who could you possibly be texting?" She scrolls through my messages. "I knew it." She holds up the phone triumphantly. "Can't take even one night off from the *boyfriend*."

"Jek's not my boyfriend," I mumble as she hands me the

phone back. “He said he might come tonight. No way I’d find him in this mob scene, so I was just—”

“Jek, at a costume party?” Camila giggles. “Now that’d be something. What would he dress up as? A chemical equation?”

I decide not to mention that Jek went as a water molecule to his eighth birthday party.

“I told him he didn’t have to wear a costume.”

Camila swats me lightly with her crop. “Of course you did, spoilsport. All you cared about was him seeing you in yours.” She eyes the plunging neckline of my lab coat meaningfully.

My phone buzzes.

Camila raises her eyebrows. “Well? Is he here?”

I check the message.

“No need to answer,” she says. “The disappointment is written all over your face.”

“He’s watching a movie.” I slide my phone into my pocket. “Might stop by later.”

“That translates to ripping bong-loads, right? Something tells me he won’t be peeling himself off his couch anytime soon. Remind me, why are you so into this loser?”

“Stop it. You could not be more wrong about him.”

“Oh, I see,” she says sarcastically. “So he’s *not* a huge pot-head?”

The truth is, Jek has all but given up weed. But since he’s mostly replaced it with even stronger substances, I’m not eager to argue the point.

“He’s not *just* a pothead, all right? He’s also a genius. I’ve seen both of you high, and I only remember one of you poring over an advanced neurochemistry text."

"Fine, fine. I get it. But you've been hung up on Jek ever since you were kids, and he still looks at you like you're his sister. I think it's time."

"Time for what?"

"Time to make a move, Lulu. Make a move or move on."

"What do you think I was doing, inviting him here tonight?"

Camila snorts. "He may be a genius, but he needs some things spelled out a little more clearly. Why are you wasting time at this party when you could be over at his house, stripping off that lab coat and unzipping his pants? Even Jek couldn't miss that signal. *Probably.*"

"Camila! Geez." I wrap my lab coat more tightly around me. "It's not like that, okay? We're best friends, we always have been, and...and if that's all he wants, that's fine. I'm not going to force myself on him."

"You wouldn't be forcing him. There isn't a boy in the world who would turn down that offer. Unless..."

"What?"

"I don't know...maybe he's gay."

"He's not gay," I say, maybe a little too sharply. Camila gives me a look and I let out a sigh. "Or, I don't know. I guess he could be."

"You of all people should know. Doesn't he tell you everything?"

I shake my head. "We don't talk about stuff like that."

"So that's it, then," she muses, leaning back against the railing. "That explains a lot, really. But in that case, Lulu, you should *really* give it up and focus on the fine-looking boys in front of you." She gestures at the throng inside the party.

"But how can you be so sure? He's never shown any interest in me, but he's never shown interest in anyone else, either. Of any gender. I think his brain just doesn't work like that."

Camila gives me a sidelong glance. "It's not the brain I'm talking about."

"Shut up. What I mean is, yeah, I've known him for ages and yeah I kind of like him, but all he cares about is science."

"Science and getting high."

I ignore her. "He's not like the other boys in this town. Doesn't have his mind in the gutter all the time. He's got other interests." Camila wraps her arms around herself, looking dubious, but I don't let that stop me. "Chemistry is his one true love," I explain, "and nothing else will ever compare for him. You want to know why I'm interested in him, well...that's why. I love his passion."

"Lulu, honey," says Camila with something like pity. "Wouldn't you rather have a boy who's passionate about *you*?"

I shrug and she shakes her head.

"You're hopeless, you know that?" She hoists herself up on the porch rail.

I don't give her an answer, but the fact is, I do know it. My feelings for Jek are just as hopeless as Camila says. I've done everything I can think of to get him to notice me, and Jek's not an idiot. He's got to know how I feel, and if he hasn't shown any interest yet, he isn't going to. The only rational response is to move on.

But I'm not quite ready to be rational yet. Maybe he needs a little more time. Maybe he just needs some encouragement. Maybe if I'm patient, he'll wake up one day and realize I'm the one he's wanted all along.

I squeeze my eyes shut, disgusted with my own thoughts. If I said any of that out loud, Camila would be the first to tell me how I've had my mind addled by too many rom-coms and fairy tales. I don't need the lecture, so I keep my thoughts to myself.

Lucky for me, Camila has stopped watching my face and moved on to more exciting spectator activities, like narrating all the town gossip while a dozen little soap operas play out through the window, as if it's our own personal flat-screen TV.

"Hmm, looks like Val and Erik are still together. Guess she never told him what she did to his car. And Brandon is *way* too drunk again. Third time this week, from what I heard."

"Quit it, Camila," I grumble.

"Come on… Don't you want to know what's going on in this sad little town?"

"I don't like gossip. People are entitled to their secrets."

"Oooh," she says, ignoring me. "Natalie Martinez, returning to the scene of the crime."

"Camila, I said—"

"Shh, I know, but this is different. It's not about what she did, it's what got done to her. If some sleazebag attacked her, don't you think it's my duty to let everyone know? For the safety of future potential victims, I mean."

I cast her a doubtful look. Camila's been known to exaggerate. "*Did* some sleazebag attack her?"

She shrugs. "Hard to say, really. It was last Saturday night, at Matt Klein's kegger. I got there late because I was…" She trails off. "Well, never mind what I was doing. The point is, when I got there, she was slipping into one of the bedrooms with this half-Asian guy. Floyd or something. Lloyd? *Hyde*. I'd never seen him before."

"That's your story? People do that all the time, Camila. *You* do that all the time."

"I'm not judging, and I'm not done! As far as anyone can tell, she went in perfectly happy and willing, but she came out twenty minutes later looking like she'd seen the devil himself. She started yelling at this guy in front of everyone, calling him a freak, saying she'd never agreed to *that*."

"To what?"

"Oh, so *now* you want to know," Camila teases.

I turn away from her, annoyed that she caught me in her trap. "So don't tell me," I huff. "You're the one who brought it up."

"Yeah, well…whatever it was, it was apparently too kinky

for Natalie to say out loud. She did say she was going to call the cops on him, though."

"Shit," I say, interested again in spite of myself. "What happened?"

"Somehow it all died out. Natalie left the kegger in tears with a friend, and I expected to hear sirens within minutes, but no one ever came. As far as the gossip mill is concerned, she never told anyone what happened. No one official, at least. But then again, Natalie's gotten around a lot since her dad got sick last year. Maybe she's afraid no one would believe her story."

"What about the guy? Hyde?"

"Beats me. At that point, no one wanted to admit to knowing him, let alone inviting him. I don't blame them… There's something funny about that guy. Something *off*."

"What do you mean?" I say, no longer bothering to hide my interest. Camila's too deep into her story to give me a hard time about it.

"I don't know…" she says, staring off at nothing as if she's replaying the scene in her mind. "He's sort of weird-looking." She shivers. "Something about his face."

"What, like a scar?"

Camila squinches up her forehead, like she's trying to remember, but after a second she shakes her head. "I don't know. Maybe." She shivers again and slides off the porch rail. "Come on, it's freezing out here. Come back inside with me and at least *try* to have fun?"

I heave a long-suffering sigh, but a few minutes later we are giggling uncontrollably at the sight of Dracula, Frankenstein and Sherlock Holmes trading keg stands, and I have to admit I am having a pretty good time—at least until Camila decides to join them, and ends our evening early by getting spectacularly drunk and puking all over Kilpatrick's kitchen table. After that, I don't have much choice but to get her as cleaned up as I can, then tug and shove her toward the front door, through a crowd that seems to have only gotten bigger and rowdier in the past couple of hours.

Once I've gotten a weakly protesting Camila through the door, I turn and give one last glance around the party on the off chance that my eyes will land on Jek. Camila's right—it's pretty unlikely that Jek would show up to a kegger, but he did say he might. But before I get a good look, I'm knocked off balance by some guy shoving his way into the house. I tip backward into Camila, and she goes stumbling down the front steps, where she wobbles a moment before pitching heavily to the ground.

"Watch it, asshole," I call over my shoulder as I hurry to her side. In return, the guy spits back a slur so vile that I spin around to face him, shock and fury pulsing through me. "What did you call me?"

The dark-eyed boy tosses a bored glance over one shoulder and opens his mouth as if to follow up on his comment. But something about my face must change his mind, because his eyes widen in what looks like panic, and before I know it he has slithered back into the crowd.

"What was that all about?" Camila asks hazily as I help her to her feet.

"I hate costume parties," I mutter. "Hard to give someone a piece of your mind when they're dressed as..."

"As what?"

I grasp at a word or an idea for a second, but it slips away from me. "I didn't get a good look at him," I tell her with a shrug. "Some kind of angel? Or a demon."

Camila giggles as I maneuver her into the car.

"Well, which was it?"

"I mean, like a fallen angel," I explain, but I can't put my finger on why I think so. I try to conjure up a mental image of him, but I don't remember him wearing anything special or carrying any props, and his face is now a muddled memory. I can't quite get a fix on whether his nose was big or small, his cheeks sharp or soft, his skin dark or light—all that stands out in my mind are those intense black eyes, and the strange fear I read in them.

CHAPTER

I can't stop thinking about that guy who ran into me at the kegger. It's weird to see anyone you don't know in a town like this, where almost everyone is connected in some way to the Research Park. London's funny that way.

No, not *that* London—London, Illinois. Up until the 1970s, it was an unincorporated farming community called Plachett, an hour and a half out of Chicago on winding country roads. It didn't even have a post office. Then Lonsanto Agrichemical Corporation bought out a bunch of the local farmers and built a major research facility right in the middle of nowhere, and people started moving in and building houses. In 1978, Lonsanto merged with Donnelly Pharmaceuticals to create London Chemical—Big Farm meets Big Pharm, people said. That's when they built the Research Park, and more housing developments, and in 1984, the town of Plachett incorporated and changed its name to London—for LONsanto and DONelly.

That history makes London feel different from most small, Midwestern farm towns. Most places grow up naturally around a river or a railroad, and they wind up a mishmash of old buildings and new, straight roads and roads that wind off into nothing, fancy brick houses and old wooden shacks. In London, the whole town was planned by the company from the beginning to attract the best scientists in the country, so it's like living in the pages of a tourism pamphlet. There's a picturesque Main Street with coffee shops, antiques stores and a microbrewery. The buildings all have solar panels, the flower beds are filled with noninvasive wildflowers, there are bike paths crisscrossing the whole town… When you go to a friend's house, you always know exactly where the bathrooms are, because every house was based on one of three different plans.

I have to admit, it's beautiful in the spring and summer, especially on the London Chem grounds, which are basically a big park right on the edge of town, with paths through the trees for bikers and joggers, free and open for anyone to use. Of course, that means us locals have to share space with protesters yelling, "GMO, just say no!" and "No more frankenfoods!" but you get used to them. It's all worth it for the botanic garden, the butterfly pavilion and the mirrored glass lab buildings in strange, fanciful shapes, all designed by famous architects. The biggest are the twin headquarters of Lonsanto and Donnelly, curved around each other to reflect the symbiosis of the companies. They tell you all this when you visit—when I was a kid, we had field trips to London Chem every semester or so.

That's another thing London Chem won't let you forget: how invested they are in education. They paid for both schools in town—the K-8 and the high school where I go now, with its state-of-the-art laboratory facilities, better even than most colleges. That means science is a huge deal at London High, and the top students are super competitive—especially when it comes to the various science fairs and competitions sponsored each year by London Chem. Monday morning after the kegger, the latest award is all anyone can talk about.

"Jayesh Kapoor won the Gene-ius Award *again*?" Steve Polaczek says, reading the morning announcements off his phone. "I can't believe it. Who the hell is this guy?"

We're in the middle of setting up another mass spectrometry lab in biochem. It's our third this semester, after Donnelly donated a hand-me-down QTOF. Now we have to use it every other week just to show how grateful we are. Really, London Chem should be thanking *us*. Sure, we get fancy lab equipment, but they get a massive tax write-off every time they toss something our way.

My lab partner, Danny Carew, claimed he can't find his goggles and is wandering the room asking people if they've seen them, which is a transparent excuse to curry votes for the upcoming student council election. He's left me to do all the grunt work of setting up, which I'm not really doing because I'm distracted by Steve's question. I'm itching to answer him, but he and his partner, Mark Cheong, are across the lab bench from me, very clearly *not* including me in their conversation.

"What do you mean, who is he?" replies Mark lazily. "He's the guy who wins all these awards."

"Yes, I *know*," says Steve sarcastically. "This time for research into—" he reads from the screen "—metabolic pathways for the artificial synthesis of (S)-reticuline."

Mark raises his eyebrows. "Impressive."

Steve dismisses this assessment with a wave of his hand. "Sure, whatever. But who *is* he? If he's good enough to win the Gene-ius Award, how come he's not in any of my classes? I've asked around before, and no one seems to know him. Does he even go here?"

Steve's got a big mouth and loves to act like he's a real player in the school's science competitions, but it's mostly hot air. He placed once as a sophomore, but that's it. Truth is, he isn't half as smart as he thinks, and he spends more time obsessing over what everyone else is working on than studying and developing his own ideas. I don't know how many times I've seen him in class with his head bent over in deep concentration, only to realize that instead of taking notes, he's recalculating his GPA in the margins of his notebook.

Mark shrugs. "It's probably some awkward loser you never even notice. Keeps to himself, you know? A silent, nerdy ghost, haunting the halls of London High," he finishes in a fake-spooky tone.

I can't ignore them anymore.

"He's not a ghost," I say, my eyes fixed on my notebook.

I can feel their stunned stares immediately. It clearly hasn't occurred to them that I might know anything about this situation. This happens all the time. I've been in classes with these kids for years now, but they still act surprised when they realize I'm in the science track with them. As far as they're concerned, the science track is for the London Chem brats—the ones whose parents work at the Research Park—not kids like me, the children of farm laborers. I've heard all the smooth comments about how great it is that London "supports diversity," as if there's no way I could have earned my spot in this class. Sure, biochem isn't my best subject, but I'm at the top of my electrical engineering and information technology classes, if any of them cared to notice.

I clear my throat. "And you do know him. It's Jek."

Before I've even registered their reaction to this information, my body tenses up with guilt. I know very well what Jek would say if he heard me: that he doesn't need or want me sticking up for him. Jek's dealt with idiots like this his whole life and he's figured out a way to handle them that works for him, which basically means letting these guys believe whatever the hell they want. It drives me nuts, but I'm beginning to understand that the alternative can be worse. But I just can't stand the self-satisfied way these boys are so sure they know everything and deserve everything, and are blind to everyone who isn't them.

After a moment's silence, Steve lets out a sour laugh. "What are you even talking about?"

I look up from my lab notebook. "You know, Jek?" I nod toward Steve's phone. "That's his real name. Jayesh Emerson Kapoor. His initials are J.E.K."

"The black kid?" says Mark, his tone incredulous.

I grip my pencil to steady my nerves, but I can feel my heart rate rising. Such an innocuous comment, but there's so much behind it. I don't know whether I'm angrier at the assumption that these two can read everyone's race and ethnicity perfectly just from looking, or at their surprise that a black person could kick their ass at a science competition, but I can't point out either one, since they didn't actually *say* any of that.

"His mother's Indian." I keep my voice calm and steady. "His father is black."

"Oh," they say in tandem, as if that explains it all. "Indian."

Let it go, Lulu. It's not your fight. Jek can handle his own battles. Not that he does. He's happy to fly below the radar and avoid drawing attention to himself. *That* kind of attention, anyway. It's been this way since middle school, when he first abandoned his real name and told people—even teachers—to start calling him Jek. I asked him about it once, and he admitted that he was sick of people assuming he was nerdy and uncool because he was Indian. Presenting himself as the only black kid in our grade made him seem a lot more exciting—

even if it came with other baggage, like people assuming he's no good at science, or automatically blaming him whenever there's any trouble.

Now, only his close friends know that he's biracial, and that he's secretly still obsessed with science. For everyone else, he just plays into their expectations: doesn't advertise his grades, doesn't talk much in class and when he gets called on, acts like he's as surprised as anyone when he gets the right answers. And so he gets to be everyone's cool friend instead of a threat. I wish he could find a way to embrace both sides of his identity and challenge people's dumb stereotypes, but Jek's made it clear he's not interested in being a crusader.

"Does his mom work at London Chem?" Steve asks.

I nod.

He smacks his hand on the lab bench. "I should have known. The guy's a ringer. His mom probably did the whole project for him."

It's the most absurd thing he could possibly say. If that's his objection, it could be true for almost everyone in the science track at this school. If anything, Jek is the *least* guilty of this crime, given that his mom sometimes comes to *him* to consult on metabolic processes or different drug absorption mechanisms. I am this close, *this close*, to blowing up in this asshole's face and telling him all about how Donnelly Pharmaceuticals has patents on *three* processes that Jek initially conceived in previous Gene-ius Award entries, but I'm saved by the return of Danny, who knows me well enough to read the dangerous expression on my face.

"Lulu," he says gently. "Would you mind checking the storeroom for extra pipettes? If we wait till we reach that step, everyone else will have grabbed them all."

I'm seething silently as I tug open the door to the supply room. I find the pipettes and grab a handful of them, still preoccupied enough to nearly mow down Maia Diaz on her way into the supply room. Somehow I manage not to drop glass everywhere, and I mumble an apology on my way out when she stops me with a light hand on my arm.

"Lulu," she says softly when I turn around. "You're friends with Jek, right?"

I raise my eyebrows, wondering why everyone is so interested in my best friend this morning. "Yeah."

"Right," she says, nodding to herself a little. "Can I ask you something?"

I shrug and gesture for her to go ahead. She glances around the room nervously, then grips my arm and tugs me back into the supply room. I'm so caught off guard that I don't even try to resist. I know I should really get back to Danny, but I have to admit I'm curious about what Maia has to say.

She flicks on the light and pulls the door shut. In the shadowy depths of the supply closet, I see the wall of boxes behind her, all different sizes, and all identically marked with a leafy vine creeping through a double helix—the company logo of London Chem, and our sports team, the Helices. They look like the bewitched brambles of fairy tales, and for a strange moment they almost seem to be closing in on us. I nod for Maia to get on with it before claustrophobia gets to me.

"Matt Klein's kegger," she says. "A couple of weeks back. Did you hear what happened to Natalie?"

I hesitate. I hate to admit I had anything to do with that kind of mindless gossip, but playing dumb won't help. "I heard something about it, yeah," I say with a nod.

"Look, this is kind of a big secret and I know Natalie wouldn't want me talking to anyone about it, but there's something weird going on and I think…I think someone should know." She pauses. "I think *Jek* should know. I'm just trying to do the right thing."

"I don't understand. Jek wasn't even at that party. What's it got to do with him?"

"I don't know, exactly," she says. "The thing is, I never knew Jek's real name before, but when Steve said it just now it sounded familiar. And I realized, I remembered it from Klein's party. Natalie was really upset that night, so I took her outside to talk. I wanted her to tell me what happened, and if we needed to call the cops or go to the hospital and get a rape kit. But that guy, Hyde, he followed us out." She shudders at the memory. "I didn't even know what had happened between them, but he gave me a bad vibe. Creepy-looking, you know? I don't know why she'd want to mess around with someone like that. Anyway, he called after Natalie, telling her to be reasonable, to let it drop. I told him to fuck off, but he ignored me. He just looked at Natalie and said, 'Name your price.'"

"What?" I say, genuinely shocked. I still have no idea what this has to do with Jek, but I'm starting to have very bad feelings toward this guy Hyde. "He just…just like that? He offered to *buy her off*?"

"I couldn't believe it, either. I started to tell him exactly where he could put his dirty money, but Natalie stopped me." Maia looks down at her shoes, then glances up again. "It sounds bad," she says. "I know. I didn't want to believe Natalie would accept cash over something like this, but she has a point. Who's going to believe a brown girl over a white boy when it comes to rape? You know how it goes—everyone'll say, oh, that poor boy made one mistake and now she's ruining his life."

"A white boy?" I think back to Camila's description of Hyde. "I heard he was Asian or something."

Maia shrugs. "Looked white to me. Anyway, Natalie's father's been sick a lot, and her uncle, too, from the pesticides they work with. So they haven't been able to work lately and they have all kinds of medical bills…"

"It's okay," I assure her, thinking of similar situations in my own family. "I understand." Health insurance for the laborers at London Chem is a joke, and *of course* the company always denies that the chemicals are harmful. But it's not like anyone has the cash for a lawyer.

Maia nods. "So, Natalie, she…she told him her price. And

it wasn't low. I thought for sure he'd drop his offer or try to bargain, but he didn't even blink. He just took out his phone. He said all he needed was her app info, and he'd transfer it right away."

"And she accepted the cash?"

"It was a lot of money."

"I guess that explains why the story died," I say, half to myself. "But I still don't see what any of this has to do with Jek."

"Because," says Maia, "the name on the account that sent the money wasn't Hyde. It was Jayesh Emerson Kapoor."

I stare at her in the dim light of the supply closet, trying to parse what she's telling me. "Are you sure?" I say. "That's not possible."

"That was the name," she says firmly.

"Jek," I say softly to myself. "What the hell? How'd he get access to Jek's account?"

"That's what I'm wondering. And I don't want to stir up drama for Natalie if I can avoid it, but I'm worried for her. Worried that if Hyde hacked into Jek's account or something, the money's going to disappear and she'll wind up with nothing. I wouldn't put it past him." She shakes her head in disgust. "Has Jek mentioned anything about any identity theft?"

"Not to me, but…we haven't exactly been close lately."

There's a knock on the door.

"Lulu? You get lost in there?" It's Danny. Shit, I almost forgot I'm supposed to be in class right now.

I put my hand on the doorknob, but at the last second I turn back to Maia.

"Thanks for letting me know about this. You're right, there's definitely something strange going on. I'll talk to Jek about it as soon as I can."

Assuming I can get him to talk to me.

CHAPTER

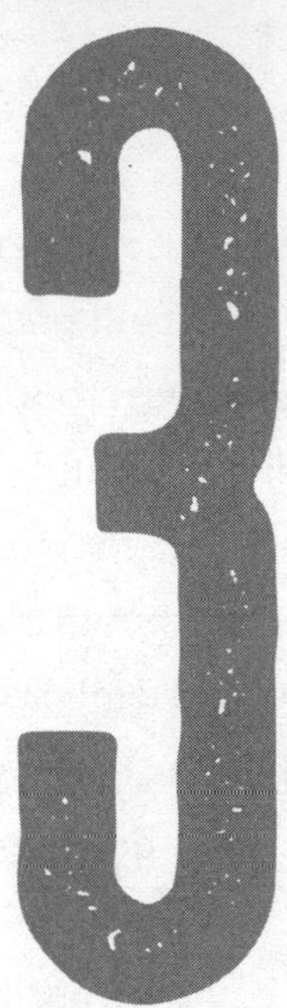

I send a quick text to Jek on my way back to the lab bench, telling him I need to talk soon.

I'm not exactly surprised when the school day draws to a close with no reply.

Even at the best of times, Jek's never been great about responding to texts, calls or any other method of communication. It's frustrating, but it's just part of his character. Even as I remind myself of this, I can't help thinking back to what I told Maia in the supply room: *We're not exactly close these days.* I surprised myself a little when I said it—I've never expressed that thought out loud before, though I have to admit that it's not the first time I've thought it. Is it true? Or am I reading into things?

Like any well-trained scientist, I force myself to consider

the evidence objectively. I don't see Jek as much as I used to, but we're both pretty busy with school and everything. Even though we're both in the science track, our schedules are totally different because he does mostly chemistry, and my focus is on computing. He hardly responds to my texts and messages, but that's not outside the realm of normal for him. I can't remember us having any big fight recently. I worry all the time that my crush on him has made him uncomfortable, but I do try to be discreet, and if he's put off by it, he's never let on.

Results: inconclusive. Researcher is too close to the subject to remain objective in her analysis. As usual.

Maia's story about Hyde has at least given me a good excuse to talk with Jek. If he's not going to answer my urgent texts, I really have no choice but to go to his house and make him listen to me, face-to-face. If it's true that Jek's name was on that receipt, then this guy Hyde could be running some kind of scam: hacking, identity theft or maybe something even worse. Jek's not great with that kind of computer stuff—if it wasn't for me, he'd leave all his databases unprotected and vulnerable to attacks.

I pull up outside Jek's house and notice that shadows are gathering on the columns and gables of the sprawling houses on this side of town. It's around 5:00 p.m. and sunset is almost an hour off, but the sky is already low and threatening, and lights are coming on across the neighborhood to ward off the darkness of an encroaching storm—a reminder that London's sunny, warm season has truly ended and we'll be in the thick of winter soon.

When I was a kid, the winters in London were snowy and bright. I'd wake up to the whole countryside under a smooth white blanket, and Jek and I would go out and pelt each other with snowballs as the sun sparkled against the landscape. We haven't had a winter like that in years, though. Instead, November to March brings nothing but a dark, gritty rain and heavy pea soup fogs that have an almost brownish cast to them. Some people say this is all part of some top secret London Chem experiment gone wrong, but others say it's just a normal part of the same global warming that's affecting everyone. Either way, it will be months before we see real sunshine again.

Up on the hill above Jek's house, the curving structures of Donnelly and Lonsanto are barely visible, their reflective surfaces blending in with the roiling clouds. I step out of the car and pull my jacket tight against a sharp wind that rattles dead leaves still clinging to the once-lush trees. I'm still not entirely used to visiting Jek here. Up until last year, he lived with his mom, Puloma, off Main Street in a smallish condo cozily decorated in a hodgepodge of styles: posters for old rock shows mixed with tin-and-brass trinkets, colorful silk cushions tossed over rickety chairs and benches. Puloma hired my mom as her cleaning lady back when they first moved to town, and I used to play with Jek while our moms worked—

that's how we became friends. I still remember waking up there after sleepovers, his mom making us breakfast of *masala dosa* while we watched cartoons.

Then last year Puloma married Tom Barrow, one of the other London Chem scientists, after a whirlwind romance, and she and Jek moved to this house where Tom lives with his three interchangeable blond sons, all somewhere between seven and eleven years old. Their house is much bigger than the old condo, and looks about as bland as all the other houses on the cul-de-sac. The only difference between this house and its neighbors is the addition that extends out from the back and down the hill a bit—originally built for Tom's former mother-in-law and where Jek lives now. This space, connected to the rest of the house by a short flight of stairs, was Puloma's main bargaining chip in getting Jek to go along with her new marriage—she promised him that he could turn the apartment's kitchen into his own personal laboratory. Tom doesn't exactly approve of him having so much freedom and autonomy, but Puloma has always had a soft spot when it comes to Jek, and she doesn't let Tom interfere.

I cross the lawn to the side door that opens directly into Jek's apartment. The addition isn't really visible from the street, so Tom and Puloma have let the upkeep slide a little: the paint is peeling, and you can see broken blinds through the windows, whereas the rest of the house has pretty lace curtains. The porch light was knocked out a few months ago by a stray baseball from the kids' afternoon game of catch and no one has bothered to fix it, so the side door remains in heavy gloom even when the rest of the house is cheerfully lit.

I'm almost to the door when it opens and a figure steps out into the thickening darkness. I start to call out a greeting, but my voice dies in my throat when I realize it's not Jek. The figure startles a little at my cutoff cry.

"Sorry," I say, stepping into the light cast by the doorway. "I thought you were… I'm looking for Jek."

The silhouetted figure regards me a long moment, a curious tilt to his head. "You've just missed him," he says lightly. "I can give him a message, if you like." His voice is husky and low, with a lingering softness on every *S*. He's backlit by the open door behind him so I can't see him well, but there's something about him that nonetheless feels off—the way he talks, or holds himself, or the strange breathiness of his voice. Or maybe it's the way he smells: a hint of citrus carried over by the wind, not unpleasant, but flat and artificial, like detergent or air freshener.

"You're Hyde, aren't you?" I say, though I can't explain what makes me so sure. He goes very still.

"I don't think we've met," he says after a pause.

"I'm Lulu," I say. "Lulu Gutierrez." I take a step toward him, my mind churning with curiosity. Those things Camila and Maia said about how odd he looked, beyond description, I have to see for myself. "Would you do me a favor?" I ask, stunned at my own daring. "Would you step into the light? I want to see your face."

Hyde hesitates, and for a moment I think he's going to laugh at my request, or get offended and tell me to get lost. I could hardly blame him if he did. But he surprises me.

"If you like," he says, and he takes a step back over Jek's threshold, letting the lamplight hit him directly.

I'm not quite surprised to discover it's the boy who ran into me at the Halloween party, but I can't help the gasp that escapes me now that I see him clearly. I can understand why Camila and Maia disagreed about his race—his features are hard to place. His eyes have a sleepy, heavy-lidded aspect that suggests an Asian background, and his skin has a sallow cast, though that could just be the light. His hair, though, falls in thick, dark curls and his nose has a slight bump to it that could be European or Middle Eastern, possibly.

None of that explains, though, why his face is so off-putting. There's something unpleasant and alien about his looks, and I search him for what is producing this uncanny effect, like one eye set lower than the other or missing eyebrows, but I can't put my finger on it. His features seem somehow out of proportion with each other—eyes too small, mouth too big, nose too prominent—but in the next moment the effect shifts, and it's his chin that seems too sharp for a mouth too soft. Just like at the party, though, the most remarkable thing about him are his eyes—as black and unreflecting as the shadows settling around us.

I know it's rude to stare, but Hyde doesn't seem offended. He just stands calm and self-possessed before me, a smile twisting his lips as he waits for me to finish my examination. Then he steps outside again and tugs the door firmly shut, casting us both in darkness.

"Now," he says, "return the favor and tell me how you knew me."

I swallow against a mounting tremor in my voice before answering. "You were described to me," I say. "We have friends in common."

I can feel more than see Hyde's sneer at this. "I'd be surprised," he says softly, again teetering on the edge of a lisp. "What friends?"

"Well… Jek, for one," I point out.

He stares at me coolly. "Jek never mentioned me to you."

Even though I never quite claimed he had, I still feel called out by this statement. But it's not like Hyde can know every conversation Jek and I have had. I shake off the creeping sensation Hyde is giving me and remind myself why I came here in the first place: to warn Jek about him.

"What are you doing here, anyway?" I ask, my voice firmer now. "Alone at Jek's place."

"What's it to you?" he replies, unperturbed. "If Jek doesn't mind…"

"Sure," I say with a shrug. "None of my business. But maybe I'll make sure Jek actually knows you're here." I pull out my phone, but Hyde makes a sharp gesture before my thumb is even on the screen.

"No," he says quickly. "Don't."

"Why not?"

Even in the dark, I can sense the prickling alertness in Hyde's body. It's gone in a flash, and his tone becomes lazy and sneering again.

"Text him if you like," he says, "but it won't do any good. Jek forgot his phone when he went out earlier. I was just on my way to bring it to him." He takes Jek's phone out of his pocket. It's instantly recognizable, thanks to its distinctive case decorated with colorfully trippy mandalas. I hesitate, still unsure. Jek forgets his phone at home all the time, which is one of the reasons he's careless about returning texts, but who the hell is this guy to be hanging out in Jek's room alone? Especially after what Maia told me about Hyde spending Jek's money as if it was his own—even close friends don't usually do that.

"All right, then," I say carefully. "Bring him his phone, and I'll talk to him later." If Hyde has really broken into Jek's house or something equally criminal, his cover story won't hold up long.

"You do that," Hyde replies coolly before stepping over to where Jek's bike is leaning against the garage—it's one of Jek's little idiosyncrasies, that he prefers biking to driving. I guess Hyde must share it, because he mounts Jek's bike and heads off toward the main road without another word.

Again, I'm weirded out that this stranger is so confidently helping himself to Jek's possessions, but I have to admit that Jek's pretty casual about his stuff, and generally shrugs it off when someone "borrows" his bike without telling him. Last year his stepdad made a point of getting him a seriously heavy-duty lock on a bright green chain so he'd stop using his missing bike as an excuse for coming home late, but Jek can't be bothered to use it, so it just hangs uselessly off the frame. Still, it's a bit weird that the bike's here, if Jek's not. The whole situation feels suspicious—maybe it's nothing, but I don't feel right just walking away.

I may not be able to contact Jek and ask him about Hyde, but I'm not completely powerless. I head up the hill, around to the pillared and porticoed front of the house and knock on the main door. Some little blond kid opens it after a minute. Jek's new stepbrothers all have names that begin with *C*, but I can't keep them straight. Conner, Cameron, Caden, Carter, Caleb? I have no idea.

"Hi," I say. "Is Jek around?"

The kid shrugs. "Try his apartment."

"I did. I was just wondering if he was in the main house." Jek still joins the rest of the family for dinner some nights, if his mom is cooking, though she clearly isn't right now—the house smells of cheap jarred tomato sauce, which means the au pair is making dinner. She cooks mostly pasta and grilled cheese and chicken fingers, since that's all the Barrows will eat, anyway. Back when it was just Jek and Puloma, their house was always filled with the smells of spices Puloma's parents sent her from the Indian markets where they live in New Jersey. London doesn't have any Indian restaurants, let alone an international grocery, so I learned to associate those smells with Jek's house.

"What about Puloma?" I try. "Is she around?"

"Yeah," the kid says laconically before wandering off toward a room where I can hear his brothers are playing video games. I show myself in and walk around a bit, looking for Puloma. I've only been in the main part of the house a couple of times, but I know the layout well enough from others in the neighborhood.

Though Puloma and Jek have been living here for over a year, I can hardly tell that either of them are part of this household. Photos of Tom's boys line the walls, and the rest has the blandly tasteful mark of a professional decorator: leather couches in neutral colors, faux-rustic coffee tables and way too many decorative throw pillows. Puloma clearly hasn't added much, and the walls still have blank spots where Tom's ex-wife reclaimed personal items.

Moving through the living room to a corridor along the back of the house, I find Jek's mom hunched over a laptop in a room that must be her study. The door is ajar, and for a moment I just stand there, taking in the familiar smell of Puloma's incense. The decor in this room feels different, like this is Puloma's space. The furniture is plainer and more grown-up than back at the old house, but it's accented by vividly colored textiles, shiny tin figurines and an intricately carved marble elephant that I remember playing with as a little girl.

I knock gently and clear my throat.

"Puloma?"

She startles a bit, then turns around.

"Lulu!"

"I'm sorry to interrupt," I tell her. "I didn't mean to—"

"Don't be silly. Come in. I haven't seen you in ages. Will you have some tea with me?" Perched on an end table is an elegant brass tea set with a slender spout and jeweled cups, but Puloma ignores this in favor of an electric teakettle and a pair of chunky mugs shoved behind the papers on her desk. She flicks the kettle on and gestures me toward a comfy-looking couch under the window.

"Are you sure?" I say.

"Please. I needed a break anyway, and I never get to see you these days." I enter and take a seat as she pours the tea. "I guess that's the downside of giving Jayesh his own door," she says, handing me one of the mugs. "You always go straight there."

It's true that since they moved, I've spent more time dealing directly with Jek, and have hardly spoken to Puloma at all. It didn't occur to me that she might miss seeing me.

"Actually," I admit, "I came here looking for Jek. Have you seen him?"

Puloma frowns. "Not since last night," she says. "He must have gone out after school. Is he ignoring his phone again? I hate that."

"No, I…I don't know. Just…there's this guy. I just saw him come out of Jek's apartment. Is it… I mean, should he be in there when Jek isn't?"

"Oh," says Puloma. "That must be Hyde. You don't know him?"

I hesitate. "Not really," I say. "I just met him outside."

"Jayesh told me they were working on a project together. Some experiment that needs to be checked at particular intervals. He gave Hyde a spare key to look in on it when he's not around."

"Oh," I say, feeling a little embarrassed that I was so suspicious. Although based on what Maia said, I'm obviously not the only one he's rubbed the wrong way. "What do you think of him?" I ask, trying to sound conversational.

Puloma shrugs. "I haven't met him, really—I just saw him leaving one day while I was unloading groceries. I suppose I could have insisted on an introduction, but I don't like to hassle Jayesh. Honestly, I'm just happy he has a black friend now—I know he's always felt so isolated in this town."

I blink at Puloma in confusion. "You think Hyde is black?"

She puts down her tea and gives a nervous laugh. "Isn't he? I only saw him for a minute, but I thought he looked..." She trails off awkwardly. "Actually, could you tell me a bit about him? Or maybe whatever they're working on in there? I know it's not right to pry, but Jayesh's life is a mystery to me these days." She gives me a wry smile.

Puloma and Jek have always seemed to me more like partners in crime than mother and child. For bedtime stories, she used to read to him from biochemistry journals, and while other kids messed around with store-bought chemistry sets,

Puloma snuck home the real thing from work. They did experiments together as he got older, and she even named him as a coauthor on two of her papers. She's always encouraged Jek's scientific curiosity, even when it led in directions other parents might have disapproved of, so he's never had much reason to hide things from her.

But then, a lot has changed since Tom entered the picture.

"Um," I say at last. "I don't think I know much more than you do."

Puloma laughs gently. "No, of course. I'm sorry, Lulu—I didn't mean to make you a spy for me. I trust Jayesh to make good choices, and tell me anything I need to know."

Puloma clearly thinks I'm being evasive to protect Jek, but I wish that was the case. I'm flattered that she thinks I'm privy to Jek's secrets, even if it's far from the truth lately.

"Did he tell you he just won the Gene-ius Award?" I offer. "You must be so proud of him, following in your footsteps."

She smiles and shakes her head. "Jayesh is nothing like me, really. But that's a good thing. When I was younger, I wanted to live dangerously. To change the world. But I've always been afraid of the consequences. So instead I came here to London, where the work is steady and the pay is good. A compromise for the sake of stability." I start to object but Puloma cuts me off. "No, don't get me wrong—I don't regret it. It's just that I want Jayesh to know that he doesn't have to make the same choices just to make me happy. I want him to feel free to be bold, take risks, make mistakes. And not always play things safe. He's more brilliant than I am, anyway—I can see it already. And the last thing I'd ever want to do is cage or restrict that kind of mind. That's the privilege of genius—never to ask permission."

I nod and look down at my tea. I'm glad Puloma has such trust and confidence in Jek, and I want to believe that he's deserving of it, but my mind turns inescapably to the strange story Maia told me about Hyde using Jek's bank account. If it's true that Jek is friends with Hyde, does that mean Jek gave Hyde the cover-up money willingly? But why would Jek want to protect this creepy sex predator he barely knows? That just doesn't sound like him—Jek has never done anything like that before, or hung around with that kind of person. It's easier for me to believe that Hyde tricked Jek somehow, like making him think the money was for something else, something innocent. Jek *can* sometimes be too trusting for his own good.

I'm tempted to tell Puloma about my fears, just to get an adult perspective on the situation. If Jek's a victim of some kind of con game, she should know. She could help. But she's right that I'm not eager to become her spy. Everyone has their secrets, and I know as well as anyone what kind of damage people can do by spreading them. If Jek is hiding his work and his friends from his mom now, maybe he has a good reason for it.

After I leave Puloma, I spend the rest of the night flipping my phone in my hand, my fingers swiping to Jek's name in my address book. I feel like I need to either warn him or reassure myself, but the last person with Jek's phone was Hyde. Sure, he said he was about to return it to Jek, but what if that was a lie? Not much point in texting my suspicions directly to the criminal. I could call—I'd recognize Jek's voice, of course, which is nothing like Hyde's—but Jek always lets calls go to voice mail, so…same problem, there.

Eventually, I put my phone down and go to bed. I can track down Jek at school tomorrow. What damage could Hyde really do between now and then?

CHAPTER

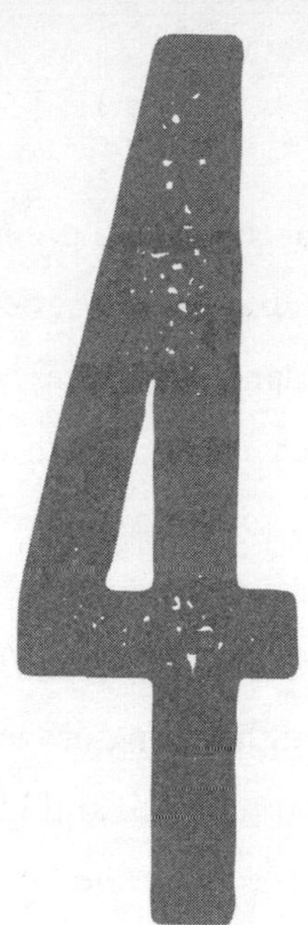

Jek is harder to get a hold of than I anticipated. I see him at various points during the school day—across the lunch room, at the other end of the hall between classes—but every time I try to catch his eye, he ducks his head and disappears behind a corner. I know we haven't been as close as we once were, but it's not like him to avoid me. I wonder if he's figured out that I want to talk about Hyde. He might be feeling guilty or embarrassed about what happened. Still, I have to know for sure. This stuff about Hyde is too important for me to just let it drop.

Over the next several days, I try Jek's house a couple of more times before, on a wild hunch, I keep driving up the hill until I reach the London Chem grounds. I pass the main buildings with their handful of desultory protesters marching across broad green lawns, then continue along the twisting, shadowy wooded paths until I break out into the open farmland stretching brown and muddy on either side of Twin Creek Road. From there, it's a careful half mile through a filmy gray fog until the hulking form of the old, disused grain elevator comes into view. My hunch about Jek's whereabouts is confirmed when I make out the burnt-orange of his bike through the fog; it's leaning up against the side of the building, the green lock and chain hanging uselessly from the frame.

The grain elevator is a relic from when London was a small farming community without Lonsanto's state-of-the-art agricultural facilities. Modern grain elevators, like the one Lonsanto currently uses on the other side of town, are smooth steel cylinders, but this one is the old kind—a rickety wooden tower, fat at the bottom and narrow at the top, like the silhouette of a giant. It hasn't been used in years, so it's gradually falling into ruin, the slats in the wall pulling free to let daylight through, and the roof starting to cave in. Signs warn people from going near the place for safety reasons, but that just makes it all the more appealing as a meeting point for kids looking to make out or get high. The whole area is littered with beer cans, cigarette butts, shell casings and the occasional used condom.

Tonight it's too grim and damp for most people to want to hang out here, but Jek's not most people. I've known him to bike out here even in the middle of a storm, if he's craving solitude. I feel a little bad, busting in on his alone time like this, but it's his own fault for avoiding me all week.

I park my car down a gentle slope so it won't be immediately obvious to passing vehicles, then follow a muddy path across the old, weed-choked railroad tracks toward the broad entrance where grain was once dropped off for storage. Once inside, I tread cautiously through the dim space, past the rusted, broken-down machinery, until Jek comes into view at the far end. He's standing in front of a fallen away part of the wall, nothing more than a dark shape outlined against the dingy fog outside. His silhouette is all ridges and angles, like a bird with its wings folded, and only a sliver of his profile is visible past the edge of his raised hood.

As my eyes adjust to the light, I'm able to pick out more details of his expression: his lips pressed firmly together, his brow furrowed. It's the way he always looks when he's deep in thought, so fixated on some knotty problem that the rest of the world becomes invisible to him. Some people find it off-putting, but I've always loved that look on him—that reminder of the incredible things his mind is capable of. I feel like I know him better than anyone, but when he gets like this, I know his thoughts are taking him way beyond anything I can understand. Maybe beyond what anyone can.

It's clear he hasn't heard my footsteps, and for a moment I hesitate to break in on his solitude, but I came here for a reason, so I announce myself with a pointed cough.

Jek springs to life as he whirls, stumbles and catches himself against the rotted planks of the wall.

"Jesus, Lu." He rubs a hand over his face, then stretches it out in front of him as if checking it for tremors.

"Hello, stranger," I say. "Feeling a little jumpy?"

He snorts, then lowers himself to sitting on an overturned crate, still panting a little. I pick my way gingerly through the debris on the floor and sit down next to him.

"Sorry to spook you."

He takes a deep, steadying breath. "No big deal," he says, flashing a friendly smile. "How've you been?"

"Not too bad," I tell him. "Except my best friend seems to be avoiding me."

Jek has the decency to look a little guilty at that. "Sounds like a dick," he says. "Want me to kick his ass?"

"Mmm," I agree, and I feel an unexpected swell of relief that we can slip so easily into our old friendly banter. "I'd like to see that."

We're not touching, but we're sitting close enough that I can feel the heat of his body through the damp chill of the air, and pick up his usual smell of smoke and chemicals, like a match that's just gone out. It might be off-putting on anyone else, but on Jek it's homey and familiar. Stretching my legs, I notice a syringe set among the usual beer cans and cigarette butts on the floor.

"Geez," I say, nudging it with the edge of my sneaker. "Since when did people start using this place to shoot up? I remember when this town was strictly smoking and snorting territory."

"Strange days," Jek agrees, eyeing the object.

"I guess it was inevitable the London Chem brats would get there eventually," I observe wryly.

Our high school is rated among the best in the country, and officially all the science-track students are serious, hardworking and committed to their studies. *Unofficially*, everyone knows that these same students take turns throwing extravagant keg parties every weekend where they indulge in the latest fashionable decadence. There's always a house available, because someone's parents are off presenting results at a conference or lobbying in Washington on behalf of the company. The parents kind of know what goes on, but by some unspoken agreement they all look the other way. As long as everything is cleaned up before they get back to town, no one ever has to acknowledge the masquerade.

"'London Chem brats'?" Jek raises an eyebrow at me, and I can't tell if he's seriously offended or just kidding around.

"You know I don't mean you," I tell him. "You're not like the rest of them. You're always too busy geeking out in the lab."

Jek laughs. "Was that supposed to be a compliment? Anyway, they're just messing around. Since when do you judge people for having a little fun?"

I give him a sidelong look. "I don't care what they get up to," I insist. "I'd just rather not know about it."

Jek nudges against me with his shoulder. "Afraid it will give you ideas?"

I feel my face heat up at the suggestion. "Nothing like that."

"No? Maybe you don't need the help. Maybe you've got enough depraved ideas of your own."

I huff out a breath and turn away from him.

"Aw, come on, Lu," he says. "I'm just kidding. I know you're not like that."

And that, of course, is even worse, as it sets me thinking of all the things I've dreamed of doing with Jek. I may not hang around with the party crowd anymore, but that doesn't mean my mind is completely pure and innocent. There are things in my head that I'd never tell anyone.

Still, it's tough to hide anything from someone who knows you so well, and I'm convinced Jek will draw the worst—and most accurate—conclusions from the way I'm squirming. But when I glance over at him, he's looking out into the fog again and I can't tell if he's noticed.

We're both quiet for a moment, listening to the soft patter of rain that just started.

"So what are you hiding from, out here?" I try after a bit.

Jek shakes his head. "Not hiding," he says. "Just...getting away. Clearing my head before I do something stupid. Stupider," he corrects himself.

I raise my eyebrows.

"My stepdad," he explains. "There was an experiment. Everything was going just as I predicted. And then it...wasn't."

I hiss in sympathy. I've seen the results of some of Jek's failed experiments.

"A very small explosion," he says. "Hardly any damage. But Tom heard breaking glass and smelled smoke, and ran down to see what was going on. When he realized I had locked the door between my apartment and the main house, he hit the roof. Said it was a safety hazard. Then he went off about me being so secretive, and how they would all be burned alive in their beds one day on account of me. Things got heated, and I had to get out of there."

"Sounds like quite a scene."

He sighs. "I don't know how much longer I can take it."

I nudge my knee against his. "Hang in there, kid. Another year and a half, and you'll be off to college."

Jek presses his lips together and stares off into space.

"Might take off a bit earlier," he mumbles.

I freeze. "What are you talking about?"

"Nothing." He shrugs. "Just… There's always Emerson, right?"

"Your dad?" My chest tightens up at the thought that Jek might leave town, that I might never see him again. "You'd really think of moving in with him?"

"I don't know. He mentioned it again the last time we talked. And it couldn't be worse than this, right?"

I give a little snort. Most people would probably think life with Jek's dad sounded like paradise. He made a bunch of money as a stockbroker a few years ago, and since then he's "retired" to a Caribbean island. But he and Jek don't exactly have a lot in common—Emerson believes a lot of odd stuff about how science and technology are instruments of state control and repression, and last time Jek visited him, they got into a big fight.

"I know, he's kind of a crackpot," Jek concedes. "But maybe it would be good for me to get to know him better. I love my mom, but between her and Tom… Do you have any idea what it's like to be one of the only black people in this town? Hell, I'm the only black person in my own house. There's this whole part of myself that's completely cut off from anyone like me."

I nod again in sympathy, but the truth is, I know I can't begin to understand his situation. I deal with plenty of racism around this town, but at least there's a big Latino population here, including a lot of people who care about me, who understand and support me. I can't blame Jek for wanting that kind of community, even though it breaks my heart to think of him leaving.

"What about your lab?" I ask. "You wouldn't have access to equipment and supplies with your dad."

Jek is quiet for a while, considering that. "Maybe it wouldn't be so bad," he says at last.

"Jek, come on. You love science. It's the only thing you've cared about for I don't even know how long. You can't seriously consider giving that up."

"Why not?" he says sharply. "Who says I can't try something new? Just because I've always been one way doesn't mean I have to be like that forever."

I stare at him. "You're serious?"

He leans back and some of the tension leaves his body.

"No," he says. "I don't know. I'm just talking. What about you? You've been tailing me all week, so I figure you must have something big to report. Finally hack that coupon site so we can get free pizza for life?"

"Nothing like that," I say with a snort. I glance up at him and find his gaze on me, warm and steady. For the first time in weeks, I have his complete attention, but for a moment, I can't help being distracted by his warm brown eyes and long lashes. His intelligence is so clearly written on his features, but it's not just that. There's kindness and generosity, too. And, caught up with it, our whole history together: laughter and games, teasing and skinned knees. Jek looks the same as ever—same baggy, practical clothes, his wild hair tucked up under his usual knit cap—but it's been a long time since I've interacted with him in nonelectronic form, and I'd forgotten how comfortably we fit together. How right it feels just to be with him.

I shake off these thoughts and focus on what I need to tell him. Now that I have him listening, I'm not sure where to begin.

"I met a friend of yours the other day, when I went looking for you," I try. Jek's gaze slides away from my face and he looks a little annoyed already. Not surprised, though. "Hyde," I say, just to be clear. "He was coming out of your place."

"And?"

"And, well..." I say, frustrated. "I've heard things about him. Not good things."

Jek shrugs. "Hyde's made some bad first impressions. Ruffled a few feathers. That's all."

"I don't know, Jek. How well do you know this guy, anyway?"

"Better than you do," he says sharply. "Come on, Lu. You of all people know better than to listen to gossip in this town."

I can't help wincing at the comment. Of course Jek knows how I once became the object of London's rumor mill. Everyone knows about it. But he hasn't made any reference to it in years—he knows how uncomfortable it makes me. For him to bring it up now means he's either suddenly transformed into a complete asshole, or he's desperate to change the subject and deflect attention from himself. But I won't let him throw me off course so easily.

"This is different, Jek," I press on. "I'm not just satisfying some prurient curiosity, I'm trying to look out for you. How do you know you can trust this guy? What if Hyde is..."

I'm not sure how to finish. I'm worried Hyde's a con artist, but Jek is the smartest person I know, even in a town of some extremely brilliant people. How can I sit next to a certified genius and tell him that some stranger has outsmarted him and tricked his way into his finances? But the fact is, there are different kinds of smart, and Jek isn't always so smart about people. Since Jek doesn't care about money or possessions, he can't imagine anyone else would. In the past, I've always been around to look out for him. Maybe the recent distance between us gave Hyde an opportunity to manipulate Jek.

I take a breath.

"Have you checked your bank account lately?"

"What?"

For the first time in this conversation, I seem to have surprised him.

"That's what I wanted to tell you, Jek. I heard..." I'm not sure how much to say. I don't want to break Maia's or Natalie's confidence. "Something happened at a kegger, with a girl. I don't know what, exactly, but I heard Hyde paid her to drop the issue. Paid her a *lot*."

Jek looks away. "What's that got to do with me?"

"Because he transferred the money from *your* account."

Jek looks up sharply. "Who told you that?" He sounds agitated, maybe even nervous. Not the disbelief and anger I was expecting.

I look steadily into his face, trying to read him.

"Is it true? Did you already know about this?"

He leans his head back against the wall. "It's fine, Lu. It's... Look, I appreciate your concern, but you don't need to worry about it. I've got it under control."

"Oh." I'm baffled. I had expected Jek to be shocked by my revelation, or to offer some totally reasonable explanation for it at least. Not to brush me off. "Okay then." I feel my temper rise along with my confusion. "I guess that's cool. I just didn't realize that your new hobby was bankrolling rapists."

I stand to leave, fuming, but he stops me with a hand on my arm.

"Lu, I swear. That's not what it is. You don't have the whole story."

"All right," I say. "So tell me."

He shakes his head. "I can't. But I… Look, just trust me, okay? It was a misunderstanding. A mix-up. It's all taken care of."

"Why can't you explain it, then?"

"Because it's none of your business!" he explodes, rising to his feet. I take a step back from him, surprised and hurt by his outburst. The pattering rain fills in the silence between us. Finally Jek lets out a slow breath and rubs his face. "Jesus, Lu," he says more quietly. "Just stay out of it, all right? If I tell you it's fine, *it's fine*."

"Fine," I mutter, moving toward the exit. "Sorry to bother you." He calls my name as I head out into the rain, but I am about 300 percent done with him right now. Why do I even bother? Let him clean up his own messes.

CHAPTER

I fume about Jek on the entire drive home, and it's only when I pull into the driveway and I'm hit with the scent of my mom's *carnitas* emanating from the house that my mood starts to improve. Whatever psychodrama Jek is involved in, it's not my problem to deal with—especially now that he's told me to stay out of it.

I park and go in through the back door, which leads directly into the kitchen. My house may not be big like the ones in Jek's neighborhood, but it's clean and comfortable—Mom always says, a small house means less to clean. I guess she would know, given how much of her life she has spent scrubbing the big houses on the hill. I used to dream of living in a house with a second story, but Jek pointed out that having a bedroom at ground level meant we could crawl in and out of my window without my mom knowing. Not that either of us have made use of that feature recently.

Moving stealthily through the kitchen, I pull a fork from the drying rack and dip it into the simmering pot.

"Lulu?" My mom's voice comes from the living room. "You better not be touching that pot before it's done."

"I'm not," I call back, then shove a chunk of meat in my mouth.

"And you're late," my mom continues. "You promised to fix my computer right after school."

With a sigh, I drop my fork in the sink and follow her voice into the living room. A couple of lamps are lit, but as usual the room is dominated by the bluish glow emanating from the large-screen TV that perpetually plays Spanish-language sports and news, thanks to a satellite hookup. My uncle is pretty much always lying on the couch in front of it under a pile of wool blankets—he says it helps distract him from his joint pain.

He's lying there now, watching a soccer game with the sound off, while my mom occupies her usual spot in the recliner, her laptop on her lap. She passes it off to me before I can even sit down in the remaining seat—a stiff-backed chair that no one likes. Sometimes I wish I'd hidden my interest in computers from the family so they wouldn't badger me all the time for help with theirs, but just like Jek's circumstances fostered his love of chemistry, I have my family to thank for my talent—mostly because every laptop, phone and tablet

I've ever owned has been a hand-me-down or a thrift-shop find. They've always been junked up with spyware when I got them, or hopelessly out-of-date. I had no choice but to teach myself how to fix them up.

"I bet you burned yourself," Mom mutters as I poke gently at the blistered roof of my mouth with my tongue. "You never learn."

"What's wrong with it this time?" I say, ignoring the dig.

"Keeps freezing," she says. "I have to shut down the whole thing, and I lose my place."

She gets up to tend to the pot in the kitchen, and I start in on the usual troubleshooting steps even though I'm almost positive she's let her hard drive get cluttered with malware again.

"Remind me why you play this game," I call out to her as I work. It's the most boring game I've ever seen: your character has to do all these real-life things like go shopping and plant vegetables and pay taxes, but my mom's obsessed with it for some reason. "You have to do all these things in real life, so why would you do them in your free time?"

"It's more fun when it's someone else's life," she calls back.

"Plus," my uncle Carlos says, "when she screws up in the game, she can just start the level over." He giggles. "Can't do that in real life."

"I heard that," Mom yells from the kitchen, and Carlos rolls his eyes and returns his attention to the soccer match. He used to be a big soccer player and thought about going pro, though you'd never know it to look at him now. He decided to stay here and put his energy into the family business instead, working his way up from farm labor to running his own feed store. But now he can't do much. He's lost so much weight that his skin sags off him, and he feels dizzy whenever he stands up. I remember how he used to pick me up and throw me in the air when I was a little girl. Now he gets winded just walking to the refrigerator. We all know it's because of the chemicals he worked with every day, but he won't talk about it. Doesn't want to admit that the business he built with his own hands is slowly killing him, and the rest of the family, too.

"Where were you all afternoon?" Mom nags, coming back from the kitchen and standing behind my chair to watch my progress with her computer. "You're always going out after school, when you know it's the only time I get to see you."

Mom used to clean for people like Puloma when I was a kid, but a few years ago she took a job cleaning the offices and labs for London Chem. It means she has to work nights, but the pay's better and it's steady. And the most important part is it keeps her away from the farm chemicals. Ever since Uncle Carlos got sick, Mom has lived in terror of all the products used on the crops around here.

"I was out with Jek," I tell her, bracing for her disapproving grunt before she even makes it.

"Always with that boy."

"What's that supposed to mean?" I say, bristling.

She strokes a hand along my hair in what's meant to be a soothing motion. "Lulu, sweetie, I've known Jek since he was a little boy, just like you, and you know I care about him too...but you're growing up now, and boys like that are only going to get you into trouble."

I crane around to look at her. "What do you mean, *trouble*?"

She sighs and leans against the chair back. "I'm not saying he'd ever try to hurt you, but things are different for him. He can do whatever he wants and the world will give him all the second chances he needs. His mother indulges him, his teachers and everyone else. He can afford to screw around. You have to stay focused and work, *mija*."

"You're wrong about him," I say, even though I know there's no winning this argument with her. This is more about her own life experiences than anything to do with Jek or me. Just because she made some bad choices, she thinks I'm destined to go down the same path. "No one I know is harder working than Jek."

Mom scoffs. "Because he plays around in his little laboratory? That's not work, that's fun. Work is what you do because you *have* to, not because you want to. Jek knows nothing about that."

"Neither does Lulu," Carlos comments idly, not taking his eyes off the screen. "Why don't you make her work? She could be useful at the store, but you keep her here like a little princess."

Mom straightens up and turns on him. "That's different.

Lulu's job is going to school, and I am not letting you talk her into going to work at that store of yours. She needs to stay focused on her studies so she can go to college and get a good job."

I've heard this fight a million times, but at least it's distracted Mom enough that I can finish up the virus check and escape to my room, leaving the continuing discussion behind.

My room at least is clean and calm, even if Mom is always hassling me about the mess. It's not *really* messy—my bed is made and my laundry pile is manageable. What Mom hates are the old computers, phones and tablets stacked on every surface, many of them with their cases forced open so their electronic guts spill out. It may not be pretty, but it's the best way for me to learn how all these parts work. Or don't work, as the case may be—at least a few of these projects of mine will probably never be anything but doorstops. Still, you never know if you don't try.

I move my latest project—overclocking the CPU of an old flip phone—from the bed and throw myself down on it, brooding over how wrong Mom is about Jek. He isn't like the other London Chem kids, who only care about drinking and sex and who's throwing the next kegger. Jek's family may have money, but he's always been marked as different, and no one will let him forget it. As one of the only black kids in town, he's had to hold himself to a higher standard.

But as I lie there listening to the argument in the other room, my thoughts turn back to Hyde. If anyone would be a bad influence, it's him. Something isn't right about his friendship with Jek. For as long as I've known him, Jek has been private and hard to get close to—his friends have all had to earn his trust over the course of years. It's not like him to become so close to someone so quickly. And even good friends don't share banking info. Since Jek is aware of what Hyde did, at least I can be sure it wasn't theft or hacking…but that doesn't necessarily mean the money was freely given. What could Hyde have possibly said to convince Jek to front him this cash? Did he tell Jek, "I just assaulted a girl and I need to buy her silence?" Jek would never support something like that, I'm sure of it. Not even for a friend.

So maybe they aren't friends, then. Maybe there's some other reason Jek is helping him out…not out of friendship, but fear. Based on what Maia and Camila have told me, not to mention my own conversation with him, Hyde seems like the type who will stop at nothing to get what he wants. It's possible he is controlling Jek somehow. Threatening him. But how? Threatening to hurt him or someone he loves? Or using some secret knowledge against him? I don't know what Jek might be hiding, but I know better than most that everyone has their secrets.

I was only nine years old when the whispers started. I didn't think anything of it at first, and even once I started to suspect they were whispering about me, I dismissed the idea as paranoia. What could anyone possibly have to say about me? Turns out it wasn't about me—not exactly. It was my mom.

Somehow the gossip had trickled down from the adult world to the schoolyard that my mom was having an affair with a client—a married man whose house she cleaned. One of the London Chem scientists.

I still don't really know if the rumors were true, or exactly how far things went between my mom and this man. I don't even know who it was—somehow the gossip never touched him, and as far as I can tell, he never paid any price. All I know is that shortly after that, my mom stopped cleaning for a while and spent most of a month on the couch, in a deep depression. We never talked about why, and I don't want to know any more details than I've already heard. Ever since the day Jessie Holbrook finally said to my face what everyone in town had been saying behind my back, I've tried to shut my ears to any and all gossip that comes my way.

But I may have to abandon that policy now if I'm going to help Jek with whatever trouble he's in. I know he told me to stay out of his business, but technically I'm not looking for information on him—it's Hyde I'm after. A guy like that must have a mile-long list of things he's hiding. If I could find something on Hyde—something illegal or immoral from his past that would destroy him if it became public—maybe that would neutralize his control over Jek and he'd be forced to back off.

These ideas comfort me enough to let me fall asleep, but by the next morning, they mostly feel silly. Identity theft, blackmail, threats...it all sounds a little far-fetched. The honest truth could just be that Jek's changing. That he isn't the same boy I grew up idolizing, sweet and brilliant and good-natured. I don't want to believe that he would so easily slip into a friendship with someone like Hyde, but maybe I don't know him as well as I think I do. Maybe I've been hanging on to a version of Jek he's left behind.

I've just about convinced myself to let everything go when Jek texts me Friday afternoon.

9 pm. My place.

It's like there's a competition between the boys in this town to see who can send the shortest texts. I want to text back a million questions—what's at 9:00 p.m.? What are we doing? Does he want to confide in me? Apologize for our little fight the other day? Are we just going to watch a movie and pretend nothing happened? Or does he have some other plan?

Instead, I call Camila to consult with her.

"Oh, my God," she exclaims when I've described his message to her. "It's finally happening!"

"*What's* happening? The message says practically nothing."

"What do you mean? You've hooked him! It's a date."

"A date?" I repeat dubiously. "Come on, Camila. When a boy wants a date, he uses complete sentences. In my experience, a message like this is a request for a hookup."

"Well, what's so bad about that?" says Camila, not disagreeing. "Don't you *want* to hook up with him? Why waste everyone's time with dinner and some boring movie?"

"You're such a romantic," I tell her flatly.

"Hey, I'm a pragmatist," she replies, unbothered. "No shame in that."

"I don't know. It just doesn't seem like Jek. I can't see him suddenly treating me like a booty call."

"Lulu, if you're waiting for him to show up on your doorstep with a dozen roses and a rented limo…"

"Nothing like that!" I insist. "I've just never known him to be into this kind of stuff. Not with me, not with *anyone.* To be honest, I think he might be completely asexual."

"Well," she says, "only one way to find out for sure."

"Mmm? What's that?"

"Show up tonight at his place. 9:00 p.m."

She has a point. With Camila's advice in mind, I stow away all the questions I still have and text Jek back. He wants brevity, two can play at that game.

K.

CHAPTER

An icy, crystalline mist slicks the pavement that night as I head over to Jek's house just after nine. I knock on his door, still wondering what he wants, why he invited me, when a thought suddenly filters up from my unconscious: *I don't know if Jek ever got his phone back.* He must have, right? There's no way Jek's been walking around for days without his phone and not noticing. Hyde said he was going to return it, and he must have done so. Besides, why would Hyde steal someone's phone and use it to invite people to the real owner's address? That doesn't make sense.

I've almost 100 percent convinced myself of this logic, but I'm just enough unsure that a little thrill pulses through me as I wait for the door to open. The thought that Hyde might be the one who texted me—that he's the one who wanted to meet me here—settles in the back of my mind. What will I do if the door opens and it's not Jek waiting for me, but Hyde?

The door opens.

It's not Jek.

"Hey, Lulu!"

Before I can respond or react, long arms are flung enthusiastically around my neck. "Long time no see. Glad you could make it."

It's Lane. Lane's been friends with Jek almost as long as I have, so I've been friends with him awhile, too. He's tall and wiry with rosy cheeks that make him look perpetually cheerful, which he basically is—a great big puppy, in human form. Even though I still think of him more as Jek's friend than mine, I've always liked him.

I greet Lane with slightly more reserve than he showed to me, then head to Jek's bedroom to drop off my coat with the others, taking stock of the scene as I return to the main room. Jek's apartment feels cozy and familiar to me, but to a stranger it would probably seem a bit odd. His aesthetic is a weird mix of druggie burnout and mad scientist, with walls covered with a mix of hip-hop posters, black light-sensitive abstractions and gently undulating mandala tapestries. The furniture consists mostly of hand-me-downs from his mom's old place, which were already threadbare and falling apart when we were kids. And where the apartment's freestanding kitchen once was is the most high-tech laboratory you could probably find outside of a legitimately funded lab. Unlike the comfortable decrepitude visible throughout the rest of the place, Jek's workspace is meticulously clean and well-ordered, with his test tubes and pipettes lined up in gleaming rows, and a centrifuge and sterilizer tucked away into neat corners. His ongoing experiments and sensitive chemicals are carefully labeled according to his own unfathomable system and stored in a locked glass-front cabinet. And in the center of it all, Jek's pride and joy: the strange, sleek machines his mother light-fingered from London Chem's retired equipment storage for Jek's personal use.

Tonight, a handful of people are milling around the sitting area of Jek's apartment and a few more are in his kitchen/lab. Of course. Not a date. Not an apology or a confession. And not a movie sleepover, like when we were little. It's Friday night, and Jek is hosting a party.

I shouldn't be surprised. I've been to quite a few of these gatherings in the past, though I've skipped out on the last couple. They're not parties like the kegger I went to with Camila, where half the school shows up to get wasted and trash someone's house. Jek's parties are much smaller, never more than twenty people, with the music low and unobtrusive and an emphasis on shared experience.

These little get-togethers, which Jek calls his *clinical trials*, are really just his way of testing out whatever new compound he's been working on. I remember when we were kids and his trials were more innocent. In early elementary school it was pretty basic stuff—baking soda volcanoes and the like.

As he got older, though, it wasn't enough for Jek to repeat experiments people had been doing for years. He wanted to do "real" science, like his mom and the other researchers at London Chem. He wanted to develop new compounds for the betterment of mankind. He worked on cleaning agents at first, sometimes with mixed results. Like the concoction he created to remove rust—it worked perfectly, except for the fact that it ate right through the metal.

Jek went on to develop bug sprays, detergents and hair products...but he didn't truly hit his stride until he started working in the psychoactive realm. After a drug prevention program freshman year, Jek learned about LSD, GHB, MDMA and DMT, and he was instantly fascinated. He found a few recipes online and started making stuff, which naturally he tried out on himself. He tried to get me to join him on these early psychotropic expeditions, but the whole idea of messing with my brain chemistry made me nervous. In fact, I kind of hoped Jek would get bored with this project and move on to something else, but from his very first dose, he was obsessed with the way chemicals could change his perceptions and thought patterns. He'd talk my ear off on grand philosophical topics, like wondering what it even meant to have an identity, if your whole sense of yourself could be shifted with the addition of a few chemicals.

While most kids would have been content to dose up on whatever was available and take what revelations came, that wasn't enough for Jek. He had to pull back the curtain and tease out exactly *how* these effects came about. Once he had identified every reaction, he had to know what other ones were possible. How tinkering with this or that carbon chain could produce new and previously undreamed-of results.

There is at least one comforting thing about Jek's little hobby: it's all perfectly legal. Well, not *perfectly* legal… It's kind of a convenient loophole, actually. The law can only restrict drugs that it knows exist. Since the stuff Jek cooks up in his lab is one of a kind, there are no specific statutes against any of it. Of course, if any one of his creations got popular enough, the authorities would probably crack down, but Jek's really good at tweaking things, switching them up, so the chemical makeup of the substances is always changing.

Though he's been doing this for a few years, and sharing recreationally with close friends, it's only been in the past few months that Jek has set himself to turning a profit, either in London's innermost druggie circles, or at clubs and concerts in Chicago. Last I knew, it was a pretty small-time operation. But that was some time ago now, and around the time we stopped being close. I wonder how things might've changed…if this new trial tonight is just about satisfying scientific curiosity, or creating a new product line.

Jek's got the usual suspects assembled for this event, plus one or two new faces. I work my way around the room, catching up with friends and acquaintances. One person is noticeably missing, though.

"Where's Jek?" I ask Lane when I bump into him again.

"He's dealing with the old man," says Lane, clearly referring to Tom. "Probably promising we'll behave ourselves tonight."

The parental factor at these parties has always been a bit awkward. Puloma's been pretty open with us about her own psychotropic adventures back in grad school and, while she'd never openly give her blessing for our activities, she, like the other London Chem parents, has quietly instituted a don't-ask-don't-tell policy.

Tom is a different situation. I'm pretty sure he has no idea what Jek gets up to in the lab, but it seems like only a matter of time before he figures it out. And I have a feeling he won't be so open-minded. Puloma has insisted that Jek is entitled to his privacy, and neither of them are to enter Jek's apartment without an invitation, but Tom doesn't exactly approve of that policy. Every time Jek wants to have people over, they have to go through this little appeasement dance.

"What about Hyde?" I ask, trying to keep my tone neutral. "Is he coming?"

"Who?"

"Hyde? Friend of Jek's? I get the impression they're pretty tight now." The fact that Lane hasn't met him is strange. What kind of friendship could Jek and Hyde have if they only hang out alone together?

"Hyde…" Lane muses. "That his first or last name?"

I have no idea. "I don't know. Maybe neither? It's what he goes by."

Jenny Vasquez has been chatting with Trevor Minkel and

Bryce Dalton nearby, but at this, she breaks off from them and nudges her way into our conversation. "Are you talking about Hyde?"

"Yeah," I say, hoping Jenny has the dirt that I've been looking for. "Do you know him?"

"Never met him," she says, a wicked gleam in her eye, "but I hope he shows tonight. From what I've heard, shit gets *wild* whenever he's around."

"Yeah?" says Trevor. "Well, that little shit better watch out, if he does come. He owes me a hundred and fifty bucks. He was taking bets on the football game last week, but he never paid out to the winners."

"I wouldn't count on ever seeing that money," says Bryce, laughing. "I heard Kevin started a fight with him and wound up getting his ass kicked."

"What?" says Trevor. "No way. Hyde isn't even that big."

"Yeah, but he fights dirty. Vicious, I mean. He would have put Kevin in the hospital if someone hadn't threatened to call the cops on them."

This is exactly the kind of gossip I've been looking for, but before I can follow up on Bryce's story, Lane's girlfriend, Hailee, comes over and passes out cups of water.

"If you're talking about Hyde, I don't think he'll be here tonight."

"Do you know him?" I ask, eager for firsthand information.

She shrugs. "Kind of. But I don't think drugs are his thing."

"What is his *thing*?"

"Everything else, pretty much," she says with a sly grin. She glances at Lane and the smile drops from her face. "*From what I hear.* That's why Jek hired him."

"What do you mean, hired him?"

"Well, I don't know for sure, but that's my impression. I met him in Chicago, at one of the clubs Jek used to hit. He was selling some of Jek's stash—I guess Hyde's been handling Jek's business for him lately."

"Really? He has Hyde doing the dealing?"

Suddenly things make more sense, and I'm almost happy to hear it. The business side of Jek's activities has always made me nervous. He started selling once his experiments got more elaborate and he needed better funding than he got from his mom's allowance, but I've never really understood it—it seems like such a huge risk for someone like him, with so much to lose. Between customers, cops, doormen and other dealers, I've always worried that Jek would get into trouble sooner or later. Whatever my feelings about Hyde, I have to admit it's safer for Jek to leave the drug dealing to him.

My thoughts are interrupted by a repetitive ringing sound, like a fork tapping against a glass. I turn to see it's actually a pipette being tapped against a beaker.

"Attention, please?"

Jek is standing on his coffee table, an Erlenmeyer flask of unappetizing reddish-brown liquid in his hand.

"Thanks, everyone," he begins, addressing the small crowd. "Thank you for coming. You know you're all doing me a huge favor by being my guinea pigs, but I hope you enjoy it a bit, too." There are a few hoots and cheers. "At this stage of the trial," Jek continues, "in a more official setting, I would normally make you all sign forms stating that I've made you aware of the risks of this study, but since this whole process is totally illegal and breaks most of the Geneva convention rules about use of human subjects…let's skip that little formality."

People laugh.

Jek holds up his flask. "This is actually not the final substance," he explains. "The compound is pretty volatile, so it's no good leaving it out all afternoon. I learned that the hard way. Best to do the final step—" Jek removes a small baggie of gray-green powder from his pocket, tugs it open with his teeth and pours it into the flask "—immediately before ingestion."

At first, the powder sinks lifelessly to the bottom of the glass container. Then Jek puts his thumb over the top, gives the flask a little shake and everything changes. The liquid begins to bubble and fume, and the flask swirls with a purplish cloud that slowly turns to a watery green before evening out into a bright yellow that fluoresces under the black light.

"This is the substance we'll be sampling tonight. Preliminary tests—on me—have produced some extraordinarily vivid phosphenic and photopsial effects. Or, in layman's terms, *bitchin' visuals.* I suspect this will turn out to have some entheogenic qualities as well, but that's harder to tell when experimenting on a single subject. Especially when that subject is also the experimenter. So that's where you come in.

"Most of you have participated in my studies before, but we do have a couple of newbies. Just to remind you all of the guidelines here—yes, you get free drugs. In return, you have to write up a report of at least one single-spaced page, and please no more than five single-spaced pages—" Jek pauses and singles out a boy with the five-foot bong "—I'm looking at you, Antonio. I don't want another fifty-page manifesto on the mushroom people." A few people giggle, and Antonio looks sheepish. "So, yeah, no more than five single-spaced pages describing your experience. I'll be messaging you all with some further guidelines for that in the morning. Please turn these in before Monday. Any longer than that and recall weakens exponentially. Failure to do so will result in a severe penalty of—" he pauses dramatically with a frightening look on his face "—not being invited back to play next time. And I'm serious about that. No excuses. This is for science, first and foremost."

A few kids raise their cups of water and call out, "For science!"

Jek raises his yellow beaker to the light.

"I like to call this little beauty…2bhx14d." Silence. "Yeah, sorry, I suck at marketing. That's just what it's called in my lab notebooks. If you have any better suggestions, let me know! There's a section for it on the survey."

Jek hops down off the table and moves toward his workspace, where he has laid out a collection of single sugar cubes on cocktail napkins. Using the pipette, he carefully saturates each cube with the liquid until they, too, are glowing yellow, then he passes them through the crowd.

As people gather around the coffee table to collect their doses, I slip into the bedroom to get my coat, then head for the door. A hand on my arm stops me. "Leaving already?"

I turn back toward Jek guiltily. "Yeah… Sorry, Jek. You know I'm not really into this stuff. Plus I have a lab report to turn in on Monday. I mean, a real one, and I need to do a lot of reading. But you have fun."

His hand is still at my elbow.

"Lu," he says softly. "Come on. Don't run off. We hardly see each other anymore."

"I know, but—"

"You know you don't have to take the drug to hang out with me, right? You can just stay and chill."

"Well, maybe for a—"

"Good, that's actually for the best, because I need a lab assistant."

"Ah, no, Jek, I told you I didn't want to do that again. Playing babysitter to a room full of *psychonauts* is not my idea of a fun Friday night."

"Come on…as a favor? You're the only one I can trust, the only one who isn't a total idiot who will screw up all my data."

"Can't you do it?"

Jek frowns. "Well," he says, "the thing is, reproducing the

experimental conditions on one subject over multiple trials helps ensure consistency of results. And given the precise parameters of this experimental design, any shift in control factors could call the whole analysis into question."

I roll my eyes. "Meaning you want to have fun and get high, so you need me to be the responsible one. Geez, Jek, is that the only reason you invited me? Because you knew I wouldn't take the drug and you could wheedle me into doing the boring part for you?"

"Lu…no." He looks offended. Hurt, even. "I invited you because I wanted to hang out with you. I thought that's what you wanted, too."

I sigh inwardly. Of course that's what I want, though I'd be happier if it was just the two of us. Still, it's been a while since Jek went out of his way to include me in his life like this, and I'm grateful for the gesture. Besides, even if all he wants right now is a lab assistant, maybe if I play my cards right tonight, I can get us back to how things used to be, before Jek got so caught up in his drugs or his new friends. I take it as a good sign at least that I'm here and Hyde isn't.

"All right," I tell him. "What do you need?"

Jek grins and pulls me into a hug. "You're the best, Lu. You know the drill—keep everyone well hydrated, make sure no one is freaking out and take note of any externally visible effects. Beyond that, check vitals, do a little hand-holding, call the EMTs if, and only if, absolutely necessary."

With that, Jek hands me a bottle of sedatives he dummied

up in his lab, which will put someone right to sleep if they seem to be having a bad time. Luckily, it's a good night, and none of that is called for. The whole thing starts out pretty slowly, and I can see people getting a little frustrated as they wait for any effects to kick in. I hear some whispering, probably about the time Jek dosed a small group with a complete dud. Some people will simply not let him forget it. I try to make myself useful by putting on music and turning off the most glaring of the lab lights. The substance Jek has created will stand or fall on its own merits, but it can't hurt to set the mood a little. I even flick on a couple of red and orange bulbs that Jek uses when he's working with photosensitive chemicals. I can't decide if the effect is more warm and cozy or "Welcome to Hell," but the partygoers seem to approve.

By the time I've finished, I can see that most of the subjects have shifted into a somewhat altered state. I note that people are lounging more bonelessly on the couches and cushions and speaking in softer voices. Sentences trail off into nothing as people become distracted by hallucinations invisible to their conversation partners. So far, pretty typical stuff, at least from the outside. I decide to check in with people and see if anything more interesting or unusual is going on with their subjective experiences.

"Hey," I say softly, sliding to the floor next to Jenny. "How are you doing?"

She grabs my hand and looks urgently into my face. "Lulu," she says, "isn't it amazing?"

"I don't know," I remind her gently. "I'm just observing. Why don't you tell me about it?"

"Oh, you have to try it sometime," she enthuses with a blissed-out smile. "The visuals are amazing, but it's more than that. I can *feel* everything. Not just touch, but light, music, air...like the whole universe is purring."

"That sounds awesome," I tell her, taking out my phone to make a few notes in Jek's electronic database. I helped him set it up ages ago to keep track of all the data from his experiments. "Anything else?"

Her brow furrows as she focuses very hard. "It's weird," she says. "I feel everything, but it's like I can *watch* myself feeling at the same time. Like part of me is standing outside myself, or it's all happening in a movie. Does that make any sense?"

"Absolutely," I say, selecting the tag for "dissociative properties." Entertaining enough, and clearly a new experience to Jenny, but pretty standard when it comes to psychoactive drugs. I'm about to move on to extract data from some of the others when I'm caught by something in her eyes. I try to blink it away, sure that it must be my imagination or the light playing tricks on me. I look at the wall, count to ten and look back, but it's still there, so I make a note in the database and move on to the next subject.

It happens to be Liam Holloway, which is a little awkward because we hooked up at a kegger last year, and I never replied to his texts afterward. But Liam's not one to hold a grudge, luckily—or at least not when under the influence of Jek's concoction.

"Lulu," he intones with a hazy smile, rolling the syllables around in his mouth. "I'm so glad you're here with me right now."

"Thanks," I say, discreetly dodging his hand as it reaches out to stroke my arm. "Me, too. Can you describe what you're feeling?"

He considers a moment, then laughs. "Not really. I don't know, my thoughts are going in crazy directions. Like some of them belong to someone else." He pauses. "Say, do you think I'm psychic?"

"Could be," I say, humoring him as I make a few quick notes. But what's really got my attention is not his words but his eyes—if what I'm seeing in him and Jenny is real, it's definitely the first time I've encountered this effect. I glance around for Jek to bring his attention to the phenomenon, but he's deep in an intense conversation with Lane now, so I make another note in the database and continue my rounds.

Throughout the evening, Jek and I somehow keep missing each other. It's frustrating, but I tell myself I'll catch him on his comedown, and try to stay focused on the task at hand. As the night wears on and people seem less chatty and more contemplative, I dim the lights some more and change the music. Some folks are having quiet conversations, while others are stroking the cushions or gazing at the psychedelic-themed wall decorations. I work some people through breathing exercises if they seem like they are getting a little anxious, refill water cups, take car keys from anyone who looks like they might be tempted to drive, but by 4:00 a.m., everyone seems to be sorted out, so I check vitals and reflexes and give them the okay to go home.

Once the last person has been ushered out with a reminder to check their messages over the weekend and fill out the response form, I finally allow myself to seek out Jek, only to find him stretched out on his bed with his eyes closed. So much for us hanging out together, I guess. I've spent all evening taking care of his dirty work in hopes of spending some meaningful time with him, and he can't even be bothered to stay up with me. I sigh and curse my weakness for him under my breath as I reach for my coat. And of course, he's fallen asleep on it.

Working carefully, I try to tug it free without waking him, but he shifts and groans in his sleep. Then he rolls over and his hand closes around my wrist.

"Lu," he slurs. "Where are you going?"

"Home, Jek. It's late, and you're half asleep."

His eyes stay closed but his voice is a bit clearer. "Stay over."

I can't help it—my heart thumps heavily in my chest.

"Stay here? With you?"

"You used to." His eyelids slip open a little. I smile down at him.

"It's been a few years."

"If you go home, you'll wake your uncle up." It's true. Carlos *is* a light sleeper, and he hates when I come in late. Jek senses my hesitation and tugs a little more firmly on my wrist. "Stay," he repeats. "Mom'll make us breakfast."

I can't help grinning. "Just like old times."

"Like old times." He shuffles to get himself under the covers, then lifts an arm, inviting me to do the same. I text my mom so she knows where I am, then slip out of my shoes and crawl under the blanket with him.

His breath is shallow and steady—he's already fallen mostly back to sleep. Propped up on one hand, I take the opportunity to admire him in the moonlight streaming in through the window, his lips slightly parted, his lashes spread against his cheek. Jek huffs a sigh and settles down more firmly into his pillow. All I wanted tonight was a little conversation—this is so much more than I was expecting. What does it mean? It's true that we used to do this all the time as kids, but we're not kids anymore. Surely even Jek has to recognize that it feels different now.

Jek shifts again in his sleep and curls his body toward mine, as if his unconscious seeks something his waking mind won't acknowledge. The very thought makes me light-headed and I'm sure I won't be able to sleep like this, so close to him that I can feel the warmth of his body, his breath against my cheek. I set my head down on the adjacent pillow and force my eyes closed, willing myself to sleep, but I'm afraid I'll spend the whole night struggling not to close the small distance between us. Somehow, though, the comforting rhythm of his heartbeat and his familiar burnt-chemical smell must work to soothe my nervous excitement, because at last I am lulled into unconsciousness.

CHAPTER

I wake up the next morning warm and comfortable, still caught up in the threads of a dream. A watery sunlight streaks through the window, apparently having broken up last night's mist. Without thinking, I roll over and snuggle closer to Jek's side of the bed.

Luckily, I'm spared the embarrassment of him noticing this semiconscious move, because Jek has apparently slipped out without waking me. For a moment I just lie there in a twist of mixed emotions, remembering how nice it was to share space with him, but also thinking about how *utterly* uninterested he must be in me if he can share a bed all night and not even try anything.

A little part of me had hoped that we would wake up together and, in the soft quiet of morning, he would reach for me like I just did for him and…no. No point of thinking about that. He's long gone without even stopping to wake me.

Camila was right: I need to get over this before my silly fantasies ruin a perfectly good friendship.

Shaking off my mood, I get up and head into the kitchen/lab. Even though I tried to clean up a bit last night, the gray daylight filtering in through the blinds reveals that the place is still mostly a mess—cups of water have been abandoned on every surface, the counters are piled with unwashed lab equipment and a box of hypodermic needles has been knocked off a shelf, strewing its contents all over the sink.

The boy himself, however, is nowhere to be found.

I consider just taking off, but if they're expecting me in the main house, I should at least say hi to Puloma before I leave.

I do my best to wash up in Jek's bathroom, though a bit of soap and a hairbrush can't change the fact that I slept in my clothes. Taking a breath, I open the door to the staircase leading to the main house and am greeted with the smell of frying *dosas*—I haven't smelled that in years, and it immediately takes me back and sets my stomach growling. I head up the stairs a little more enthusiastically and find Jek sitting on a stool at the counter, a cup of coffee in hand, while Puloma is busy at the stove. The kitchen is bright and airy, the appliances shiny and modern. One wall is dominated by a big window overlooking the backyard and the fields beyond as they slope up toward the London Chem buildings, just visible behind a wall of trees.

"Good morning," I say as I slide onto the stool next to him. Puloma jumps slightly, fumbles her spatula and spatters a bit of grease on her thumb. She turns around, sucking it.

"Lulu," she says. "This is a surprise." She's smiling but there's something else in her expression—confusion? alarm?—and I notice her eyes dart over to Jek. I turn to him, as well.

"Seriously? You didn't even tell your mom I was here?"

Jek shrugs as he pours me a cup of coffee from the pot cooling on the table. "Mom's pretty bright. I knew she'd figure it out sooner or later."

I look back at Puloma, an apology on my lips, but she stops me.

"No, no, Lulu. Stay, it's fine. It's more than fine. It's…nice. Really nice. Jayesh never tells me anything about his life… He prefers his dramatic little scenes, right?"

"Hey, I'm not dramatic," says Jek, but Puloma ignores him.

"He came to me this morning, out of the blue, and asked for *masala dosas*," she tells me. "I guess that was supposed to be my hint. No time to make them from scratch, but luckily I had some mix in the pantry from the last time I got a package from my mom. I haven't made them in ages—Tom's boys won't eat anything like that. It's frozen waffles for them or nothing."

"Where are the boys, then? Still sleeping, or…?"

"Oh, no," says Puloma, turning back to the stove. "They're long gone. Big junior soccer tournament this weekend. Jayesh only crawls out of his hole when he knows everyone's out of the house. It's like living with a mole person," she teases. There's something a little weird in her tone, though, like nervousness combined with barely disguised excitement. And she keeps glancing over her shoulder at me. It's unnerving.

It's only once I've had a few sips of coffee that it hits me. Oh, *God.* Of course. What would a mom think if her son shows up first thing in the morning with a girl who clearly spent the night? She'd be an idiot not to assume that we… Does Puloma really think I'd be so brazen as to have sex with her son and then sit down to breakfast with her? There's no way I'd be able to look her in the eye if we had really done… *that.* Of course, now I can't look her in the eye anyway, just knowing that she thinks it.

I feel desperate to correct her assumption, but how? She hasn't *said* anything that would need correcting. I glance over at Jek who, as usual, looks totally oblivious. Because, of course, to *him* I'm not a potential girlfriend at all. I'm still little Lulu who sleeps over on the weekends. Whatever his mom is assuming, Jek doesn't think in those terms.

"So," Puloma says at last as she puts down plates full of food for us all. "How was the party last night?"

"Good," I say, grateful for even a slight shift in attention. "I think everyone had a lot of fun." I hardly get the sentence out before I receive a kick under the table. I shoot a glare at Jek, who is too-innocently scooping up chutney. As if I need the reminder that Jek doesn't discuss his experiments with his mom anymore.

"How about you, Jayesh?" she says. "Did you have a good time?"

Jek rolls his eyes. "Mom. I don't want to talk to you about my parties."

Puloma huffs an exasperated sigh and throws her hands in the air, while I feel almost as awkward as before. Back in the old days, there wasn't so much tension between Jek and his mom—they always got along great. Clearly, I'm not the only one frustrated with Jek's recent secretiveness.

"Fine," she says, sitting down across from us. "How about *you* make some conversation, then."

They stare at each other for a long moment before Jek breaks.

"How's work, Mom?" he says grudgingly, but there's a hint of a smile. He's teasing her a bit, and she smiles back a tentative truce.

"It's fine," she says, then laughs at herself. "Now *I* sound like a teenager. Work is..." She sighs out the rest of her answer. "You know. The usual frustrations."

"What about that thing we were talking about last week... the Alzheimer's trial? Any progress there?" Instantly, Jek has dropped his sullen adolescent pose. There's nothing like shoptalk to get him out of his shell.

Puloma shakes her head. "Hard to make scientific progress when there's all this bureaucracy and red tape to dig through first. Sometimes I envy you, Jayesh—getting to throw together whatever you want without anyone looking over your shoulder. Once you grow up and go to work, science turns into one long waiting game."

"But all that red tape and stuff," I say, "isn't there a reason for it? To make sure everything is safe and ethical?"

Jek snorts and Puloma waves her hand airily. "Sure," she says. "The regulations are well-meaning, for the most part. But these days, they tend to be written by politicians and bureaucrats, not scientists. The work we do here at London Chem is so complex…what could some senator possibly hope to understand about it? And their policies are all so reactionary. Mistakes have been made in the past by a few scientists who got carried away, but when it gets out, the public panics and winds up listening to paranoid idiots like those protesters outside my lab." She nods in the direction of London Chem. "The restrictions they put in are based in fear, not logic. They gum up the works unnecessarily and slow down our progress.

"It would all be much more efficient if they let the scientists self-regulate. Scientists are the ones who work with this stuff every day. They know far better than lawyers and politicians and busybody nonprofits what safety measures should be in place for a given drug. Which ones are more radically experimental, which ones are only a tweak on something already working well." Puloma lets out a self-conscious laugh. "Sorry," she says. "I let myself get carried away there. Jayesh has heard this rant a million times…guess I was just excited to have a fresh audience." She glances at her phone. "Oh, the morning's half gone! I should go do my run now or the whole day will be wasted."

And with that, she finishes her coffee and heads off to change. Jek waits until he's sure she's out of earshot before nudging me.

"So," he says. "Now that my oversight committee has taken off, does my favorite lab partner have a preliminary report on last night's experiment? I think it went pretty well, but it's important to have an objective perspective on—"

"Relax, Jek," I reassure him with a grin. "It went great. From what people were describing, the new drug sounds incredible."

He heaves a sigh of relief, and I'm reminded that these little events of his are more than just parties. He really does care about the success of his experiments.

"Thanks, Lu. It meant a lot to me to have you there. There's no one else I'd trust with this kind of data. Speaking of which..." He looks at me meaningfully.

"Ah, right," I say. "The data." I pull up the database on my phone and go over my observations with him, describing the things people said and did the best I can remember.

Jek nods through it all and makes a few notes of his own. "Anything else?" he asks when I'm through.

"Yeah, actually," I tell him. "There was one thing. At first I thought it must just be a trick of the light, but I kept noticing it, even under the bright lab light. It seemed like...like people's eyes had changed color." I shake my head, feeling a little embarrassed. "I know that's impossible, but… I noticed it on Jenny first. Doesn't she normally have brown eyes? But they were flecked with green. I wondered if she was wearing contacts or something, but I kept noticing it on other people too… Liam, and Bryce… Maybe I was remembering everyone's eye color wrong, but I looked at Lane, and I *know* his eyes are gray. I made him stand under the bathroom light and everything, and they looked…dark brown."

Jek taps the table thoughtfully. "Hmm," he murmurs, half to himself. "There must have been some cross-contamination. But I wouldn't have thought, at such a low dose…"

"You mean you've heard of this kind of thing?" I say dubiously. "A drug that can change people's eye color? That would be pretty huge, wouldn't it? Changing someone's gene expression with just a pill. Are you saying you've seen this effect before?"

"What?" he says, distracted from his own chain of thoughts. "Oh…well, there's never been any documentation of it." He stands up and starts piling plates to carry to the sink. "Von Hoyrich proposed a mechanism in a paper last year, but that was purely hypothetical. I showed it to Mom and she declared it totally impossible."

"Well, I don't know what that was," I say, "but it looked like a pretty amazing high all the same. I think you've got a hit on your hands. Could be your greatest triumph yet," I offer. Jek's always been a sucker for having his genius flattered.

He smiles in acknowledgment of the compliment, but shakes his head. "No," he says, "not my greatest."

"Why, you've got something else in the works?"

He shrugs. "Too early to say, really." He's trying to play it cool, but I can see from his expression that he's bursting with it, so I hold my tongue, and soon enough he elaborates a little. "It could be big," he goes on, unable to repress his enthusiasm. "Like, seriously big. Once people hear about this..." He gives a low whistle. "It's going to change everything. The practical applications are out of this world, but even just the pure science of it...it's a thing of beauty. People will *never* forget my name."

I have to admit, Jek looks positively smitten with his new creation, whatever it is. If only he ever talked about me that way. But all of his energy is directed at his work; there's nothing left for mere humans.

"Sounds amazing," I say, leaning forward. "Do you think it will be ready soon?"

A furrow appears in Jek's forehead and he sits back down. "I don't know," he says. "There've been some...difficulties. It's still at an unpredictable stage. Temperamental."

"Why don't you talk to your mom about it? I know she keeps her distance more these days, but she always used to be a big help to you."

"This is different," he says sharply. "I can't talk to her. I tried to tell her about what I was working on back in the early days, but she made it very clear that she didn't approve.

She's…she's too set in her ways. Too accustomed to the standard methods."

I frown. "Puloma? That doesn't sound like her."

"Mom's a brilliant chemist, but she lacks vision. *Ambition*. She always has. That's why she's settled for a comfortable job here in London, where the company owns all her research and she's a slave to their corporate needs instead of her own imagination. I can't take the risk of her mentioning it to anyone at London Chem. This needs to be kept top secret for now… It's much too sensitive to share. No one's going to know anything until I have more data. Until I have all the possible kinks worked out."

"Except Hyde."

Jek raises his head sharply. "What?"

"Isn't he working with you on this project? After I saw him coming out of your door the other day, your mom said he'd been helping you out with some experiment that requires him coming and going at all hours. It's the same experiment, isn't it?"

Jek doesn't answer and I fix him with a look.

"So this project is so top secret that you can't trust anyone with it—not me, not your mom—but Hyde, who you've known…how long? You're working with him on it, trusting him to take care of it when you're not around… I've never known you to do that before. Even giving him a key to your apartment? He must have done something pretty impressive to earn that kind of trust."

"Lu, I told you—" Jek begins, but I'm not ready to let it go.

"Or is this even about trust? Jek, is something else going on? Hailee says Hyde's mixed up in your *business.* And I know you're giving him money. But no one else in town seems to trust him at all."

"I thought we agreed to drop this, Lulu." He looks a bit pale, but his eyes are flashing with anger. I hold up my hands in surrender.

"I'm not trying to... Look, all I'm saying is, if you're in trouble, if this guy is threatening you in some way, or he knows something about you, whatever it is...you know you can talk to me, right? I'd always have your back, Jek, no matter what."

He nods and looks down guiltily.

"I appreciate that, Lu. Really. But I can handle this. And if it makes you feel any better, I'll tell you one thing—the minute Hyde becomes a problem, I can get rid of him. And he'll never bother me or anyone else again."

"'Get rid of him'?" I repeat. "What are you, a gangster?"

Jek huffs out a breath. "Not like that," he says. "Just trust me, okay?"

"All right," I say doubtfully. "As long as you're sure..." I grab my coat and stand to leave. "I better be going. I still have that lab report to work on." He nods and walks me to the front door. At the last moment, he stops me with a hand on my arm, and like an idiot, I can't help the little shiver of pleasure his touch still produces in me.

"Lu," he says softly, hesitantly. "If Hyde ever comes to you…like, for a favor…would you do it?"

I laugh, surprised. "What? No. I don't even know the guy."

"No, but… I'm asking you, actually. If he ever needs anything, and he comes to you, I want you to help him. It would mean a lot to me."

I look at him, trying to read his expression. "Jek, I'm sorry. You do what you need to do, but to me, he seems like a creep. I'm not going to help him out."

"Fine, just…" He squeezes my arm. "Hear him out, okay? That's all I ask. If he ever needs something from you, or just wants to talk, and you can't get in touch with me…remember that I'd want you to help him. Okay? Just treat any favor to him as if it were a favor to me."

I give him a long, searching look. None of what he's saying makes any sense. Why would Hyde ever need a favor from me? And why wouldn't I be able to get in touch with Jek? I have no idea what he's implying, but it scares me a little.

"I don't know if I can do that," I tell him at last. "I don't like the guy, and until he gives me a reason to like him, I don't see that changing. But I promise to keep what you said in mind. Will that be enough?"

Jek nods and gives me a half smile. "Yeah," he says. "That's all I'm asking. Thanks."

CHAPTER

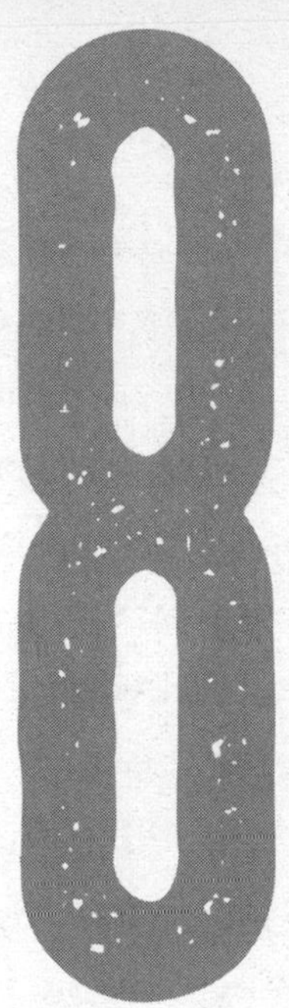

I hoped hanging out with Jek would resolve some of my concerns about him and Hyde, but if anything, I only have more questions now. For a while it felt like I was hanging out with the same old Jek again, who I've known since forever. But the stuff he was saying before I left has got me worried all over again.

One thing is clear: I'm not going to get any more information than I already have out of Jek. If I keep badgering him on the subject, I'm only going to wind up pushing him away again. Jek knows he can talk to me, knows I won't judge him, whatever is going on. When he's ready to confide in me, he'll find me. In the meantime, I do have another option—check back in with the town gossip and see if I can find out anything more about Hyde. Digging around in people's personal secrets makes me feel gross, but with Jek stonewalling me, I don't know what else to do.

I try not to think about the way I'm compromising my principles as I approach Alexis Dupuy and Olivia Bradley a couple of weeks later in the cafeteria. These two are always in everyone's business, so I figure they're a good place to start. And while I may not be BFFs with them, Alexis does owe me a favor.

"You still backing up all your files every night, like I told you to?" This is my opening gambit: a not-so-subtle reminder to Alexis of how I helped her out in her time of need.

"You're my savior, Lulu," she replies. She turns to Olivia. "The hard drive on my laptop died the week before finals last year. I thought my life was over, but Lulu worked her magic and somehow recovered all my data. Hey, maybe she can help with your problem, too."

Sighing inwardly, I turn a politely inquisitive gaze to Olivia.

"My parents," she says with a groan. "They installed some nanny software on my computer, so they see everything I do online. Can you help me get around it?"

"Sure," I say. "No problem." At that point, the conversation stalls out as Olivia and Alexis stare at me expectantly, and I try to think of a smooth way to segue into my own request.

"So, um… I have a question," I say finally, just to get past the awkwardness.

"Oh, my God," says Alexis. "It's about Javier, isn't it? Are you guys getting back together?"

I sigh inwardly. Javier and I only dated for about a minute last year, but he's asked me out like a dozen times since we broke up. He's a perfectly nice guy, but he got way too serious too quickly, and it spooked me. I wasn't up for any big commitment.

"Nothing about that," I tell them. "Actually, I was looking for Hyde."

The two exchange a meaningful look and start to giggle. "Who isn't?" says Olivia.

"Yeah," Alexis agrees, "you're going to have plenty of competition there."

I want to tell them it's not what they're thinking, but it's not like I want to get into the real reason why I'm looking for him. Maybe it's best to let them draw their own conclusions.

I shrug noncommittally. "What do you guys know about him?"

Olivia giggles. "I know what Tanya did with him last Sunday, but she swore me to secrecy."

"I don't know," says Alexis, more serious than her friend. "I'd stay away from him. I've heard some seriously sketchy shit about that guy."

"Like what?" I ask, trying not to sound too eager.

"That he's a real creep—he'll invite people over to his place to watch a movie, and then it turns out to be all these fucked-up torture videos. And not like, scenes from movies—real people being legit tortured. It really freaked some people out."

"Oh, come on," says Olivia. "How can you tell for sure

that they're real? And where would he even get something like that?"

"You can find anything online," Alexis assures her knowledgeably. "But the really creepy rumor is that he makes them himself—that he finds people in the city and films them torturing each other. Then he pays them off to keep quiet. That is, the ones who survive."

Olivia shakes her head. "Who told you that? Someone was messing with you."

They bicker back and forth a bit, but I can tell I'm not going to get anything more useful out of them. Clearly neither of them knows Hyde well, and it's impossible to tell whether their stories have even a grain of truth to them, or if it's just the lurid bullshit people always make up about the "new guy."

"Do you guys know who he hangs out with?" I ask. Maybe they can at least get me closer to the source. "I never see him around school."

Alexis laughs. "Of course you don't. He doesn't go here."

"What do you mean? There's no other high school for miles around."

"I mean, he doesn't go to *school*," she elaborates. "I heard he's a dropout who ran away from home."

"No," Olivia corrects her. "Someone told me he got kicked out of boarding school."

"Then what does he do all day?" I interject before they can dig into their disagreement. "Does he have a job?"

Alexis shrugs, and Olivia is apparently just as uninformed.

"I've never seen him around anywhere," she says. "Only at the keggers."

Of course. I hate those dumb parties, but it makes sense that they're the most likely place to find Hyde and his circle.

"Any idea where the party is this weekend?"

"Andrew Chang's," says Olivia. "His parents are at a conference or something."

I make a mental note of it and take my leave. I don't relish the idea of going to another one of these massive house parties, but right now this is my best shot at getting the information I'm looking for.

Friday night I put on a little lipstick and head over to Andrew's house. These keggers are always overcrowded to the point of claustrophobia, so I'm a little worried whether I'll even be able to spot Hyde. I start by making the rounds of some smaller lounge areas, chatting with some casual friends, though my mind keeps wandering from the conversations. I make my excuses and keep moving from room to room, more focused on my mission than on the drunken antics around me, but the minute I enter a smaller sitting area furnished with leather couches and a massive entertainment center, I know he's here. I can't quite explain it—before I even see him, it's like there's a change in the air pressure that gives me the same creeping chill I felt the last couple of times I met him. Finally I spot him lounging on the couch, partially obscured by people leaning over and around him cooing appreciatively at the device in his lap.

"Wow," says Melanie Hooper, pressing up close against his arm. "You got the rose gold finish."

"Sure, but that's just the packaging," says Jason Donovan, who's in my electrical engineering class. "Can it track RFID?"

A football bro named Alex Spade leans across the others. "Let me see," he says, making a grab for it. Hyde snatches the object out of his grasp.

"See with your eyes, sweetheart," he murmurs, giving Alex a once-over. "Unless you want to ask me nicely."

Typical. In this town, I guess I shouldn't be surprised that people are obsessed with fancy gadgets: the London Chem brats love to one-up each other with their electronics. Although it's a little strange because I didn't think Hyde was one of those rich kids. I'm pretty sure I'd know if his parents were associated with London Chem at all, and the fact that he's been borrowing money from Jek suggests that he isn't swimming in the stuff himself. So what's he doing with this fancy new phone? Hailee mentioned that he was dealing for Jek these days… I wonder if this means business is especially good. Or if Hyde's been helping himself to more than his cut, which doesn't seem unlikely, given everything I've seen.

Hyde must sense my attention on him because he looks up at me before I can decide what to do next. He doesn't say anything—his expression doesn't even shift, but something in his eyes glitters so coldly that it almost makes me lose my breath. That same uneasy feeling I had when I entered the room seems magnified twenty times by having his black eyes fixed on me, and for a moment I'm frozen to the spot. When I do manage to tear my eyes away from his, I've completely forgotten about my mission to learn more about Hyde—all I want to do is get out of there as quickly as possible.

My first instinct is to leave the party and head straight for my car, but once I'm out of the room, my head clears and I manage to pull myself together. I feel like an idiot, fleeing from the very person I came here to find. What I need is a minute to regroup, prepare myself, and then I can go back in there. In the meantime, I head into the kitchen, hoping a cold drink will soothe my nerves.

In the corner, a couple is making out noisily against a counter, but I ignore them in favor of fixing myself a screwdriver.

"Lulu!"

I recognize the voice immediately and can't help cringing a bit.

"Camila," I say, turning toward the couple and trying to manage a convincing smile. She steps forward and gives me a big hug, even though it's only been a matter of hours since we saw each other in school. A couple of drinks have made her more effusive than normal.

"It's so good to see you!" she coos. "Oh, but Jek's not here. I haven't seen him all night, if you're looking for him."

"I know," I snap back before I can stop myself. "Why would I be looking for him?"

I hear the defensiveness in my voice and wince. Given my history, it's not exactly surprising that Camila would assume I'm looking for Jek, but it's not like he's the only reason I ever leave my house.

"I'm sorry," I tell her, still feeling a little rattled. "I just need to get some air."

I leave her in the kitchen and make my way to the porch, desperate to get away from the crowds. I remember now why I never go to these things. Too many people I know, who know me. Too many people watching, talking, spreading rumors. No one has any secrets in this town.

Outside, the misty night air makes everything look a little fuzzy around the edges, and the lights of the commercial strip outside town are nothing more than colorful blotches on the horizon. Ignoring the chill and the damp, I take a deep breath and try to get a hold of myself.

"If you're not looking for Jek," comes a low, rasping voice behind me, "then who are you looking for?"

I spin around and look directly at Hyde. He's leaning casually against the sliding door, his hands tucked into his pockets.

"Who says I was looking for anyone?" I spit back, but from his expression, he knows I'm on the defensive. I hardly know this guy, so why does it feel like he can read me so well? "Can't a girl go to a party without an ulterior motive?"

Hyde licks his lips and smiles.

"Some girls," he says. "But you don't normally show up to

these things." He pushes back from the door and takes a step toward me, removing his hands from his pockets.

"How would you know?"

He takes another prowling step toward me. I can smell him now: that strange, off-putting citrus scent, pleasantly sweet but with a slightly bitter undercurrent.

"Because," he says, "I do come to these things. And I don't see you."

My grip tightens on the rail behind me. "You're taking an awful lot of interest in my comings and goings, considering we've only spoken once."

"Oh, Lulu," he murmurs, crowding me up against the porch rail. "I could be wrong, but I think you've taken an interest in me, too."

I can't help it—my cheeks burn at the comment. This is all backward. I was supposed to be the one in control of this encounter. I was going to dig up some way to manipulate Hyde into leaving my friend alone. But somehow it feels like he knows my every move before I make it.

I look up into his face, only inches from mine now. I remember his hair as dark, but in this light I see that it's threaded with strands of gold and copper. His complexion, too, is paler than I remembered, with a smattering of freckles I didn't notice before. The one thing I definitely haven't forgotten is his eyes—so intensely black, they seem to be all pupil.

"There's something about you," I say, and I realize my voice has slipped into a whisper. "I can't place it. Something so—"

"Yes?" he says, his breath steaming between us. He feels so close I can hardly breathe.

"Familiar."

Hyde doesn't move but I sense his muscles stiffen, and he looks at me with an unreadable expression.

Alex Spade comes careening out of the house brandishing Jason Donovan's T-shirt, breaking the stillness. He fumbles and slips on the wooden porch, slippery with mist, and breaks his fall against Hyde's back.

For a moment, Hyde is forced up against me, the heat from his body a shocking contrast to the cold air. Less than a breath later, Hyde has reared back and turned on Alex, one fist gripping the front of his shirt, the other battering against his ribs and stomach. Hyde's face is white with rage, and Alex looks too surprised to even register what is happening.

"Wait," I manage to shout. "Stop."

But he doesn't. Hyde delivers two more solid punches before grappling Alex off the porch and into the yard. Alex manages to land a couple of swings of his own, but it barely slows Hyde down. He shoves Alex onto the wet grass, straddles him and starts beating him with both fists, all before anyone else at the party has even made it outside.

"Stop him," I shriek, louder this time. "Someone call the cops!" Finally people start to swarm out of the party. Hyde's hands are now around Alex's throat. He looks crazed and furious, and the thought comes to me not as a fear, but a fact: *He's going to kill him.*

At last a couple of the guys break free of shocked paralysis and step forward to wrestle Hyde away from his victim. But it's only when the distant sound of police sirens starts up that Hyde seems to come back to himself and let the guy go, leaving him gasping and sputtering. For a second, Hyde stands there in the yard, sweaty and shaking with adrenaline, then he breaks out running toward the empty fields and disappears in the mist.

Things move quickly after that. With the cops on their way, no one really wants to risk being reported to their parents. The party pretty much evaporates within the next couple of minutes, and I follow the sea of people out only to find myself shivering next to Camila, watching the *swoop swoop* of red-and-blue lights.

"God," I say, still thinking about the scene in on the lawn. "What a psycho. I don't know how he even gets invited to these things."

Camila shrugs. "Hyde's got a temper. Most people know how to avoid it."

"Yeah, well, I'm guessing he's worn out his welcome with that move. Even if the cops don't pick him up for assault, no one's going to want him around now."

Camila only "hmms" in response, so I pull out my car keys. "Want a ride home?"

She hesitates a second, then checks her phone. "Nah," she says. "I'm good."

"You have plans with that guy you were hooking up with?"

She shrugs, a little embarrassed. "Maybe, I don't know. There's a thing after this, so we're probably headed over there."

I shake my head, laughing a little in amazement. "This crazy town. Some guy nearly gets killed right in front of us, and all anyone can think about is where they can go to get fucked up next."

"Yeah, well, not everyone keeps as strict a bedtime as you, Lulu," Camila teases.

I make a face, but the truth is, I'm still feeling keyed up from the fight.

"Where is it?" I ask on a whim.

"Where's what?" Camila is distracted by her phone again.

I roll my eyes. "The after-party."

She looks up. "Why? You don't want to go, do you?" She's suddenly nervous, and I feel like the mom who just invited herself along on her daughter's night out.

"What, is it like super exclusive or something?" My tone is joking but I can't help feeling slightly hurt. It's true that I don't hit London's nightlife as hard as some people, but that's always been by choice. It never occurred to me that people might not *want* me at their parties.

"No, it's...it's not that," says Camila quickly. "It's just... you know...not your scene."

"My scene?"

"You might not be comfortable. The parties get pretty wild." She gestures vaguely.

"I go to wild parties!"

But Camila is adamant. "Really wild, I mean. Trust me, Lulu—you don't want anything to do with these parties."

I stare at her. "You think I'm a prude," I say, comprehension dawning. "Jesus Christ, Camila. I may not go out every night, but I'm not some goody-goody. Sex and drugs don't shock me."

Camila gives me a pitying look, but before she can answer, we're both startled by a car horn off to the right.

"That's my ride," she says. She gives me a peck on the cheek and then she's gone.

CHAPTER

I'm in my room the following morning, working on rooting my uncle's phone to clear room on it for his favorite apps, when I get a text from Camila—she's inviting me out to brunch at the Double Dutch, a greasy diner just outside town that's equally popular with truckers and teens. She must feel bad about blowing me off last night, and while I'm still a little peeved, pancakes on her dime will go a long way toward soothing my ruffled feathers.

An icy rain has slicked the roads so I get there a little late, but Camila has gone ahead and ordered for me—the waiter is just setting down my favorite cinnamon pancakes as I walk in. The place is busy this morning, and I spot at least a few people from the party last night, medicating their hangovers with lavish servings of bacon. I make my way across the room toward Camila, dodging harried servers and pushed-out chairs the whole way.

"So?" I begin, sliding into the booth across ripped vinyl. I have to raise my voice a little to compete with the ice pellets rattling the windows. "How was it?"

"How was what?" Camila replies, but even she's aware of how unconvincing she is. I give her a look. "It was…fine," she admits. "Fun." She huffs a breath. "You know, I wasn't trying to ditch you. I swear. It's just that Hyde's parties are kind of an acquired taste, and—"

"Wait, *Hyde*?" I say. "That's who threw the after-party?"

Camila bites her lip. "Stupid hangover," she mutters. "Always kills my brain-to-mouth filter…"

"How could you, Camila? Right after you watched him almost strangle someone to death?"

"See? This is why I didn't want to tell you. You always overreact."

I lean back in my seat, annoyed. I can feel myself being boxed into playing the prude again, and I'm not in the mood. I force myself to take a calming breath. "Fine," I say. "Explain it to me, then."

"Explain what?"

"Hyde's appeal. From everything I've heard, this guy seems like a sketchy creep. But you said he's an acquired taste. So… help me acquire it."

Camila gives me an exasperated look. "I don't know, Lulu," she says. "Maybe people are curious. Not everyone can be satisfied by sexless relationships with their childhood BFF, you know," she adds pointedly.

"What's that supposed to mean?"

"Nothing," she says, holding up an appeasing hand. "Nothing. I'm just saying, when it comes to relationships, some people are looking for safety and comfort." She nods delicately in my direction. "And other people want a little…excitement. Danger." Camila leans in close with a wicked smile. "And maybe they want to know just what it was that shocked Natalie Martinez so bad."

I purse my lips and mull this in silence. My first impulse is to roll my eyes at the predictability of humanity—of course they all want to satisfy their prurient curiosity about Hyde's sexual habits. But, then again…isn't this exactly what I was looking for? I went to that kegger because I wanted dirt on Hyde. I wanted to know what his game is, what makes him tick, so I can better understand the pull he has over Jek. So I can get him to leave Jek alone.

Cautiously, I lean forward in my seat.

"All right," I say. "What is it? What exactly is Hyde's big kinky secret?"

Camila grins and drops her voice. "That's just the thing—it's not one kink. Everyone's story is different. This kid's got a new perversity for every night of the week, and double that on Sundays. The filthy imagination on that guy…" She leans back in her seat and lets out a low whistle. "You have to wonder how deep the depravity goes."

I stare at her for a minute, turning this information over in my head. "Nonsense," I say at last, crumpling my napkin into my plate.

"What do you mean, *nonsense*?"

"This is typical gossip mill stuff. Each story is different because none of them actually slept with him. They're all just making up the craziest thing they can think of, and spreading it around to boost their own image."

"It's not just gossip, Lulu."

"How can you be so sure?"

Camila raises her eyebrows as she sips her coffee. It takes me a minute, but I've known Camila long enough to pick up on her meaning.

"You," I say, and I can feel my eyes getting bigger in spite of myself. "You had sex with *Hyde*?"

Camila shrugs and pushes a bit of pancake through her syrup. "I thought the same thing you did. And what do they teach us here except to be scientists? It was vital to run my own experiment, collect some data."

"But that was dangerous and...and not very smart, Camila." I can hear the Goody Two-shoes squeak in my voice even as I say it, but I don't care about my image right now. "The guy sounds like a complete psycho. What if he had hurt you? Or drugged you? What if he dumped your body somewhere and left you for dead?"

Camila drops her fork in her plate. "Relax, will you? I'm

fine. I knew what I was getting into, and Hyde…well, let's just say I'm not disappointed."

I raise my eyebrows. "Meaning?"

Camila blushes. And Camila *never* blushes.

"Forget it," I say. "I don't want to know. Christ… So where do these parties happen?"

"He's got a place over at Hidden Ponds," says Camila, gesturing to the waitress for more coffee.

"Hidden Ponds. You mean that trailer park outside town?"

"The one and only."

"Wow," I marvel. "So Hyde is *actual* trailer trash."

"Geez, Lu," says Camila, narrowing her eyes at me. "You're awfully quick to judge the guy. You don't even know him."

"Yeah? And how well do *you* know him?"

"What do you mean?"

"I mean…who the hell *is* this guy? What is his story? He hangs out with a bunch of high school kids and seems to be our age, but he lives alone and he's not enrolled in school. He's got cash for the hottest new phone on the market, but he lives in a trailer. Where are his parents? Do they live in town, too? Where did he come from, and how did he wind up here? As far as I can tell, he's got no ties to anyone in town. Hell, I can't even figure out his race—you said he was Asian, Maia figured him for white and Puloma thinks he might be black. Do you even know if Hyde is his first or last name?"

Camila shrugs, indifferent. "What does any of that stuff matter?" she says. "I thought you hated gossip, and now you're the one spreading rumors. So I don't know his ethnicity, or what his parents do for a living... I don't care about that. He throws great parties, and he isn't afraid to get a little wild. That's all I need to know. Why are you so interested in all this superficial shit?"

I lean back and cross my arms defensively, feeling called out. Which is totally unfair—it's not like I *judge* people on their race, or where they live, or who their parents are. I don't even know why I'm ranting about this stuff, except that I don't like Hyde and I don't want other people to like him, either.

"Come on, Lu," says Camila gently after watching me stew for a minute. "Don't be jealous. Just forget about Hyde, okay? Believe me, you don't want anything to do with his kinds of parties."

"Why?" I say, feeling rebellious the way I always did when we were kids and Camila tried to boss me around. "Because I'm too innocent? If these parties are so wild and dangerous, why do you go to them?"

Camila puts her coffee down and looks at me seriously. "Really, Lulu? You know why. I graduate this year. And what happens to me then?"

I shift uncomfortably and look down at my plate. It's something we never talk about—what our plans are when we're done with high school. It's too awkward to acknowledge that we're on different paths. "You could go to college," I offer without much confidence. "Or move to the city."

Camila shakes her head. "My grades are crap, and there's

no money for anything like that. I'm going to work for the family, here in town."

I raise my eyes to hers and see something terrible in them: fear. No, not fear—dread. Dread of the inevitable, because we both know what working for the family business means. It's only a matter of time before Camila is sick like Carlos—a ghost of the person she is now. No wonder she wants to squeeze as much pleasure as she can out of life, while she has the chance.

Camila puts out one hand and rests it over my own. "That's not going to happen to you, Lulu," she says softly. "You get good grades, and you're in all those smarty-pants science classes. You're going to get a scholarship and get out of this town. Make us all proud." She squeezes my hand. "You can't let anything distract you from that."

"Fine," I say, pulling my hand away. I'm not convinced, but I don't want to have this argument with her. Still, there's one more piece of info I need, though I'm afraid of the answer. I take a deep breath. "About these parties…"

"Yeah?"

"Does Jek go to them?"

Camila stares out the grimy, rain-streaked window, considering. "No," she says. "Not that I can remember. I'm pretty sure I've never seen him at one."

I let out the breath. So there's that at least. If Jek hasn't been attending Hyde's wild orgy parties, then maybe Jek hasn't changed as much as I'd feared. But if Jek isn't into that kind of stuff, why is he friends with Hyde at all? Why is Jek giving him money and a key to his house? Why is he lying for him and protecting him? Hailee said they were business partners, but there must be more to it than that. Whenever Hyde comes up, Jek seems…jumpy. Nervous, even. Whatever the truth of their relationship, there's something sinister about Hyde's power over him. I know it.

I'm still turning these thoughts over later that day as I drive around town through a mucky drizzle, running a few errands for my uncle. I have to stop at his feed store just outside town to look at their computer system—apparently the inventory database is all out of whack—but when I pass through the door I hear Jek's voice, almost like I was thinking so hard that my imagination conjured him from thin air. This is a small town, so it's not really surprising that I would run into someone I know as I do my errands, but it's still a bit weird, given that he's not part of the farming community.

What's even weirder is that he seems to be having some kind of argument with the cashier, Manuel, another one of my cousins.

"No, I don't want the smaller size. I told you, I'm going to need all of it," Jek is saying, gesturing at an industrial-size jug of biochemical pesticide in a nearby display.

"What exactly are you trying to do with it?" Manuel counters. "Because a little of this stuff goes a long way. The EPA's ignoring it, but you could get really sick if you use too much. My dad and my aunt both—"

Jek cuts him off.

"It's none of your business, all right? What's it to you what I'm doing with it?"

I step over to the counter.

"Jek?" I say, getting his attention. "Is everything okay?"

I give Manuel a nod of greeting, and he takes the hint and wanders off. I turn back toward Jek, who looks nervous and a bit guilty. We've texted and messaged a few times in the past couple of weeks, but I haven't actually seen him in a while. I notice that he has some bruising on his jaw and his lip is scabbed.

"What happened to you?" I ask.

"What?" he says. Following my sight line, he lifts a hand and gently passes it over the bruise. "Oh, that. It's nothing. You should see the other guy."

I stare at him, speechless. Jek, in a fight? He's never been the type in all the time I've known him. Instantly my mind goes to Hyde. Has Jek been picking up more of Hyde's bad habits? Or, worse, is that psycho the one who hit him? The thought makes me sick to my stomach.

"Relax, Lu," he says, hauling the jug of biopesticide up onto the counter. "It was a cabinet door. Opened it right into my face. I shouldn't be trusted with such complex machinery before I've had coffee."

I swipe at his arm disapprovingly. "Not funny, Jek." As he

peers around, probably looking for Manuel, I look him over, trying to decide which of his stories to believe. Only then do I notice that his eyes are bloodshot and his skin has a yellowish tint. "Did you ever get that coffee? You look like you could use a cup."

"Yeah, I'm fine," he says, rubbing his hand over his face. He still looks exhausted. "Just…rough night."

I nod, but I can't help wondering if there's more going on. If he and Hyde are fighting, maybe now is a good time to press Jek to see the dangerous disadvantages of this new friendship.

"Where are you headed after this?" I ask as Manuel returns to ring him up.

Jek looks away as he fumbles with his wallet. "Just home. Why?"

"If you're not doing anything tonight, maybe we can grab some food," I suggest. He hesitates a moment. "My treat," I add with what I hope is a disarming smile.

Jek raises an eyebrow. "You're inviting me to dinner on a Saturday night?"

Put that way, it sounds like a date. Is that what he's insinuating? Or is he totally deaf to such conventions? With Jek, it's always hard to tell.

"I—I didn't mean—" I find myself stuttering in reply. "I'm not trying—I just meant, you know…dinner. Between friends."

Jek continues to look intently at me, but doesn't say anything to stop my hopeless babbling.

"I'm not suggesting anything more than that, I swear."

Jek nods at that and puts his wallet away. "Right," he says cautiously.

"Look, I'm worried about you, okay? I just want to check in, find out how you're doing. And what's going on with…"

Jek tenses up. "With what?" he says as he starts for the door with the jug in his arms.

I follow and hold the door for him. "Hyde," I say as he steps out into the rain. "Look, Jek, I know you don't want to talk about it, but from everything I've seen, the guy's a total creep. And if he's hurting you in some way, or—"

Jek puts the jug in the back of his mom's car and slams the door closed. "This again?" he says, turning to me. "You never used to be like this, Lu. What ever happened to your philosophy of live and let live? Of respecting people's privacy? Is your life so boring that you have to stick your nose into everyone else's?" He wipes the rain from his face with his sleeve and stares down at a growing puddle in the gravel. "I'm sorry," he tries, more gently this time. He looks up at me, squinting through the rain. "I know you're just trying to look out for me. But I don't remember needing your permission to make new friends."

"Fine," I say, backing off a little so he can open his car door. "You're right. You're free to be friends with whoever you want. But if you're such good friends, how come you're never at Hyde's parties?"

Jek gives me a sharp look. He shuts the door again without getting in. "How do you know about Hyde's parties?"

"So you've been to them?"

"I didn't say that." He takes a deep breath and leans back against the car. "No," he says. "I don't go Hyde's parties. And neither should you. Shit, Lulu...you have to promise me. If Hyde ever invites you to one of those parties, don't go."

"How do you know he hasn't already?"

"Just don't, okay?"

"What the hell, Jek? So I'm not supposed to be concerned about your shady new friends, but it's fine for you to tell me who I can see, where I can go? Nice double standard there."

He shakes his head, scattering raindrops on his shoulders. "That's not what I—"

"I don't get it," I interrupt. "Last time we talked, you told me that I should look out for Hyde and do whatever favors he asks. That I should help him. That he wasn't as bad as his reputation. Now you're telling me to stay the hell away from his parties, acting like you don't trust him. Which is it? Are you his friend or not?"

Jek flops his arms in frustration. "I'm his friend, yeah. But...look, Lu, you don't belong at those parties. Neither of us does."

"That's pretty weird advice coming from you. Have you conveniently forgotten about the parties *you* throw? Some outsiders would call those pretty debauched."

Jek looks guilty, and glances around to see if anyone is listening, but no one else is foolish enough to be hanging around the parking lot in the rain.

"How much worse could Hyde's parties really be?" I ask.

"Worse," says Jek firmly. "Just trust me, Lu. It wouldn't be safe for you."

I roll my eyes. "You know what, Jek?" I tell him, heading back over to my own car. "You're right. It's none of my business what you do or who you're friends with. Thanks for making me realize how patronizing I sounded. Maybe we can just agree to back off each other's personal lives and let us both make our own decisions."

Jek doesn't exactly look happy with this resolution, but I have said all I care to on the subject, so I get in my car and drive off, completely forgetting about Carlos's database bug.

CHAPTER

Later that night I'm still annoyed, though my fury has been tempered with regret that I let my conversation with Jek turn into a fight again. It seems like every time I see him these days, we wind up pissing each other off.

It would have been nice to get dinner with him tonight, maybe go back to his place afterward. Not like a date, just to watch a movie or something. Talk. Mess around in his lab, like we used to when we were kids…

Camila's offhand comment from lunch pops into my head, interrupting this fantasy. *Not everyone is satisfied by sexless friendships with their childhood BFF.* I was offended at the time, but now I wonder if that isn't a fair assessment of my situation. Is it true that I only like Jek because he feels comfortable and familiar? That I'm afraid of what might happen if I hooked up with someone who actually wants me?

I'm not exactly satisfied by my relationship with Jek, but it feels *safe*. Stable. Predictable. What am I missing out on by never taking any risks? Exploring other possibilities?

I flop back on my bed and stare at my dark, silent phone. Unfortunately, the problem with being a homebody with a fixation on your best friend is that when you suddenly realize you want to branch out and try something new, everyone's already made plans without you.

Or worse yet, I've developed such a reputation as a Goody Two-shoes that I'm not even wanted at the cool parties. Camila made that pretty clear last night. Unlike Jek, I don't get to choose whether to attend or not. I just have to sit at home moping on a Saturday night, while everyone else gets all the excitement.

My phone buzzes and almost gives me a heart attack. It's 1:15 a.m. Who would text at this hour?

I check the text. It's nothing but an address in the Hidden Ponds trailer park.

My heart thumps in my chest.

Who is this? I text back.

The response is almost instant.

Hyde.

What the hell? I sit up in my bed and text back.

How did you get my #?

The reply comes a few seconds later.

Is it a secret? Then: Come over.

I stare at the text for a minute, wondering why the words seem to blur before my eyes. Then I realize my hand is shaking. I drop my phone on the bed as if it might bite me, and try not to imagine the possibility that Hyde can read my mind.

Five minutes later, I'm still staring uncertainly at my phone. Hyde hasn't texted again. Why did he text me? We're not friends. We're not really even acquaintances. If anything, Hyde has every reason to hate my guts. So why would he seek out my number? Why now?

He must be having one of his parties…the ones that half an hour ago I was so desperate to be invited to.

I should go. Just to show Jek that he doesn't get to tell me where to go, who to hang out with. To show Camila, too, that I'm not such an innocent. I can be as wild as any of them.

Except… Camila and Jek were both just looking out for me, weren't they? Last night I saw exactly how dangerous Hyde can be. Why would I want anything to do with that? I don't have anything to prove.

With sudden inspiration, I pick up my phone. If Jek's so adamant that I not hang out with Hyde, he can hang out with me instead. I don't care if Jek is the "safe" option—I'd rather see him than Hyde anyway, and he's always up at this hour.

Hey. Sorry I blew up this afternoon. Wanna hang out, watch a movie?

A minute or two passes before he texts back.

Busy.

I growl in annoyance. That's a pretty terse blow off, even for Jek. What's he busy with at this hour? Unless…

You're at Hyde's, aren't you? Hypocrite.

No, he texts back instantly. Busy.

I throw my phone at the laundry pile and roll over to stare at the wall. He's lying. He's with Hyde. Why is he lying? What does he do with Hyde that he wants to keep me away from? Or, if he's not lying, what's he up to that he can't just tell me? We used to tell each other everything.

The buzz of my cell phone jolts me awake from deeply disturbing dreams. I'm still in my clothes, with a lamp on, and it's…4:10 a.m. What the hell? I dig into the laundry pile and find my phone. It's Jek again.

Hey. You should go to Hyde's party.

I stare at it in confusion, wondering if I'm still half asleep. But a minute later, it still reads the same. Jek…is telling me to go to Hyde's party…at 4:00 a.m.

Why? Are you there?

No, he texts back instantly. That's even weirder.

Another text comes fast on its heels.

Because Hyde wants to fuck you.

I fumble a moment but manage not to drop my phone.

Is this some kind of prank?

The next text is disgusting. So disgusting I shut off my phone and crawl back into bed, the covers up over my ears, my fingers trembling, my skin burning. Jek has never…he would never say something like that. Not to me. Not to anyone. I can't even picture him thinking it. What the hell is going on?

I shut my eyes tight and try to get back to sleep, but I can't. I can't stop thinking about Jek and why he would text me that, and about Hyde, and whether Hyde really said anything about me to Jek, and all the things Camila told me about Hyde and what he does.

Hyde put Jek up to this, somehow. Or got him drunk or high enough to…but even that seems far-fetched. My brain keeps coming back to the image of Hyde standing in front of Jek's door, holding Jek's phone in his hand. But that was ages ago, and Jek definitely got his phone back since then. But is it so unlikely that Hyde might have swiped it again? Maybe Jek was there earlier and left it behind. Maybe Hyde took it from him. Maybe Jek's passed out or is disoriented, and Hyde thinks it's all a big joke.

I open my eyes and look at the clock. 4:33 a.m.

Jek could be in trouble. But he told me to mind my own business. But that was before he texted me at 4:00 a.m., instructing me to have sex with his friend. Which effectively makes this my business, I think. Whether or not Jek really sent that text.

I get up and grab my car keys.

Hidden Ponds is outside London city limits, a short drive along the town's commercial strip past the multiplex, the chain restaurants and big-box stores, their signs all blazing through the darkness even at this hour of night. Farther on, the big-boxes turn smaller, their illuminated signs dimmer and plainer, and tucked among the pawn shops and palm readers is the easy-to-miss turnoff for the trailer park.

The park itself is hardly lit at this time of night, and I have to creep through to read the numbers pinned haphazardly to aluminum walls. At last I find the one I'm looking for: a dingy single-wide with a slick muddy patch where the front yard should be. Maybe it does make me judgmental like Camila said, but I still can't believe all those rich London Chem brats are showing up to parties at a dump like this.

Not that it seems like much of a party—other than a few dim lights in the windows, it doesn't look like there's much going on inside. Through the door, I can hear the low thump of music and not much else. But then, it is pretty late. I'm starting to feel like an idiot for coming at all—at this hour, everyone has surely gone home, and Hyde is probably passed out in bed.

I'm about ready to turn around and head back to my car when the door swings open to reveal Hailee, her face streaked with running mascara. I'm stunned into silence at the sight, and so is she it seems. Then my shock shifts into annoyance: Is *everyone* I know hanging out with Hyde behind my back?

"Lulu?" says Hailee, squinting out into the darkness. "What are you doing here? I didn't think this was your scene."

"Oh, um…" I sputter. "I was looking for Jek, actually. Do you know if he was here? Earlier, I mean? I just…" I trail off, flustered. If she asks me why I showed up to a party at four thirty in the morning looking for Jek, I really don't know what I'm going to say.

"Jek? Here?" Hailee looks puzzled by the question. In fact, she looks a little wobbly, her eyes hazy and disoriented. "I don't remember seeing him."

I step inside the doorway and wrap an arm around Hailee, surreptitiously glancing around the room. The cramped space is bathed in a blue half-light thanks to a large television screen propped against one wall. The sound on the TV is muted, and it takes me a moment to make sense of the grainy images flickering across its surface; when I recognize a close-up of flesh and wire and sharp metal, it reminds me of what

Alexis and Olivia told me about Hyde's home movies, and I look away with a shudder.

Around the TV, mismatched couches and cushions are shoved tightly into all the available space, and sprawled across them are various acquaintances of mine from school or around town, plus a few strangers. Some are passed out, some are watching the scene in the video unfold with dull, glassy eyes. And some of the human piles are…moving.

My mind isn't prepared to parse what I'm looking at, so I gently guide Hailee toward a kitchenette in the corner. It's none of my business, anyway.

"Are you all right?" I ask her as I fill a cup with water.

She gives a sort of hiccup-laugh-sob in reply, but she accepts the cup and takes a long drink.

"Am I all right?" she repeats when she's finished, as if bewildered by the question. "Not really," she says at last. "But I only got what was coming to me."

My chest tightens at her words, as I think about what Maia told me happened to Natalie. I'm almost afraid to hear what Hyde might have done to Hailee, but I can see that she needs someone to talk to right now.

"Hailee," I say firmly, trying to get her to focus, "what happened? Whatever he did to you, you can tell me."

She gives another bitter, choked laugh and shakes her head. "God, it's so embarrassing." I hand her a tissue from my purse, and she wipes fruitlessly at her smudged makeup. "Hyde and I were…" She breaks off, looking ashamed, but I urge her on. "We'd been fooling around a little, the past couple of weeks. Nothing serious. I know that's shitty of me, because of Lane, but..."

She glances at me guiltily. I almost can't believe what she's telling me, but at the same time I'm ashamed at my own naïveté. Hailee is here by herself, at Hyde's place. Based on what Camila told me this afternoon, that can only mean one thing. But how could she do that to Lane? Sweet, trusting Lane. I feel a ball of anger welling up in me on his behalf, but I tamp it down. Whatever is going on between Lane and Hailee, that obviously isn't the issue right now. Hailee and I have never been that close, but she needs a friend, and I'm the only one here for her. I nod at her to go on.

"I just figured what he didn't know wouldn't hurt him," she says with a helpless shrug. "And I was going to break it off, really I was, but then Lane said he was busy tonight, so I came here, thinking 'one last time.' Then I get here and find—"

Another sob cuts her short. A part of me is still shocked and angry that she would betray Lane, but I can't help being touched by the depth of her misery and self-recrimination. I pull her into what I hope is a comforting hug.

I'm still holding her when a door opens behind her and Hyde steps out. He's not wearing a shirt, and the top button of his jeans is poorly done up. I let go of Hailee and turn away, embarrassed, then feel even more embarrassed at my looking away. *Pull yourself together, Lupita.*

I lean into the counter as Hyde walks past, trying to make

myself invisible. But Hyde ignores me as he scans the various surfaces around the room. Finding what he came for, he moves smoothly toward a half-empty bottle of whiskey and tosses it from hand to hand as he heads back toward what must be the bedroom. It's then that he spots me.

"Well," he murmurs, running his eyes down my body, "if it isn't sweet little Lulu Gutierrez. I knew you couldn't stay away." Distantly I'm aware that Hailee has left me, though I couldn't say whether she's moved a few feet away or headed out the door. That would probably be the smartest move at this point, but I feel locked in place by Hyde's gaze. He puts the bottle down and lounges easily against the counter across from me, his hips canted forward. "So. Come to take me up on my offer? I'm afraid the bed's occupied at the moment, but I'm sure we can improvise."

I shake my head, both to reject his suggestion and clear the fuzz from my brain. "Th-that's not why I'm here."

"No?" he says, and arranges his face in an expression of mild disappointment. "Then what did you come for? Whatever you want, I'm sure it can be arranged." He's not leaning against the counter anymore. I realize he's moving closer to me, so slowly that I could easily slip away, if I wasn't frozen in place. He bows his head a little and his breath comes warm on my neck. "No rules here, Lulu," he says, his voice so low and rough I can feel it in my bones. "All you have to do is ask."

"I—" I begin, but my mouth is suddenly dry. The scent

of him, sweet and bitter like the pith of an orange, is almost overwhelming. I lick my lips and try again. "I want—"

A familiar voice breaks me from my trance. "Hyde? Are you coming back to bed?" I whip my head around to match the name to the voice and there it is. Lane is standing in the bedroom doorway, his eyelids heavy, his pupils big and dark, and a sheet clutched loosely around his hips. Hyde doesn't answer him. Instead, he lifts a hand to my cheek and gently nudges my face back toward his.

"Go on, Lu," he says softly. "Tell me what you want."

My heart is pounding and I swallow hard as I stare into his inky black eyes.

"I want to get out of here."

CHAPTER

It's still dark when I get home, though the black sky overhead is just beginning to shade into a damp gray over the London Chem buildings up on the hill. I close the front door behind me as quietly as I can, but before I can slip into my bedroom I hear a hiss from the living room.

"Where the hell have you been?"

With a sigh, I turn and follow the sound to its source. Mom is sitting in her usual chair, her laptop on her lap. Thanks to her work schedule, she can never sleep at night, even on the weekends. Over the past few years, I've gotten used to waking up on Sunday mornings just as she's getting ready to go to bed. I think she likes her video game mostly because it makes her feel less lonely during those dark hours. But now, with all the room lights out, the cheerful cartoon characters of her game cast her face in an eerie pink-and-green glow. I move to turn on a lamp, but she stops me.

"You'll wake Carlos," she says in a low voice as she nods toward a lump of blankets on the couch. "He was up coughing most of the night, he needs his rest."

She pauses her game and directs me back into the kitchen.

"What were you doing out in the middle of the night?" she demands, still keeping her voice down.

"Nothing, Mom," I insist. "Just…a party."

Mom flicks on the bright overhead light and pulls me under it as she examines my eyes.

"Were you driving drunk?" she asks fiercely. "High?"

"Mom, no!" I pull away from her. "Nothing like that."

She hums her disbelief.

"A party that gets out at 5:00 a.m., and no one is drinking or doing drugs? Lulu Gutierrez, you must think I was born yesterday. It was one of those London Chem brats, wasn't it? I don't like you going to those parties," she goes on before I can correct her. "They're not good for girls like you."

"Girls like me? What's that supposed to mean?"

She clucks her tongue at me. "You know what I mean. The rich boys invite the poor girls to their parties, act like you're all friends. Then they pass the girls around like toys. I watched it happen with your cousin, and I don't want to see it happen to you."

"You think *Camila* is anyone's toy?" I let out a sharp laugh at the thought. I don't know anyone more in control of what she wants than Camila. "What makes you think that she's not using those boys as much as they're using her?"

Mom presses her lips together. "Come on, Lulu…you're not so naïve. You need me to tell you the difference between them? The difference is, when all this is over, they're going to go off to fancy East Coast colleges, and Camila will still be here. And you'll be no better off if you do what she does."

I want to argue with her more and defend Camila, but a part of me recognizes some truth in what she's saying. I think not just of Camila, but Natalie, and Maia, and all the other girls I grew up with who now spend every weekend flirting with the London Chem brats on the kegger circuit. Everyone's having fun together now, but come graduation, I know it will be a different picture.

I collapse into a chair, having lost all energy for this fight.

"It wasn't like that," I explain weakly. "I wasn't doing anything. I was just looking for Jek."

She narrows her eyes, clearly not finding this story a big improvement over the other. "Did you find him?"

"No," I sigh. "Nobody had seen him."

"Yeah?" She sits down across from me. "Is that good or bad?"

"I don't know. I'm worried about him, Mama," I say, calling her by a term I haven't used since I was a baby. "I don't like the people he's hanging out with, and I think he might have gotten himself into trouble."

"Well, what do you expect? I told you that boy was just like the rest of them."

"Mom!"

She sighs. "Lulu, I know you care about him," she says more gently. "I know how it is. You think if you worry enough, if you take care of him and rescue him, that will make him yours. But you'll never keep a boy like that. Just look at me and your father."

"Jek is nothing like Dad," I say, offended.

"Sure," she says. "If you say so. But *I* was a lot like *you*. I thought I could tame him. I found him a job, gave him a family. And what did he do? Ran off to the city the first chance he got. Listen to me, Lulu." She leans across the table and puts out one hand. "You're never going to be the most important person in Jek's life, so you've got to be the most important person in *your* life. It's okay to worry, but don't mistake his future for yours."

I'm too tired to mount an argument, so I just nod blearily and give her my hand to squeeze.

"Good," she says. "Now, go get some sleep."

I go to my room and fall into bed just as the first rays of pink cut through my blinds. My last thought before sleep takes me is to hope I have a text from Jek when I wake up, explaining what happened.

Six hours later when I check my phone, there's nothing. I don't hear from him the rest of the day, either.

I'm not sure if I would trust a text from him at this point, anyway. Who knows where his phone is now, and who's controlling it? In the evening, I stop by his house but he doesn't answer his door, and Puloma says she hasn't seen him since the previous night. She tells me he's been in and out a lot lately, and she might have just missed him.

I don't really start to worry until Monday morning when he doesn't show up to school. No matter what he's gotten up to with his various extracurricular entertainments, Jek always shows up for his classes. The last time he missed a day was for food poisoning in eighth grade.

By second period, I'm flipping my phone in my hand, again considering whether or not to text him. Instead, when the bell rings at the end of my English class, I make an impulsive decision and duck out toward the parking lot, my palms sweating. I can't remember the last time I ditched a class—probably not since middle school, when I faked a stomachache to get out of a test I hadn't studied for. I try to look inconspicuous as I hurry through the parking lot toward my car, and I nearly jump out of my skin when I hear my name called. *The vice principal*, I realize with a sinking stomach. Dana Jones. The school district hired him a couple of years ago, in the wake of a scandal about how few teachers and administrators of color there were at London High. As a result, he's one of the few other black men in town besides Jek. I haven't dealt with him much since I mostly stay out of trouble, but he has a reputation for being firm but fair.

"What are you doing out here?" Mr. Jones calls as he approaches, sounding more curious than accusatory. "Don't you have class right now?"

"Yes," I admit. "I should be in PE, but..." I feel around

in my mouth for a believable lie, but nerves have driven every useful thought from my head. "I—I'm worried about a friend," I confess when nothing else comes to mind. "Jayesh Kapoor? He's not in school, and I can't get in touch with him..."

I'm positive that with every word I'm just sealing my doom, and Mr. Jones will send me back to class and give me detention, too. But as I watch his face, his large brown eyes look more sympathetic than strict.

"He's not answering his phone?"

"No, sir."

Mr. Jones doesn't speak, but instead gives me an appraising look.

"You're not in trouble much," he says, and I'm not sure if it's intended as a question. "Have you ever been sent to my office?"

"Only once," I say honestly. "I overslept and didn't have a note from my mom."

Mr. Jones gazes off toward the school, then turns back to me with a decisive tug to his tweed jacket.

"Go look after your friend," he says. "I'm sure gym class can survive one day without you."

I smile gratefully and rush off toward my car before he can change his mind. I kind of can't believe I just got permission to cut class, but I guess this is one of the privileges of being a "good girl" at school. I can't help thinking Mr. Jones would react differently if he knew I'm headed not to Jek's house, but back to the trailer park where I recently attended an orgy party. But I'm not going to be the one who tells him.

I'm not totally sure what I hope to find at Hyde's place—all I can figure is that if Hyde is controlling Jek's phone, he probably knows where he is. Or if not, maybe I can at least catch him off guard and get some real answers out of him. The night of the party, I freaked out and ran off without getting the information I went for, but I promise myself that I won't let that happen again. I want to know why Jek was texting me about Hyde, and why I haven't seen or heard from Jek since then. If Jek won't talk, maybe Hyde will.

I park my car across from the trailer and pull my coat tight around myself as I get out.

It's not actually raining, but the air feels heavy and pregnant with moisture and it leaves a rusty film on everything it touches. The trailer in particular manages to look even grimmer and more desolate than it did the other night.

I grit my teeth as I prepare myself for another conversation with Hyde, but before I've even crossed the street, the front door opens and out comes Jek. He's tugging a T-shirt on over his head, his backpack slung from one arm.

At first I'm too relieved to make sense of what I'm seeing. "Hey," I call out. "What are you doing here?"

The moment he hears my voice, Jek freezes. Even from across the street, I can see his whole body stiffen in alarm. After a moment, he recovers himself and manages a weak smile.

"Lulu," he says as I approach. "Shouldn't you be in school?"

"Shouldn't you?" I point out lightly, but one look at his face brings back the concern that had sent me searching for him in the first place. "Are you all right?" I ask. "You don't look so good."

Jek rubs a hand over his face. "It's nothing," he says. "Hangover."

I take a moment to process that, and as I do, the concern drains from my body and is replaced with something else entirely.

"You were with Hyde last night," I observe. "Getting fucked up." I squint at him through the mist. "On a school night. While I was worried sick about you."

"Yeah?" says Jek, looking about as pissed as I feel. "And who told you to worry?"

I don't even know what to say to that, but I don't get a chance to say anything before Jek is darting a look at his phone. "Shit," he says, "I better get going." He slips away from me and grabs his bike from where it's leaning unchained against the trailer.

"Jek, wait," I call after him. "Come on, I'll give you a ride." But he ignores me and takes off down the bike path.

I don't hear from Jek again all day, and I tell myself that's fine by me. Mom was right—Jek doesn't deserve my concern. While I was lying awake worrying about him, he was out doing God knows what with his new *friend*. Well, that's just fine. Let him have his fun; I have other things to worry about.

I'm in my room researching scholarship leads when I hear a gentle tapping at my door. Jek pushes it open as I look up.

"Your mom let me in," he explains. "Though she didn't look too happy about it…" He raises his eyebrows at me, his question unspoken.

I don't answer him, though I do sit up a bit from where I'm lounging in bed. He closes the door behind him and leans against it, as if he's not quite sure he's allowed in. Such a change from a few years ago, when he would have immediately started fiddling with the old laptops and cell phones scattered around my room, poking at my projects and asking me questions about them. But it's been ages since he came to my house—usually we meet at his, since he has so much more space and privacy. I've dreamed of him showing up here, a couple of times. In those scenarios, it was always a thrill to know he had sought me out. But after what I saw this morning, now I can't enjoy the experience.

"What are you doing here?" I say at last.

Jek swallows as he gauges my mood. "Apologizing?" he tries. "I don't know. Should I not? You seem—" he waves a hand in my direction, as if to encompass all the ways that I seem "—angry."

"Oh?" I say tightly. "And why would I be angry?"

"Um…" he says. "Right. Look." He pushes off from the door and moves aimlessly around the room, picking up an old MP3 player and fiddling with it a moment before setting it down again. "I just wanted to explain. About this morning."

"Why would it make me angry," I continue as if he hasn't

spoken, "that my best friend is running around with some weirdo pervert? That he gave said pervert my number? And then sexted me on behalf of the pervert? What part of that might I not be totally cool with? According to you?"

Jek sweeps over and perches on the edge of the bed near me. "That wasn't me," he says, his eyes pleading. "Come on, Lu…you know I'd never do that. You *know* me."

I turn my face away from him. "I'm not sure I do. Not anymore."

Jek sighs and squares his shoulders. "He had my phone," he explains. "Hyde's idea of a joke. You've got to see that."

I look down at my hands. "Yeah," I say, nodding slowly. "Yeah, I thought that. I was really sure that was the only explanation that made sense." I look up at him. "Until I saw you coming out of his house this morning, so embarrassed you couldn't even look at me. You looked guilty as hell, Jek. *And* you had your phone in your hand." Jek at least has the decency to look sheepish. "Now you come here and you want me to believe you had nothing to do with all that. You lied to me, Jek—you told me you never go to Hyde's parties, but you had to have been there."

Jek stands up from the bed and rounds on me. "So what if I was," he says. "What about you? If you were so offended by Hyde's text, why did you show up that night?"

"You think I went there to see Hyde?" I say. I can feel my voice and my temper rising. "I was *worried*," I tell him. "Worried about *you*."

"Of course you were," he says with bitter sarcasm. "Such a

hero! Saint Lulu who has never had an impure thought in her life. You're telling me you weren't curious? That you weren't desperately hoping to be invited to that party?"

"No," I say, standing to face him down. "I honestly don't care if I never see that piece of trailer trash again. But apparently I'm the *only* person Hyde doesn't have under his spell."

"What's that supposed to mean?"

I stare at him hard. "Jesus, Jek," I say, my voice lowered now against the snooping ears of my family. "Do you think I'm an idiot? The first time I met Hyde, he was coming out of your room. And this morning I see you coming out of his half-dressed. Ask anyone who's met Hyde, they'll tell you exactly what it means." Jek steps away from me but says nothing, so I go on. "I'm only embarrassed I didn't see it sooner. Hyde was never helping you with an experiment—that was just a story you told your mom to explain why you were spending the night together. Why else would you give him money, make excuses for him, practically let him get away with *murder*? I thought blackmail at first, or he was threatening you, but then why would you be so quick to defend him? To protect him, even when you know he's done awful things?"

Jek is shaking his head. "Lulu, no, you've got it all wrong. It's not—"

"Stop it," I say, putting out my hand. "I don't care, all right? You don't have to explain yourself to me. You don't owe me anything. I just thought..." I sit down on the bed and pull a pillow into my lap. "For God's sake, Jek. How long have we known each other? And in all that time, I have *never* judged you." No longer able to hide my hurt, I hear my voice cracking with emotion. "I never tried to change you. I've defended you more times than I can count. What made you think you had to hide this from me? You know I love you the way you are…however you are. And if you're—"

I don't get to finish the sentence before Jek pulls me to my feet and cuts me off with a kiss. A brief kiss, just a firm press of his lips against mine. I don't know what to make of it. I look up into his face, bewildered.

"Lu," he says, soft and serious, "I'm not sleeping with Hyde. I don't *want* Hyde." His eyes search my face. "Do you?"

"What?" I ask, still dazed from the unexpected kiss.

"Saturday night," he says, still holding me close. "You answered his text, you went to his house. What did you want from him? What were you looking for?"

"I told you, Jek—you. I went there looking for you."

He kisses me again, and this time it's slow and deep, his body pressed close to mine, his familiar smoky scent filling my senses. The kiss doesn't feel fake, it doesn't feel for show; it feels like everything I've wanted for such a very long time. At first, I don't know how to react—for all that I've dreamed of this moment, now that it's happening I'm mostly bewildered. Questions whirl through my mind but I can't focus on them. My blood feels warm and sluggish, almost as if I've been drugged, and for a moment or two, my brain shuts off and I surrender myself to physical sensation—the sweetness of his breath, the warmth of his body, the shivery effect of his fingers just under the hem of my shirt, slowly stroking my skin.

My mind snaps back into control and I break free, pushing him away.

"I can't," I say, retreating back to the bed. "God, I can't, Jek. There is so much you're not telling me, so much I don't understand." I look up at him, desperately wanting him to contradict me, but knowing he can't. "I've trusted you for so long, but I don't right now."

Jek looks down at me, his anguish mirroring mine. "I know," he says. He reaches out and touches my face. "And you're right. There are things I have to hide. I want to tell you…at times, I've come so close, you have no idea. And I will. I promise I will someday. Can that be enough for now?"

I turn my head away from him. "I don't know," I say. "I don't think so. I need to think."

"Okay," he says, as he moves toward the door. "I understand." He has his hand on the knob, but he doesn't turn it. After a moment, he turns around, and his eyes have a new light in them.

"Wait," he says. "Lulu. What if I got rid of him?"

I stare at him, not following.

"Hyde," he explains. "What if Hyde disappeared? Left town? That would solve everything."

"But why would he leave? He seems pretty happy here, Jek."

Jek dismisses my concern with a wave of his hand. "I told you before, Hyde is under my control." He's moving around the room now, a strange excitement taking hold of his body. "I can't explain, but the minute I tell him to get lost, he will."

I shake my head. "That's... Look, I don't know what kind of arrangement you have with the guy, but what you're saying kind of misses the point. I don't care what Hyde does, or where he does it. It's you I'm worried about, Jek. All these secrets... I feel like I don't know who you are anymore."

Jek turns sharply toward me, his face all but glowing with his new idea. "But don't you see? I'm the same as I ever was—it's Hyde who's the problem." He's looking at me with that mixture of elation and frustration he gets sometimes when he can't make me understand his latest scientific discovery. Then, as usual, he seems to give up on making me understand. "Don't worry about it, Lu," he says, taking my face in his hands again. "The important thing is that you were right. I should have listened to you before. I can get rid of Hyde, and I will."

He kisses me once more, quickly, and then he's out the door.

CHAPTER

For the rest of the night I am mostly numb, wondering at what I have done. I've been wanting Jek for so long, it feels like a part of me. Even when I dated other boys now and then, in the back of my head I was always wondering, hoping, wishing that Jek would show interest in me. I never really thought he would, and it never occurred to me that I might turn him away if he did.

Still, I can't help thinking I made the right choice.

I thought getting together with Jek would be simple, but everything between us is mixed-up and complicated. The Jek who came to my room last night wasn't the Jek I grew up with. His face, his eyes, his voice are all familiar, but the rest? I don't know, because he won't tell me. Ever since Hyde came to town, Jek hasn't been himself.

Of course, now he has promised to get rid of Hyde. Given what I know of him, Hyde doesn't seem like the type to ride off into the sunset just because someone asks him nicely. But I'll be happy enough if Jek just stops hanging around with him. The less Jek sees of Hyde, the better off he'll be.

As days go by, stretching into one week and then two, I hear less and less about Hyde. It seems he's lying low after all. It's hard to believe he's gone for good, but whatever Jek said to him must have worked. When I ask around about him, no one has anything new to add to the old stories, and Camila says he hasn't thrown any parties lately. In fact, it seems like no one's heard from him since the party I sort of crashed.

I know I should be happy, but…something about the whole situation makes me squirm. What exactly happened to Hyde? Did he mean so little to everyone that no one but me even wonders where he went? And what did Jek do to drive him off so suddenly and completely? Threaten Hyde with some kind of exposure? Pay him off? Beat him up, or worse? I try not to let my mind go down that path. I don't want to believe my best friend is capable of anything violent…but I can't deny the circumstances are strange.

But maybe strangest of all is how Jek's been acting toward me—like he's my boyfriend. Sweet, attentive, flirtatious, even, like he's *courting* me. It's wonderful…but somehow a little disconcerting, too.

On Tuesday it's blustery but not raining for once, so he talks me into a walk after school to the Twice-Loved Thrift Shop so we can poke around, looking at dusty old lab equipment. It's like old times—until I'm in the middle of spinning some silly story about how a Victorian phrenology bust wound up in a junk shop in rural Illinois and he slips his hand into mine. He definitely never did that before.

My sentence trails off as my brain stutters to a halt.

"What?" he says. He squeezes my fingers and casts a cautious look in my direction. "Is this not okay?"

"No," I say. "It's fine. It's…nice. Just, I don't know. New." I look down at our interlaced fingers, then back up at him. "What changed?"

"What do you mean?"

I tug him a little toward the back of the store, away from the too-interested ears of the salesclerk.

"We've been friends for years now," I explain, "and that was great. But you seemed…" I trail off, not sure how to describe the puzzle Jek has always presented to me. I take a breath. "I mean, you never seemed to want anything more than that. And I—well, I did. And I think you must have known that…" I look at him cautiously, and he nods. "Right," I say. "But I didn't want to pressure you, so I just let things coast. And now all of a sudden…" I lift up our hands as evidence of the change. "Why now?"

Jek looks away and runs a finger along the carved head of an old walking stick. "I don't know," he says, not meeting my eye. I know he isn't exactly comfortable with these kinds of conversations, but I feel like I need some kind of explanation, so I squeeze his hand, silently urging him to go on. "I guess I just always felt…out of sync with you," he says with a sigh. "We were close, and then… I got caught up in my own stuff. My experiments and everything. And I just kept counting on you to be there." He glances at me. "Then one day I looked up and you weren't. There were these other guys, and they all wanted you, and you moved on. And I didn't. And after that, you—you had all this experience, and I…" He stops again and swallows. "I didn't know if I had enough to offer you."

"And now?" I say, my throat catching a little.

"I don't know," he says, looking into my eyes at last. "I guess it stopped seeming so important."

A giggle bubbles up from my chest before I can stop it.

"What?" he asks, his brow furrowed.

"No, nothing, just…" I look down, embarrassed but still smiling. "I can't believe you kiss like that, when you've never done it before. But I guess that's all part of being a genius, huh?"

Jek laughs and tips my chin up, brushing our lips together. "Must be."

We kiss a little more until the salesclerk clears his throat.

"Why don't you come over tonight?" Jek suggests as we separate and turn back to a crate of vinyl records. "We could watch a movie, hang out."

I feel the hairs on my neck prickle: excitement and warning, all at once.

"Jek," I sigh.

"What?" he says, all innocence. "We used to do it all the time."

"Yes," I agree carefully. "But…is that what you mean? Watch a documentary, eat some popcorn, look at funny pictures on the internet. Then you wander off to poke at your experiments while I scroll through hacker forums on my phone?"

"Maybe," he says quickly. "If that's what you want." He hesitates, biting his lip. "Is that what you want?"

No, I think. That's not what I want. And that's what I'm afraid of. That thanks to a buildup of years' worth of unrequited longing, I'll fall all too easily into bed with Jek, only to realize that the person I thought I knew is actually a stranger.

I slip away from him to the other side of the crate, and he nods shortly to himself.

"Right." He takes a breath. "Okay."

I shake my head, not wanting him to get the wrong idea. "Jek, wait, I…I just think it's a good idea to take things slow. We've known each other for ages, but this…" I make a vague hand gesture to encompass whatever is happening between us. "This is really new. And for the past few months, you've been—"

"What?"

I blow out a breath. "Difficult," I say honestly. "Confusing. Secretive."

"Jesus, Lu," he says, pushing away from the record crate and letting his voice rise a little. "Did it ever occur to you that maybe you're the one who's changed? You used to respect people's privacy and stay out of their business. When did you become so obsessed with knowing everything I do, everything I *think*, even when it has nothing to do with you?"

I stare at him, stung. But there's an uncomfortable truth to what he's saying. Experience once taught me the damage you can do by digging around in a person's secrets—not just to them, but to everyone around them. And yet here I am, obsessing over snippets of gossip and acting like I'm entitled to know every detail of Jek's life.

"Okay," I say, forcing my voice calm, "maybe you're right. Look, I'm not trying to force you to tell me what's going on, and I'm not giving you some ultimatum. But right now… obviously we don't trust each other very much. Doesn't that matter to you?"

He takes a minute, rubbing at a dingy brass candlestick with his thumb. "Fine," he says at last, exhaling slowly. "I get it. So…no movie. It's cool." He starts to head out of the shop, but I follow him and tug on his jacket sleeve.

"Hey," I say. "I'm not trying to push you, but anytime you want to talk, I'm here. You know that, right? Whenever you're ready…you *can* trust me. No judgment."

He turns back to look at me, and there's something in his eyes this time. Hesitation. Like there's something he wants to say, but he doesn't quite dare. I hold my breath, waiting, but just as his mouth opens, there's a jingle of the bell on the door, announcing someone else has come in the shop. Jek's face goes blank at once.

"Come on," he says. "I'll walk you back to your car."

I'm worried after that conversation that Jek will retreat back into his shell, but I wake up that Saturday morning to a text from him, suggesting a trip to the butterfly pavilion on the London Chem grounds. I guess he took my message to heart and is trying to keep our dates as innocent as possible. I haven't been there since I was a little kid. I did love it then, though, and it might make a nice break from the dreary sludge of winter around here.

We meet up at his house and walk together up the hill in a dull drizzle, past the soggy-looking protesters at London Chem headquarters, its pale gray towers reflecting the flat, featureless sky. I'm looking forward to warming up amid all the plants in the pavilion, but once we step inside, I'm not so sure I made the right decision. The place is almost entirely filled with overstimulated children tugging bored parents around. The shrieking and giggling sounds are somehow louder in the enclosed space, and the hot, humid air makes me instantly cranky and uncomfortable. I give Jek an uncertain look, but the one he returns is so anxious and hopeful that I can't bear to disappoint him, so we both strip off our heavy winter coats, leave them on a rack by the entrance and head into the exhibit.

We make our careful way along the curving path, doing

our best to avoid the toddlers hurtling past every minute or so, and at first I'm so distracted that I forget that this pavilion was ever meant to be something other than a sweltering, overcrowded swamp. Then Jek nudges my elbow and points, and I lose my breath because right in front of us are five beautiful butterflies lined up on an overripe banana in a feeding tray, their velvet wings pulsing to a languid beat. It's pretty much impossible to be cranky when faced with a sight like that.

After that, my eyes feel different, almost as if I've been given special butterfly-viewing glasses. Everywhere I look, I see the delicate creatures, now that my vision is attuned to them, and some even seem to stare back at us with their eyelike wing markings. I'm so fixated on the butterflies, I don't even notice the other beasts sharing their space—not until Jek points out an adorably fuzzy little guy hanging from a leaf just above my head.

"Oh," I exclaim, "a caterpillar." I reach out carefully to trace a fingertip along its downy back, and it curls away from me a little.

"Let him be," says Jek softly, and he nudges me over to a display of pupae in a glass case. They're lined up next to each other, some just plain green cylinders, but in others I can see the beginnings of wings, still damp and tightly furled.

"'Metamorphosis occurs when the caterpillar passes through a pupal stage,'" Jek reads from the sign, "'during which its tissues and cells are broken down and reconstructed into the form of the adult insect, or imago.'"

"How strange," I murmur half to myself as I gaze into the case. "You see caterpillars and butterflies all the time in the world, and you take them for granted. It's easy to forget how amazing the transformation really is."

I turn back to Jek to find him looking at me with a bizarre intensity. I can't put my finger on it, but it feels like there's some kind of static charge in the air. Or maybe it's that the pavilion is now weirdly silent.

"Where did everyone go?" I ask, glancing around the place. Somehow without my noticing, the whole pavilion seems to have emptied. Apparently Jek was as lost to his surroundings as I was, because he gives a start when I point it out.

"I don't know," he says softly.

I peer around in all the corners, but I catch only the occasional flash of color.

"Even the butterflies have disappeared."

Jek looks up at the glass dome over our heads. "Storm," he says succinctly. I follow his gaze and sure enough, the sky above us has turned dark and threatening while we've been wandering. "The butterflies think it's night."

The place has an eerie feel to it, and I shiver despite the heat. "Maybe we should get going before it hits," I suggest.

Jek agrees, so we find our coats and head out into a dark gray fog intermittently pierced by a needlelike drizzle. We've hardly made it a few yards down the road before a massive crash startles us, and the drizzle turns into a sudden downpour. The gutters flood immediately, and eddies form around our sneakers.

"Back inside," Jek shouts. He takes my hand and tugs me back into the pavilion.

Once inside, the heat of the enclosure seems to hit me twice as hard, the air wet and thick with the sickly sweet smell of rotting fruit. A minute ago I was shivering, soaked to the bone from being out in the rain, but now I can't wait to peel off my sodden coat and sweater. Jek follows my lead and strips down to a thin white T-shirt. We leave everything in a soggy pile near the door and head back into the exhibit.

I've never been here before during a storm. The rain beats noisily against the glass structure, and the light is dim and greenish through the dense, overhanging branches with their fat, heavy leaves. Condensation beads up on every surface.

"It's kind of creepy in here, all alone like this," I say.

"Yeah," says Jek, glancing at me shyly. "Sorry our date kind of took a nosedive."

"No, it's fine," I assure him. "Nice, in a way." Even though there's not much to see now, we make our way dutifully around the little path as if on autopilot. "It beats sitting at home, researching scholarships."

Jek "hmms" noncommittally, and I realize we've never talked before about his college plans, even though it's a subject on everyone's mind this year.

"What about you?" I prod tentatively. "Any thoughts on where you want to apply?" I try to make the question sound casual, but the truth is my heart beats a little faster to have aired this concern.

I know it's too soon, our relationship too new, to be thinking about long-term plans together, but that hasn't stopped me from fretting and fantasizing a bit. A little part of me likes to dream about us ending up at the same school, even though I know it isn't likely. Jek has the brains and money to go to the very best places, and there's no way I could swing that. But if I knew what he was picturing—Harvard? Berkeley?—then maybe I could aim for something in the same city. No matter what happens with our relationship, it would be nice to have a familiar face nearby when I'm dealing with college stress.

"I don't know," says Jek after a long pause. "To be honest, I'm not sure I want to go to college."

I stop and stare at him.

"Not go? What are you talking about?" I know plenty of people who probably won't make it to college after graduation, but only because they don't see it as an option. As my mom says, Jek lives in a different world. And if there's anything I know about his world, it's that *everyone* goes to college.

Jek shrugs and continues a little way down the path. "It just seems like a waste of time," he says hesitantly, as if he's expressing aloud something that, until now, he told only himself. "I don't know if I have much to learn from books and professors. Maybe it makes more sense to travel for a while. To see the real world for a change, instead of the inside of a lab."

Put that way, I have to admit it makes a certain amount of

sense. And Puloma is enough of a free spirit, she'd probably approve this plan. But I can't help feeling my heart sink as I realize there's no way for me to include myself on this adventure. I don't have the money for that kind of thing, and besides, I can't skip college. My own dreams depend on it. My mother would never forgive me if I gave up all that for some boy. I'd never forgive myself.

The thought dampens my mood a bit, and I trail behind Jek on the path by a few steps. After a minute or two, he turns to look for me, and a strange expression crosses his face.

"Stop," he says quietly but firmly. "Don't move."

"What?" I ask, though I do as he says. "Why?"

"There's...wait." He walks toward me, slowly and carefully as if approaching a skittish colt. Once he's not more than a couple of inches from me, he snaps a twig off one of the nearby branches and moves it toward my head.

"What are you—" I start, but he puts a hand on my arm. "Shh. Don't move."

He slowly lowers the twig in front of me, and that's when I finally see it: a huge, iridescent blue butterfly with a deep violet "eye," almost like a peacock.

"Look at that," I breathe, afraid to move a muscle. "I've never seen a butterfly that big." With its wings fully extended, it's almost the size of a paperback book, folded open.

"I know," says Jek, still holding out the twig. "You've got to wonder if the scientists here have been slipping their experimental by-products into its food."

The butterfly gives its wings a tentative flap, then flutters away into the branches. I turn to Jek and take his hand.

"It's hard to imagine something like that could come from that fuzzy little caterpillar we saw," I say as we continue down the path.

"Which do you like better?" he asks, his tone light. "The caterpillar or the butterfly?"

I glance over at him and laugh. "Silly question," I say. "You can't have one without the other. And it's the metamorphosis that makes them interesting."

Jek stops short and pulls me up close to him.

"What?" I say, surprised. I look up into his eyes. He's gazing at me intently, an unplaceable expression on his face. I can't tell if it's the way he's looking at me, or the damp heat of this place, but I start to feel a little light-headed and rest a hand against his chest for support.

Somewhere distant, I'm aware of thunder growling and a shuddering flash of light, but I can hardly think of that because suddenly Jek is kissing me, hard and breathless, and my arms are full of the boy I have adored for most of my life. He pushes me up against the nearest surface, and I gasp from the chill of the wet glass against my steaming skin.

"Jek," I say, between frenzied kisses. "Wait." I slide a hand down his chest and push gently. "We agreed..."

But Jek only crushes himself up against me more forcefully, hitches my leg up over his hip.

"Don't fight me, Lu," he says into my neck, his voice

wrecked with desperation. “Please. I know you want this, too.”

For a moment, I let myself succumb to this temptation, my skin prickling from the electricity in his lips, his touch, in the overheated air, my whole awareness swamped with him. But as much as I want to let myself go, I know neither of us is prepared for this.

“Jek, no,” I insist, squirming in his grasp. “Stop it.” I push harder, and he breaks away from me, breathing heavily, sweat glistening on his skin. He rubs the collar of his T-shirt over his face.

“I’m sorry,” he says, his eyes wide, chest heaving. “Jesus, I didn’t mean to…” He looks down at his hands, which are trembling slightly, and tightens them into fists. “I don’t know what got into me.”

I glance up through the glass panels at a patch of lightening sky.

“It’s letting up,” I say. “Maybe we should go.”

CHAPTER

We walk home together from the date in silence, and even when I leave him at his door, Jek seems barely willing to look at me. A sour end to what had been a near-perfect afternoon, and I feel like I ruined things just when they were starting to work. I want to fix it, but Jek doesn't answer any of my texts the rest of the night. I figure I can give him some time to cool off, but when he's still not responding the next day, I get angry. Is this supposed to be punishment for pushing him away? That's shitty and immature. Maybe my mom was right about him—that he's no different from the other London Chem brats: only interested in girls for what he can get out of them.

But my indignation turns to concern when Jek fails to show up for school on Monday, and again on Tuesday. Maybe something else is going on? Maybe he caught a cold from that storm, but I can't help but think that it has something to do with Hyde.

When my phone does finally ring Tuesday evening, it's not Jek calling, but Puloma. "Lulu," she says, "I was just hoping…" Her voice is calm, light, but I know her well enough to detect the beginnings of panic in her tone. "Have you heard from Jayesh?"

A half hour later, I'm in her study as Puloma pours tea for us both.

"Jayesh was in a terrible mood when he came home Saturday," she explains and I feel a renewed twinge of guilt.

"Did he tell you why?" I ask. Puloma looks up, but if she notices or guesses that we fought, she's too discreet to say.

"No," she says. "Just a lot of slamming doors and being uncommunicative. I was trying to leave him alone, let him work out whatever it was, but Tom wouldn't let it be." Puloma fiddles with her teacup, not meeting my eyes. "It was my fault, in a way," she confesses. "The day before, I texted and called Jayesh about something and he never got back to me. You know how he is—absentminded. He tells himself he'll reply in a minute and then forgets all about it. But that day I was already annoyed because of something at work and I needed to talk to him, and when he didn't respond, I wound up complaining about it to Tom. Tom was just being protective," she explains. "He hates to see anything upset me, including Jayesh. But Jayesh came home in such a mood, and Tom started lecturing him about answering his phone…"

Puloma puts her cup down without taking a sip.

"They've had these disagreements before," she says, "and it blows over. But this time… I don't know. Somehow it kept escalating, no matter how much I tried to calm them both down. One minute Tom was shouting, then they were shoving, and the next thing I knew, Tom was across the room with a bloody nose."

I gasp. "Is he okay?"

Puloma nods absently. "He'll be fine. But…" Puloma stops herself and stares down into the cup in front of her. When she looks up again, there are tears gathered on her lashes. The sight sets something off in me, and I feel my own chest tightening. I move to sit on the couch next to her and take her hand.

"I'm sorry," she says, reaching for a tissue. "It's just…this isn't like Jayesh at all! You know him, right?" She looks to me for confirmation, as if needing reassurance that she knows her own son. "He's not violent. He'd never hurt anyone, even in anger," she continues. "We were all so shocked. Even Tom. No one did or said anything. No one even moved. And Jayesh, he looked as horrified as anyone. Then he disappeared into his room, and a few minutes later we heard his door slam.

"Tom was upset, but I told him to just let it be. I figured Jayesh needed to let off some steam, but that he would come back by morning and we would settle everything. But he didn't. And when he still hadn't been in touch on Monday, and I got the call that he hadn't shown up at school, I started to worry.

"Ever since we moved in with Tom and the kids, Jayesh's been more distant, but I figured it was to be expected, under the circumstances. As long as he was staying out of trouble and keeping up with his schoolwork, I didn't worry too much. I knew he didn't always sleep at home, but I figured he was spending the night with a girlfriend and wasn't ready to tell me. To be honest, I assumed it was you."

I look away and shake my head silently. The fact is, for all that Jek and I have been seeing more of each other lately, I have no idea where he's been spending his nights.

Puloma sighs. "Tom always said I was giving him too much freedom, and too soon, but I told him to stay out of it. Jayesh and I understood each other well for years. I didn't think I needed Tom's input. But I guess he was right. If I had listened to him, set more limits, given Jayesh a curfew and expected him to be home every night…"

"No, Puloma," I say, laying my hand over hers. "Don't. None of this is your fault." I hate to hear her talk like this, partly because I've always thought Puloma was an awesome mom, and I know Jek loves her and values their relationship, despite his animosity toward Tom. But it's also out of loyalty to Jek. My own blood boils in sympathy to think how furious Jek would be at his stepfather laying down rules and interfering in his life. I feel sure that if Puloma had encouraged that, it only would have made Jek rebel a thousand times more.

Puloma squeezes my hand and smiles weakly.

"When he didn't come home, I thought maybe he'd gone to his dad's. Emerson's always inviting him to move in, and it would be natural under the circumstances for him to seek out his father. But he said he hasn't heard from Jayesh in over a month. I don't want to overreact and dwell on nightmare scenarios, but I'm his mother. If I knew where he was, or even just that he's safe—"

"Have you checked with all his friends?"

"I started with you. What about Hyde? Do you think he might know?"

I shake my head. "I don't know. Last I heard, he and Jek had some kind of falling-out, and Hyde hasn't been around since."

"Can you try him? I don't have his number, and if there's even a chance..."

I hesitate. I don't really want to speak to Hyde, not after my last interaction with him. Thinking of the way he looked at me, the way he touched me that night at his party, still gives me chills, and all I want is to keep as much distance between us as possible. But this is Jek, and Puloma is desperate. Her next move will probably be to call the cops, and I know Jek would definitely prefer *not* to have the police digging around in his lab, asking questions.

I call the number, but I'm not exactly surprised when it goes straight to voice mail.

I take Puloma's hands in mine again. "Don't worry, okay? I'll ask around, find out anything I can. And I'll let you know as soon as possible. I'm sure it's nothing."

I don't exactly have a plan in mind, but I head to Hidden Ponds, anyway. I'm not sure what I'm hoping to find since I'm pretty sure Hyde is long gone, but something keeps nagging at me about the way he disappeared so suddenly. Is there a connection to Jek's current vanishing act? Have they gone to the same place? Or else… The truth is, I've never been able to shake the feeling that Hyde wouldn't have gone willingly. Part of me is still convinced that Jek must have *done* something to get rid of him. And it's always possible that Hyde did something *else* for revenge…

A dense, cottony fog encases my car as I drive, dulling the usual sights and sounds of the commercial strip. Against the blankness of it, images flash through my mind: a broken window. A pool of blood. A makeshift weapon. A rotting corpse. But when I pull up across the street from the trailer, the place looks more or less the way it did last time I was here, and I breathe out a sigh of relief. I park my car and try the front door, but it's locked, so I stand on tiptoe and peek through the windows. Again, there's nothing terribly remarkable inside—just clothes strewed around here and there, a TV and a video game system. It looks like a sloppy bachelor pad—not all that different from Jek's place, actually, or any teenager's room.

In fact, if there's anything strange about it, it's that it looks so normal. It's been two weeks since anyone has seen Hyde, so why hasn't this place been cleared out? Is he still paying rent? Or if he really left town, why didn't he take his stuff?

Unless he left in such a hurry that he couldn't. Or if he never left at all.

I try to see if there's any obvious sign of recent activity, like leftover food or take-out containers, but there's nothing visible in the kitchenette. Impossible to tell if it's not being used, or if Hyde just cleans up after himself.

I go around the back, checking for any further clues, but the trash is empty and the back windows are all sealed tight. The only thing of interest is a deep tire track cutting through the mud behind the house—a bicycle tire. I can't say what it means, though. It could just be some kid taking a shortcut.

I take one last look at the scene and head back to my car. I can't get distracted wondering what happened to Hyde—Jek is more important right now.

I text Lane, but he hasn't heard from Jek lately, either. But he's at least willing to help brainstorm.

He's hanging out at the Double Dutch diner, doing homework while Hailee waits tables and keeps him supplied with a bottomless cup of coffee. It doesn't hit me until I walk through the door that I haven't really spoken to Hailee since that night at Hyde's. Not that I've given it much thought, but I guess in the back of my head, I assumed Hailee and Lane must have broken up that night. And yet...here they are, still together and chatting quietly during a lull. It makes me feel oddly hopeful, like maybe the damage Hyde is inflicting on this town can be healed.

I scoot into the booth across from Lane and we spend the next few minutes tossing around theories of what might have happened, but since there's no way to check them, they're pretty much dead ends. Eventually Hailee takes her break and joins us. She listens to a few of our aimless ideas about Jek's disappearance before tossing in one of her own.

"Do you think it could be work related?"

I frown at her. "What do you mean? Like, his experiments?"

"Like his drugs," she explains. "He'd been working on that psychedelic we tested a while back, right? Maybe he decided it was time to market test it."

"What makes you say that?"

"I don't know," she says carefully. "It could just be a coincidence, but I hang out on a forum where people talk about clubs in Chicago. Folks don't usually talk openly about drugs, but there are code words you can pick up on, if you know what to look for. They post about what they bought at this or that club, or from such and such dealer."

"And people have mentioned Jek?"

"Not in so many words, but I've seen some references to Kymera." Lane and I exchange blank looks, so she explains. "Jek didn't have a name for the drug he gave us, remember? He had some alphanumeric gobbledygook for his own records, but nothing that would work as a street name. He asked us all to suggest something, and I suggested Kymera. He never got back to me about it, and I just assumed he either picked something else or hadn't given it any more thought. But just the other day I noticed people referring to something called Kymera being dealt at a club called The Glass Horse, and what they described sounds a lot like what we experienced. It might just be a coincidence, but…" Hailee trails off into a shrug.

"It's the best lead we've got," I agree, grimly. "But why would he skip school to deal drugs in a club in Chicago?"

"Who knows?" says Lane. "Maybe he really is sick of his stepdad and planning to set out on his own. Maybe he needs to set himself up with some cash first."

"Okay," I say, pulling out my phone. "It's not much, but it's a possibility."

"Wait," says Lane. "What are you doing?"

"Calling Jek's mom. I told her I'd let her know if I found out anything."

"Lulu," he says, placing a hand over mine, "maybe think twice about that. Are you sure you want to tell Jek's mom that you tracked him through his illegal drug empire?"

"It's technically not illegal," I point out weakly.

Lane snorts. "Yeah," he says, "tell yourself that. And his mom."

"Look," says Hailee. "It's just a hunch, we don't even know if he's been there. You want to rat him out over a hunch?"

I slide my phone back into my purse. They have a point. But in that case, there's only one thing to do. I turn to Hailee.

"That club you were talking about. Do you have an address?"

CHAPTER

My first stop is Camila's to borrow an outfit at least vaguely appropriate to this kind of club, plus her fake ID. Thankfully we look similar enough in dim light. When she asks what it's for, I tell her I have a date and feign shyness to discourage any more questions from her. I hate lying to my cousin, but if Camila knew my plan, she'd only tell me to stop playing guardian angel and leave Jek to his own problems. Maybe she's right, but I can't do that. I have to help him, if I can. And even if I can't, I need to know where he is and what he's doing. I won't be able to rest until I've found out.

With the club's address plugged into my phone, I drive into the city. It isn't long before I'm in a neighborhood I've never been to before—an abandoned industrial area, all empty lots and shadowy smokestacks that have long since gone extinct.

Street numbers are hard to come by in this deserted maze, and streetlights even more so. I'm almost convinced I've missed the place entirely when I see a line of outlandishly dressed people extending into the dark, their outfits clinging and glittering in the light cast by a pink neon sculpture. As I get a little closer, I realize the sculpture is meant to be an abstract horse's head, and it's the only sign over an otherwise undistinguished-looking door.

This must be the place.

I park the car and line up with the others, feeling self-conscious at being by myself and conspicuously underage. When I get to the door, I hold my breath as I hand the bouncer Camila's ID, but he barely glances at it. He seems a lot more interested in Camila's dress, and the parts of me that are not perfectly covered by it. It's gross, but it gets me a nod, so it's worth it.

The room I walk into is so dark that I spend a few moments blinking helplessly before my eyes adjust and I can get some sense of my surroundings. The only lighting as far as I can see is a series of neon tubes in a rainbow of colors, snaking along the ceiling and walls like glowing pipes. By their dim light, I can just barely make out the boundaries of the huge, open space. It must have been a warehouse at some point, but now the vast empty space over my head makes it feel like an underground cavern, and adding to that impression is the odd, shimmering quality of the walls. From the way they reflect back the glowing neon colors, at first I'm convinced they are damp, but as I approach, I realize that they're actually covered with a jagged mosaic of broken mirror shards.

The largest part of the space is taken up with the dance floor, on which bodies move almost robotically to a throbbing beat, their faces oddly lit by the reflected light, while in the void above their heads, metallic balloons bob around on currents of air, directed by giant chrome fans in each corner. My plan was to move through the crowd searching for Jek, but I realize right away that this is hopeless. There's no chance I could ever shove my way through this mob, let alone find Jek in the middle of it.

Instead, I head to the bar in the opposite corner of the room, but I don't fare much better there. The music is so loud that I can't even hear my own shouted questions, plus there's something about the crowd that makes me nervous. I didn't really notice outside, but I definitely don't seem to be the only underage person in this club: a lot of the faces I see look around my age, some even younger. Even more disturbing, everyone else looks at least forty. And the two groups definitely seem to know each other. That alone is enough to make me want to turn around and leave, but I remind myself I'm here for a reason, so I catch someone's eye and lean close to ask about Jek. That, unfortunately, gives them the wrong idea, and I find myself pushing hands away.

Feeling helpless, it finally occurs to me to try the bathrooms, which are at least quieter. I ask some of the women there if they've heard of Jek and show them some photos of him on my phone, but no one recognizes him. I get a better reaction when I mention Kymera, but although people seem to know the name, it doesn't lead anywhere.

I'm on my way back to the bar when I notice a small group of people disappearing into a dark corner of the space. I wonder if there might be a chill-out room back there where I could talk to people in a quieter environment, so I follow them down a dimly lit corridor where the sounds from the dance floor are significantly dampened. Up ahead of me, the group slips behind a black velvet curtain, but when I step through it, they've disappeared. All I see is a dented metal door, probably the entrance to an old storeroom. I'm searching the door for a handle when a towering woman with a shimmery acid-green frock coat, silver hair and elaborately shaped eyebrows steps forward from the gloom.

"You can't go in there," she says smoothly.

"But I just saw some people—"

"It's private," she insists with a cold smile. "Invitation only. The dance floor and the bar are in the other direction."

"Fine," I sigh, pulling my phone from my purse. "But can you at least tell me if you've seen my friend here? I've got some pictures—"

The request gets stuck in my throat as I feel a hand grip tightly at my elbow. "Lulu, darling," says a rough, insinuating voice in my ear.

Hyde.

"I heard you were looking for me. Diana? Do you mind?"

He presses something into her hand, and though she gives him a dark look, she accepts it and pushes the door open. "Thank you," he says as he nudges me over the threshold. The door clangs shut behind us and I shake free of his grasp, turning to look at him. He's dressed normally compared to the other people in the club, in dark jeans and a fitted gray T-shirt, his dark curls casually mussed. The only odd element is a strange black necklace worn tight around his throat, with a single silver ring at the center.

"I wasn't looking for *you*," I practically spit. "I was looking for Jek."

Hyde raises a delicate eyebrow. "Well, you found me. Surprised?"

I rub my elbow, feeling sure a bruise is already forming.

"A little," I say. "I thought you were long gone. In fact, I'd half convinced myself that Jek murdered you."

Hyde grins, his teeth glinting in the dim light of the corridor. "Jek doesn't have it in him. Besides, aren't we supposed to be best friends?"

"I don't pretend to know what you are to each other."

"Hmm, very wise," he says. "I, for one, prefer not to label things." Hyde starts down the hall at a quick pace, then stops after a few feet. "Aren't you coming?"

"Why should I?"

"You said you were looking for Jek. Have you got any better leads?"

He bats his eyelashes at me provokingly and I grit my teeth, but I have no answer for him.

"I thought not. You'd better follow me, then."

He guides me down another dim, anonymous corridor that looks like it could exist in the bowels of any industrial plant. At some point, we pass a door that's cracked open, giving me a glimpse into what looks like an otherworldly grotto with a violet waterfall spraying lavender foam. I pause a moment to gape, but a heavily eyelinered boy hisses at me and slams the door closed.

When I look ahead, Hyde is inserting a key-card into a door at the other end of the hall, and I hurry back to his side. This room, it turns out, is even stranger—it's as small as a monk's cell, but the walls are made of flat, featureless panels that glow with warm, shifting colored light, like the effect of bright sunlight through closed eyelids. The only furnishing in the room is an oddly shaped settee in a plush synthetic fabric, and I can pick out a soundtrack of trip-hop overlaid with muted conversation and giggling, but I can't tell if it's being piped in somehow or is just overflow from a neighboring chamber.

Three people are already in the room: an older woman in burgundy silk with very long fingernails, a boy maybe my age with intricate tattoos across his bare back and a vivid-colored Mohawk and another young person whose gender I can't be sure of, pale and wearing nothing but an oversize man's dress shirt. The two younger ones are aimlessly cuddling and nuzzling at each other in one corner of the couch, while the woman looks on lazily and gives the occasional slurred direction.

"Sorry to interrupt, but I'm afraid I'm going to have to ask you to leave for a bit," Hyde says, but they hardly seem to register our presence. Hyde's supercilious smile shifts into a snarl. He crosses the small, close room and smacks the pale one on the thigh. "Scat," he hisses. "Now."

The pale one makes a muffled noise of annoyance and rolls over. The woman raises her eyebrows imperiously, but nudges the punk with the toe of her furred slipper.

"Darling, help me stand," she says, reaching out one long, elegant arm. He gets to his feet and tugs the others off the couch, the pale one listing a little and in need of support. They shuffle around me toward the door, and the woman stops and leans in to whisper something to Hyde. While they're occupied, the punk boy jerks his head to indicate that I should follow him out.

In the hallway, the pale one is leaning against a wall with his eyes half closed, but the punk seems more alert.

"You're here with Hyde," he says, and it doesn't seem to be a question. I think about correcting him, but at the moment, it's close enough to the truth. The boy huffs out a breath.

"Be careful," he says.

I offer him a grim smile. "Don't worry. I know not to trust him."

He glances over at the pale one, who is slipping inch by

inch down the wall, then back at me. "I'm serious," he says. "I know the drugs are hard to refuse, but that guy…he throws so much money at this place, they'll never kick him out. But he's dangerous. There's a button by the door if things get out of hand. Someone will come right away."

Inside, the woman gives a sinister laugh, then steps out into the hall. She holds the door open and looks at me expectantly. I swallow hard and go in.

Hyde is seated on the couch, one arm along the backrest, his legs crossed at the knee. "Can I get you anything?" he asks, his voice low and sweet again. "A drink, maybe? Or something stronger?"

He gestures to the seat next to him, inviting me to sit down, but I keep my feet planted firmly where they are.

"You mean Kymera?" I ask pointedly. "That's how you've got everyone in this place eating out of your hand, isn't it? I came here because I thought Jek might be dealing it, but of course, Jek stopped distributing his drugs long ago. He has you for that."

Hyde lifts one shoulder carelessly. "Jek's drugs open a lot of doors, as you just saw."

"Yes, how convenient for you," I say, trying not to let fury shake my voice. "So where is he?"

Hyde smiles, showing his teeth. "How do you know he isn't here?"

"Jek wouldn't be caught dead in a place like this. He's not like that."

Hyde hums thoughtfully to himself. "Maybe not," he grants. "But you would."

"What? No I wouldn't."

He uncrosses his legs and leans forward, resting his elbows on his knees. "You're here now, aren't you?"

I take a step backward, hardly conscious of the action. "That's different. I'm just here looking for someone."

"That's why everyone is here." Hyde stands and closes the distance between us. "We're all looking for someone. Or something. Some people just don't know what it is yet." He wraps a hand around my wrist and pulls it toward him. "What are you looking for, Lu?"

"You know what," I say tightly. "Stop playing games."

"Oh, but we were just starting to have fun."

"Tell me where Jek is. You must have heard from him."

Hyde leans closer, his hair brushing my skin, his scent like overripe fruit and bitter almonds filling my senses. "I'll tell you a secret, Lu," he whispers. "I don't really want to talk about Jek."

I can't suppress the shiver that runs through me. "I should go," I say firmly. "Jek's obviously not here, which means I'm wasting my time. If you won't tell me where he is, then I'll just have to try something else."

I step away and try to yank my hand free, but he grasps it more tightly.

"What if I told you," he murmurs, "that there's nothing you

can do for him now, but Jek will be home, safe and sound, by tomorrow night?"

That stops me. "How do you know?"

Hyde shrugs delicately. "I know a lot of things."

"If that's true, then there's no reason for me to be here. I should go home before my mom starts to worry."

Hyde tugs gently on my hand. "Your mother isn't worrying," he says, his eyes on my face. "She's at work, and won't be home for hours. She'll never miss you."

I stare at him. "How can you possibly know that?"

Hyde tugs a little harder, and I have to step forward or lose my balance. "Am I wrong?" he says. He takes a step back and sits on the couch, letting his hand slide from my wrist down to my thigh. "Come on, Lulu," he says, his fingers tickling and teasing just under the loose hem of my dress. "You're not expected home before morning. Wouldn't it be terribly wasteful to leave now?"

I feel my knees wobble, and I sit down beside him. "Why are you doing this?" I whisper, my skin prickling. "You could have anyone, *anyone* in London, or even here in the city. And you don't even know me."

"Teach me, then. Help me know you."

I shake my head. "Why, so you can trick me into fulfilling your sick fantasies? I've heard about the vile things you make people do."

"Is that what you heard?" Hyde laughs, cold and clear. "Would you like to know the truth? It's not my perversions that shock and appall people. It's their own. The only thing I crave is knowledge and experience. All I've ever done is ask people what they want."

"And then?"

"Then I give it to them. Go on, Lu." Hyde slides forward off the couch and kneels in front of me. "I know you try so hard to be good," he sighs, resting his hands lightly on my thighs. "To be responsible and trustworthy and loyal. But, sweetheart..." He leans in close and takes a deep, slow breath, his eyes slipping half closed. "No one is good all the time."

I sit there before him, my body so lax I could almost believe I'd been drugged. Hardly knowing what I'm doing, I lift my hand and tangle it in his curls, and he rubs into the gesture, practically purring. His face is no longer as strange and alien to me as it once was, but there's something *different* about it now. Maybe it's just a haircut, or that he hasn't shaved. Maybe it's the weird lighting of the room. But it feels like more than that.

He reaches for my hand and guides it to the black strap around his neck, looping my finger through the silver ring.

"There, now," he says, his voice low and soft, but with something of a growl underneath. "I'm yours for the night. You have complete control. Are you really going to walk away?" He looks up at me, his eyes as black as oil slicks. "Or are you going to settle down and tell me what you want?"

CHAPTER

It's storming. A violent wind beats at my bedroom window, thunder and lightning making a show of the night. I'm in bed with the lights off but I can't sleep. Earlier I was trying to keep my mind occupied by streaming videos, but I couldn't focus on anything, so I shut off my computer. There's too much on my mind. I've been anxious all day, snapping at my mom over dinner because I can't tell her what I'm worried about. I'm sick of being lectured by her about my relationship with Jek, maybe because a part of me knows she's right. I should have minded my own business and left Jek to his devices, but now I'm in too deep to extricate myself. I just wanted to help him, but now I'm afraid that whatever trouble Jek's in, I'm going to get dragged down, too.

And I feel terrible that, with all my amateur investigating,

I still have nothing satisfying to tell Puloma. Where could Jek have gone? I assumed that if he disappeared, he must be with Hyde, but he wasn't. Hyde did seem to have some idea where he was, but that's not much consolation. Does he have Jek imprisoned somewhere? Is he hurt or unconscious? Hyde said Jek would be back tonight, but I still haven't heard from him. And it's not like I have much reason to trust Hyde.

Normally storms lull me to sleep, but tonight the air crackles with electricity, my room flashing bright every few seconds. Amid all the wind and rain, I hear a tapping, rattling noise at the window. A sudden burst of lightning illuminates a dark face peering through the glass and I just barely manage to stifle my scream.

It's Jek. I move to the window and shove it open, letting rain spatter on my desk as Jek hauls himself in. He used to crawl in my window all the time when we were kids, but that was usually summer afternoons, during games of hide-and-seek. He hasn't done this in years, and never at night.

"Sorry," he says, halfway through and grunting with exertion. "I didn't want to wake your uncle."

"Oh, my God, Jek," I say, tugging him the rest of the way inside and clutching him to me. He's cold and dripping wet, but I'm so happy to see him that I don't care. I burrow my face into his neck, kiss his skin and inhale the homey scent of lab chemicals, my relief stinging at my eyes. "You're okay, you're okay," I repeat, my hands tangled in his hair. I pull back to look at his face in the dim light from the window. "Your mom was so worried. Does she...?"

Jek nods. "I've been home."

I pull away and dry my eyes, embarrassed at my excessive display. "And Tom?"

"Pissed," he admits.

I wince sympathetically. "Are you grounded?"

"You could say that," says Jek with a humorless laugh. "The asshole put a padlock on my door. I have to use the front now, so he can monitor me. Just what he always wanted—his own little police state."

"Jesus. But then how—"

"I snuck out," he says, leaning casually against my desk and sounding a little proud of himself. "Even fascists have to sleep sometime."

"So now you'll get in even more trouble," I point out, frowning. "You could have just texted me you were home."

Jek is silent a moment, his expression unreadable in the dark.

"I needed to see you," he says at last.

"Jek," I say, throwing my arms around him and burying my face in his shoulder as the storm roars outside. "I was so scared for you."

Jek's hands are on my shoulders, gentle at first. Then they grip tighter and push me away.

"Were you?" he says in a strange tone of voice. Lightning flashes outside and it makes his eyes glitter coldly.

At first I can't figure out what he means. "Of course I was!" I tell him. "We all were. Your mom was in a panic, and—" Then it hits me. "You spoke to him." My heart thuds in my chest. "You spoke to Hyde. And he told you..." But I can't go on.

"You," Jek says, his voice low and dangerous. "You wanted to wait. *You* said we should take things slow. Then the minute I turn my back..." He stops, but I can hear his breathing, feel his eyes hard on me. "Jesus Christ, Lulu," he says hoarsely. "I thought if I got rid of him, that would solve everything. That you'd be happy. But you *missed* him. I was an idiot not to see that it was Hyde you wanted all along."

His words hit like a fist in the gut. I sit down on the bed, feeling sick.

"So, how does it work?" I say at last, trying to sound light even as my voice is quivering with rage and humiliation. "You guys get together and...*discuss his conquests*?" Jek is motionless, a dark shape in front of the window. "And Hyde," I continue. "He tells you—*describes* to you—everything he does with everyone he fucks." Thunder rumbles and the room is daylight bright for a split second. "Or just when it's me?"

Jek is still and silent a moment. "Would that be better or worse?" he asks at last.

I let out a hysterical laugh. "I don't know. God, you prick. Both of you. What makes you think he isn't lying, anyway? How do you know he's not just talking big, like guys do? Trying to impress you."

Jek huffs out a breath. "Is that what you want me to believe?"

"I don't care what you believe," I say, my fury boiling over. I'm through with playing the good girl, protecting Jek's fragile ego. "You want to know what really happened? Fine. He did everything I asked for, and I *loved* it."

"Of course you did," Jek spits, looming over me. "That's what girls really want, isn't it? Guys like Hyde. Psychopathic, amoral, sex-obsessed—"

This brings me to my feet.

"You should talk!" I say, my voice too loud for the late hour. Luckily the storm must be drowning us out, or else Uncle Carlos would be banging on the wall. "He's *your* friend. Or whatever you are to each other. You're seriously going to give me that pathetic crap about how girls only go for assholes and ignore the nice guy? Jek," I continue, forcing my voice low, "I've been hung up on you for years and you never so much as looked in my direction. I love that you're a nice guy. *When* you're a nice guy...which you haven't been lately. In case you hadn't noticed, you take me for granted, you keep secrets, you ignore me to follow up on whatever shiny thing has your attention. So, yeah, maybe I got sick of waiting around for the 'nice guy.' Hyde may be an asshole, but at least he never pretends to be something he isn't. He knows what he wants, and he cares enough to ask what I want."

I'm breathing fast and hard, daring Jek to disagree with me. He reaches out and takes my arm, yanking me close.

"I know what you want," he says low in my ear.

"What?" I feel off balance, both physically and mentally. "What do you mean?"

"You're lying," he whispers. "I know what you want, and Hyde didn't give it to you."

I watch his face through the shifting shadows, not understanding. Then it hits me. "No," I say softly, not wanting to believe it. But why shouldn't I? Only an idiot would trust Hyde's honor. "He told you. Hyde told you what I said, that little shit." I start to pull free, but Jek's grip on me is firm.

"I think it was only fair," Jek says, his voice smooth. He sounds amused, almost, which is disconcerting. "Given that it involved me."

I pull my arm free at last and curl up on my bed, hiding my face in my arms.

"Oh, God," I moan. "I can't believe he told you." I hug my knees tighter and turn my face to the wall. "He laughed at me, you know. Did he tell you that part? He said to tell him anything, whatever I wanted, and he'd do it," I say, rocking slightly. "And I told him and he laughed. He laughed and said anything but that."

Jek sits on the bed and puts a hand on my back, but I tense up at the touch.

"So which is it?" I ask bitterly. "I can't believe that Hyde's not willing. He'd do anything, he told me. So it must be you. You wouldn't. You would never. And now you know I thought about it and—"

I twist away from him and bury my face in a pillow. I don't think I've ever been so humiliated in all my life. A moment later, I feel his arms around me and the weight of his body against my back as he whispers in my ear.

"Lu," he says, so softly I can hardly hear him. "I would."

For a long moment, we lie there together breathing, listening to the rain against the windowpanes. I turn my head toward him. He kisses me gently, then pulls back to look in my eyes.

"I'd give you everything."

I stare at him through the darkness, tracing his features in the pale glow from the window. The storm must have calmed by now, and there's a sliver of moon showing. I'm so confused about everything between us, and I know I should demand more time to think things out, to make peace with the secrets he still won't share. But he's here with me, in my bed, and I've never wanted anything so much in my life.

I kiss him again, briefly. "Is this okay?" I ask, one hand clutched in his shirt. "Are you sure?"

"Yes," he says. I tug him closer against me and he buries his face against my neck. "Only this time," he whispers into my skin, "please…don't think about him."

"Are you jealous?" I say, petting his hair.

"Yes," he breathes, almost inaudible. "Which is crazy."

I press him close. "Not that crazy," I admit.

He pulls back a little, brushing the hair from my face.

"Oh, Lu," he says, "you have no idea."

CHAPTER

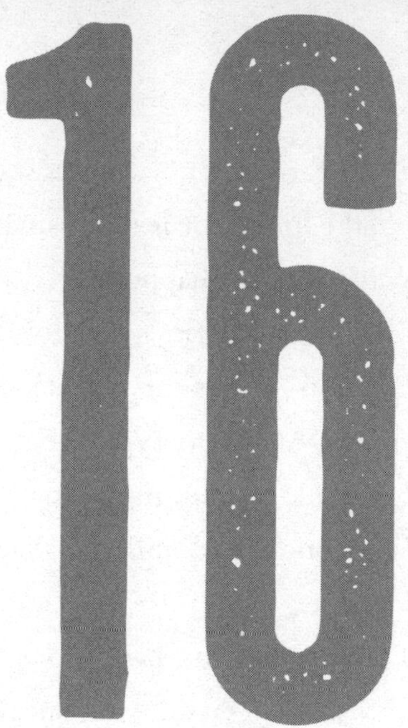

My first thought in the morning is that my alarm clock is going off, which is weird because I just hit the snooze.

The second thought involves a ton of curse words hurled at Jek, who isn't in my bed anymore. He's not in my room at all, and probably not anywhere in the house.

When you dream about your first time with the boy you've been pining over for years, having him sneak off in the middle of the night without leaving so much as a note isn't usually part of it.

I'm feeling around for my phone so I can call him and tell him how completely pissed off I am when I notice that my room looks like a tornado hit it. It was pretty neat last night, since I clean when I'm nervous, but now my things have been thrown all over, Jek's jacket is squashed up under my desk and my makeup mirror is lying smashed on the floor.

What the hell happened?

I realize my alarm is still going off, but after glancing at the silent clock, it hits me that it's not my alarm, but my phone. Ringing. At six thirty in the morning.

I scrabble around in the mess until I find the phone under a pile of books and spilled makeup. It's an unfamiliar number.

I answer.

"This is Inspector Newcomen of the London Police Department," a voice says. "Am I speaking with Lupita Gutierrez?"

I stare at the wall in front of me, my brain still sluggish. Why are the police calling me?

"What?" I say, my voice still sleep-rough. It's the best I can manage.

"Is your name Lupita Gutierrez?" the voice on the other end repeats slowly, as if speaking to an idiot. "This is the police."

"I don't—I...yes, that's my name," I offer.

"Miss Gutierrez, we need your help with an investigation. Are you over the age of eighteen?"

I rub a hand over my eyes. None of this is making sense. "No," I tell the voice on the phone. "I'm seventeen."

Inspector Newcomen gives a soft sigh, as if this is a nuisance she didn't need this morning. "You have the right to have a parent, guardian or lawyer present when we speak to you. Do you understand?"

"Yes," I say, because these are the first words she's said that make some sense. I look at the clock again. Mom's still at work, and her manager always docks her pay if she leaves early, even for an emergency. There's Uncle Carlos, but he's hardly strong enough to get the mail these days. "Do I *have* to have someone there?" I ask.

"No," says the inspector, and she sounds as relieved as I feel. "Legally, it's not required. It's at your discretion."

I wonder if this is true, or if Inspector Newcomen is simply too eager to bother with correct protocol. Since I'm just as happy not to involve any of the adults in my life in this, I let it slide. "All right then," I say. "What do you want from me?"

The inspector takes a breath. "We need you to identify a body," she says, her voice calm but with a buzzing excitement just underneath. "There's been a murder."

I sit down hard, but miss the bed and wind up on my bedroom floor.

"What? Who?"

There's a pause on the other end. "We don't know, miss," Inspector Newcomen explains carefully. "That's why we need you to ID."

"But why would I—"

"Your number," she says. "The victim texted you. Your number was the most recent one in his phone."

That wakes me up completely.

I start pulling on a T-shirt and sweatpants from the mess

Jek has made of my room, and I promise Inspector Newcomen I'll be there as soon as possible.

The whole drive over to the morgue, I can't help running through a mental list of the last people I received texts from: there's Camila, of course, but I'm pretty sure they said the body was male. It can't be Jek, I tell myself over and over, because he hasn't texted me since before he disappeared on Saturday. Unless he hasn't texted anyone else in that time, either. Or if he deleted texts in between. Shit. Shit. Lane? I heard from him a couple of days ago. My cousin, Manuel? When was the last time my dad texted me? But why would he even be in town?

A plainclothes cop is waiting for me when I get there.

"Miss Gutierrez?"

I nod, already trying to look past her at the body on the slab.

"I'm Inspector Newcomen—we spoke on the phone. Please," she says, trying to get my attention, "I need to you to listen to me."

I take a deep breath and nod again, looking at her this time, forcing myself to take her in. She's surprisingly young, and dressed boldly yet precisely, in a way that seems designed to project confidence but actually suggests an overeager beginner. Her expression is serious and composed, but just like on the phone, there's a strange undercurrent of excitement emanating from her, as if she is secretly thrilled about the whole situation.

"Thank you," she says with a tight-lipped smile. "Now, please try to focus. The victim was found without ID. He appears to have been out for an early-morning run and left his wallet at home. We need you to identify this body, if you can, but I want to prepare you first. The attack was extremely violent, with severe facial trauma. Do you need to take a few moments before you go in?"

"No," I insist. I'm aiming for reasonable and calm, but my cracking voice betrays me. I take another breath and let it out, trying not to hyperventilate. "I'm fine. Please, just let me see."

Inspector Newcomen hesitates a moment, as if she is wondering whether she should give me more time or insist on the presence of a guardian. But her own eagerness to get this investigation moving clearly wins out, and she steps aside to guide me through to the body.

She wasn't kidding about the violence of the attack. He's been beaten with a brutality that makes me wince: one eye has been yanked free from its socket, loose and missing teeth give him a crazed, jack-o'-lantern grin and over his left temple, the skull is caved in like a deflated basketball. Still, even through all the mess, there's no question who I'm looking at.

"Danny," I say, my voice shaking with relief. "Danvers Carew. He was my lab partner." I noticed last night that he texted me to ask a question about the lab report, but I'd been way too preoccupied to get back to him, and I'd forgotten all about it.

Inspector Newcomen makes a note. "I know this must be

very difficult for you," she says, not succeeding in making it sound like anything but a stock phrase. "You can take a minute if you need to, but any information you can give us about Carew would be helpful to the investigation. Do you know of any enemies he might have had? Any kind of trouble he had been in recently?"

I shake my head, bewildered. "Danny was one of the most popular kids in school. Baseball team, student council. Not the type to start fights."

The inspector looks a little disappointed by this answer. Murders like this don't happen much in small towns like London, and I can see she's desperate to prove herself by getting the investigation wrapped up expeditiously. She recovers her poise quickly, though.

Guiding me to another room, the inspector directs my attention to a table nearby where a few objects are laid out and marked with labels.

"We found this at the scene," she says, pointing to one in particular. "It appears to be the murder weapon. Have you ever seen it before?"

At first, all I can see is a messy and undistinguished heap on the table, but as I get closer, the object takes shape and my breath catches in my throat at the sight. Under a smear of blood and brain and hair is a bright green bike lock—exactly like the one Tom gave Jek last year. The one Jek never uses but always keeps strapped uselessly to his bike.

I can feel Inspector Newcomen's sharp eyes on me as I stare

at the object, and I wonder if I can still pass off my gasp as one of horror and not recognition. I'm suddenly gripped with fear of what this could mean for Jek. Newcomen, probably faced with the first serious crime of her career and anxious for a speedy solution, might be all too willing to accept the first likely suspect that falls into her path. And Jek would make such an easy, satisfying target—the cops in town have always been too quick to believe the worst of him. Once they had him in custody, would they even stop to sort out the details? Jek's not exactly my favorite person right now, but I don't want to see him in jail.

"Miss Gutierrez?" prompts Inspector Newcomen.

Before I can come up with a response, we're interrupted by a knock at the door. We both turn as it opens, revealing a young and nervous-looking uniformed officer leaning tentatively into the room.

"Inspector?" He clears his throat. "Sorry to interrupt, but we have the witness to the attack. The one who called it in this morning? We just tracked her down."

"Thanks, Jim," says Newcomen. "If you'll just show her into the—"

"Is that her? Are you the inspector?" A small woman in a red trench coat, her bright white hair cut in an elegant bob, pushes her way in past the officer. "I'm very sorry," she says with the confidence of someone who is used to dominating a room. "I was in such a panic this morning when I called, I didn't think to leave my name. But I saw everything that happened." She launches into her story before anyone can stop her. "I was out walking my dog this morning—she's a puppy, can't make it through the night—and the poor young man was jogging through the London Chemical grounds when someone came tearing through on a bicycle. The jogger told him to watch where he was going. Then the biker stopped and got off his bike and..." She stops and shivers dramatically. "It all happened so fast. He didn't even seem to think about it. He grabbed the lock from his bike and started beating the other boy. The boy fought back at first, but he was no match, and he fell to the ground screaming. It was awful. Even after the screaming stopped, he kept beating him with that chain. The sounds it made..." The woman stops and takes a steadying breath. "I was too stunned to think at first. When my mind came back to me, I took my dog inside and called emergency services."

Inspector Newcomen steps forward and places a hand on the woman's arm.

"Can you describe him, ma'am? The assailant?"

The woman nods shakily. "It was only twilight, but after the assault he got back on his bicycle and raced right toward me, so I saw him clear enough. A young man, maybe a teenager. Tall."

"Okay," says Inspector Newcomen, pulling out a notebook and jotting down the information. "How about his race?"

The woman considers a moment before speaking. "White,"

she says. "Or…he could have been Hispanic. Or some kind of Native American?"

Inspector Newcomen sighs. "But he was light-skinned?"

The woman shakes her head. "No, he was— That is—" She closes her eyes tightly, trying to focus on a mental image. "I'm sorry," she says at last. "I can't say for sure."

"I thought you said you saw him clearly."

"I did," the woman insists. "I can picture him in my mind, I just—" She breaks off in frustration. "I don't know. My memory must be playing tricks on me. All I can remember now is that there was something off about his face. Something odd and out of place. And his eyes…such strange, black eyes…"

That's all I need to hear.

"I know who that is," I tell the inspector, for the second time this morning feeling almost weak with relief.

She gives me a dubious look. "You can identify someone from *that* description?"

"I'm sure of it. His name's Hyde."

"Hyde," she repeats, making a note in notebook. "Is that a first name or last name? Does he go to your school?"

I shake my head, frustrated at how useless my information is. I hardly know anything about Hyde, but I need for Inspector Newcomen to accept this lead. Then inspiration hits. "I know where he lives," I tell her. "I can take you there."

Again, the inspector hesitates, probably concerned that this doesn't quite follow standard procedure. But her ambition wins out. "All right," she says. She rips a sheet out of her notebook and hands it to the uniformed cop. "Give this to Sarah and tell her to notify the victim's parents. Then get us a warrant—wake a judge up if you have to—and meet us there."

Inspector Newcomen drives and lets me have the passenger seat as we make our way along the now-familiar path to Hidden Ponds under low, dark clouds. I'm grateful that the inspector doesn't seem prone to small talk, as my mind is racing, trying to sort out everything that has happened in the past few hours. I know my evidence is shaky right now, but based on that woman's description, Hyde just *has* to be the murderer—I feel it in my bones. But last time I saw him, he was in Chicago, and he didn't show any inclination to return to London. What brought him back here? And why the hell would he go after Danny Carew, of all people? Worst of all, where is Jek in all this? Can it be coincidence that he skipped out on me around the same time Danny was killed? And what was Hyde doing with his bike? Is Jek back to his old ways, jumping whenever Hyde calls, protecting him and helping him cover up even the most heinous of crimes?

Out the car window, I'm startled to notice that we're almost there. The outer edge of London's commercial strip strikes me as even grimmer than usual with its seedy businesses and false neon cheer. The trailer park itself takes on an almost nightmarish quality, the shabby dwellings huddled together against a grittily driving rain.

We pull up in front of Hyde's place, and Inspector Newcomen practically leaps from the car. I take a deep breath to settle my nerves before following her.

The uniformed officers are just behind us, and Newcomen tells me to stand back as they rap three sharp knocks on the trailer door. When there's no answer, they try the handle, and to my surprise the door swings open.

The officers enter with their hands on their weapons, but once they give the all clear, I follow the inspector inside. The last time I was here, peering through windows for anything out of the ordinary, the place just looked like a normal teenager's slightly messy living space. Now it has clearly been ransacked. As I follow Inspector Newcomen around the trailer, I see that closet doors stand ajar and drawers have been flung open, their contents disgorged all over the bed and the floor. Couch cushions are heaped up, and the mattress is sloping off the bed at a weird angle.

"It looks like he was in a panic," says Newcomen, her eyes sweeping the scene. "Like there was something he was looking for." She turns to me. "Miss Gutierrez, you've been here before?"

I nod.

"Walk me through it, then. Describe everything exactly how it was last time you saw it, and what has changed. Maybe we can reconstruct what he was thinking."

I cover the whole trailer with her, pointing out everything I remember about how the furniture was positioned and what has been moved since then, but I don't think I'm adding much to what she has already surmised. At one point, one of the other officers comes over to give a report.

"The kitchen's all clear, Inspector," he says.

"Nothing suspicious?"

"Not exactly, ma'am… I mean there's nothing at all. The cupboard, the fridge, the sink… It's strange, but from the looks of them, they haven't been used."

Inspector Newcomen frowns. "What about ID?"

"Nothing, ma'am," says the officer. "No identity documents, no mail addressed to anyone but 'resident.' No photos, no computer. Nothing in the whole place with a name or picture on it."

The inspector rubs her head and sighs, then turns back to me. "Do you have photos? Could you find any online?"

I shake my head. "The parties Hyde threw…they weren't the kind people want records of. And he wasn't the type to hang out on social media."

"Sounds like he was trying to keep a low profile," she says, nodding to herself. She gives instructions to the other cop about the APB they have out, and I pull back, hanging nervously by the door and trying to stay out of the way. That's when I notice a familiar glint of pinkish gold reflecting from a pile of junk emptied from a drawer onto the surface of a desk. I step a bit closer to it and it gleams more brightly, as if calling to me. The inspector has already told me not to touch anything in the trailer, but somehow I can't resist the urge to nudge it gently with the edge of my hand. The pile shifts a bit and I can see it clearly now: Hyde's phone.

My first thought is to point it out to the inspector. Maybe the phone is what Hyde was looking for—the reason he turned this whole place upside down and inside out. There could be something incriminating on it. But who would it incriminate? My thoughts turn back to Jek, and how close he's become to Hyde…there could be messages between them about Jek's drug business, or worse. And what if Jek is protecting Hyde right now? If Jek left me this morning to go help Hyde, he could be considered an accessory after the fact to Danny's murder.

My fingers seem to do my thinking for me. I pluck the phone from the pile and slip it into my purse. Then I clear my throat.

"Inspector Newcomen?"

She glances at me over one shoulder.

"Do you still need me, or…?"

"Oh," she says. "No…just let me get your cell number, in case we have more questions for you. Then Officer Mitchell will drive you back to the station to get your car."

I'm writing my number down in her notebook when another uniformed cop comes in.

"Inspector," he says, "I spoke to the property manager of the park. He says the trailer was being sublet by a guy who matches the witness's description. But the name on the rental agreement and all the checks wasn't Hyde."

"What was it?"

"Some kind of Indian name," he says, pulling out his notepad.

"Like Running Bear?"

"No, not that kind of Indian. Like Gandhi. Hold on..."

I hardly even register the grotesque racism of this little exchange, because my mind has already moved ahead to more pressing concerns. I finish leaving my number and follow Officer Mitchell out the door without waiting to hear the rest. I'm not halfway down the walk before my phone is in my hand, texting Jek.

Expect the cops at your place within 20 minutes. Hyde's in trouble and they're tying it to you.

CHAPTER

Twenty minutes later Jek hasn't responded to my text.

I drive aimlessly around town in a wind so fierce it seems to have blown everyone off the streets. I don't know what to do with myself. Should I talk to Puloma? To my mom? I could go home, but she'd just want to know why I'm not in school, and I'm not sure I'm ready to face her lectures about the mess I'm in.

None of this feels real yet. My brain doesn't know what to do with the image of Danny Carew, beaten and bloody on that slab. I don't think I've even fully registered that he's dead. I want to go back in time, to that moment when my biggest problem was that my sometimes-maybe-boyfriend flew the coop the first time we had sex. I want the space and time to be angry at Jek about that, and hurt, and to think about whether I can stand to speak to him ever again. But I can't focus on anything like that with Danny's murder on my mind, and knowing that Jek might be implicated in Hyde's savage act...and me along with them, now that I've obstructed justice by taking that phone.

It's all too much to process right now. I feel disjointed and unreal, and without quite knowing what I'm doing, I find myself turning into the school parking lot. I'm overcome by the need to be around normal people who know nothing of what has happened. To surround myself with their obliviousness.

The school is silent as I walk the main hallway except for the wind screeching through the gaps in doors. It's the middle of third period, and everyone is in their classrooms. I consider going to my third period calculus class, but I don't want to draw attention to myself by entering late. I decide to head straight for my fourth period class and wait there for it to begin. But that's not where my feet take me. Instead, I find myself walking down a different hallway entirely, and I don't know why until the bell rings and Camila walks out of her classroom.

Camila. Of course. She's exactly who I need to see right now. She'll help me figure out what to do.

To my surprise, Camila's neutral expression turns to dismay as soon as she sees me, and I wonder to what extent today's trauma is written on my face.

"Lulu," she says, "I'm so sorry." She pulls me into a tight hug.

"Oh," I say, bewildered. "You've heard. News travels fast in this town."

"I found out first thing this morning from Karina, Lane's sister. I called her to see if she wanted a ride to school, and she broke down. When I saw you weren't in school today, I figured you'd heard, too."

I squeeze my eyes shut, trying to clear away the fog from my brain. "I can't really believe it," I say into her shoulder. "Poor Danny. He never did anything to hurt anyone."

Camila pulls back from our hug and gives me a strange look. "Danny?" she says.

"Danny Carew," I tell her, hardly considering my words. "He was murdered this morning in the park."

I realize my mistake when I see Camila's eyes go big.

"Holy shit!" she exclaims. "What the hell happened? How do you know?"

I shush her quickly—clearly whatever happened to Danny isn't public knowledge yet, and I don't want to be the source of any wild rumors. "Come on, in here," I say, pulling her into a nearby bathroom. I check the stalls for potential eavesdroppers before telling her about my early-morning phone call from the cops, and my trip down to the morgue to identify Danny's body. I don't tell her about spending the night with Jek—it's not relevant to the issue at hand. At least, I want to believe it isn't.

"Christ," she says once she's heard me out. "Danny Carew,

of all people. He could be annoying, sure, but who would kill him? Everyone loves Danny. Do the cops have any leads?"

I'm about to tell her about the witness description and how I led the cops to Hyde's trailer, but at the last moment I bite my tongue. It seems wiser at this point to keep some information to myself. No point in having gossip and conjecture floating all over town before the cops have even started their investigation. I shrug and shake my head, but Camila knows me too well to let that slip by. I see her eyes narrow, and I rush to cut off any more questions.

"I don't understand, though," I say. "If you didn't know about Danny, then what were you babbling about when I ran into you?"

"Oh," says Camila, suddenly reminded of the other drama of the morning. "That was about Lane! You mean you haven't heard? I thought for sure you would have, you're better friends with him than I am."

My heart seems to still. "What happened to Lane?"

Camila hoists herself up on the bathroom sinks. "No one knows, really," she says. "He left the house early this morning. Woke his sister up to ask her where their dad keeps the bolt cutters, then told her that he had to run an errand. Next thing she knows, her mom's getting a call from the highway patrol. They say they found him just outside town, near that old grain elevator. He was sitting in his car by the side of the road, and the trooper figured he must have a flat tire or engine trouble, so he pulled off to check on him. But he was totally uncommunicative. He wouldn't roll down his window or even look up. Just kept mumbling incoherently to himself."

I shake my head, unable to make sense of this information. It doesn't sound like Lane at all. "What…" I begin, my mouth dry. "What happened to him?"

"The cops said they sent a couple of officers to the spot to see if they could find any clues in the area, and they came up with a recently used syringe. So they're thinking it must be drug related."

I gasp and Camila fixes me with a look.

"Come on, Lulu. You can't act like you didn't know Lane was a druggie."

"What? No, I…of course, I guess he was, yes."

What I don't say is, *but he didn't have a problem*. Shooting up? That's what the kegger-circuit kids are getting into, not my friends. Lane was a dabbler, an experimenter…not an addict. But then, maybe I'm not the best judge of that anymore. I think of the box of spilled hypodermics I saw in Jek's sink. At the time, I just assumed they were for transferring chemicals or something. Maybe my familiarity with Jek and his little experiments has made me blind to what addiction looks like.

Still, it's hard to wrap my head around.

"Lane, shooting up? Alone? I've never seen or heard of Lane doing anything like that."

"Well," says Camila, "obviously he had let things get further than any of us realized. I don't know what drove him to it, but for now, he's a real mess. They've got him in the hospital under observation."

"Is he going to be okay? When are they going to let him out?"

"I don't know," she says, giving me a sympathetic look. "All I've heard is that it's too soon to tell."

That's all the info Camila has, so we head back to class. But I've hardly had time to seat myself when an announcement comes over the PA saying that we're to be dismissed early due to the tragic loss of one of our fellow students, Danvers Carew. All around me I hear expressions of shock. *Just wait until they find out it was murder*, I think grimly to myself.

Camila texts me about going over to her house, but I just want to be alone right now, so I go straight home. I lie down on my bed, trying to shake off the horrors of this morning by losing myself in sleep, but every time my eyes close, Danny's bashed-in head appears in my mind, vivid and gruesome. When I try to force myself away from that image, my thoughts turn to Jek and how he disappeared just when I most needed him. Then I think about the fact that I still haven't heard anything at all from him, so I can't tell if I should be more furious or worried. Then there's Lane and his mysterious breakdown this morning—the image of him, all alone on the highway and babbling incoherently to himself, chills me to the bone. And from that, my mind has no place to go but back to Hyde and my conviction that somehow he must be to blame for all the ways my once-predictable world has been shattered.

It's all too much. I feel like a bubble is about to burst inside me, so I shove it down as far as I can and focus on the only thing I can find to calm my nerves right now: the facts. Everything I've learned this morning is jumbled together in my head and it's making me feel crazy. But if I can just pull it all apart and look at the individual pieces, the way I do with the busted electronics in my bedroom, then maybe I can find the pattern.

I sit up on my bed and force myself to think. It can't be coincidence that Lane went nuts, Carew got murdered and Jek ran out on me all on the same day, can it? But what does it all mean? And how is Hyde mixed up in everything?

I keep sifting through all the data, but it doesn't add up. My fingers slip into my purse and draw out my phone—maybe some old texts can help jog my memory—when I catch a flash of gold and remember that I impulsively snagged Hyde's phone from the crime scene.

I still can't quite believe I did that. I was convinced that something on this phone would incriminate Jek, but what if it's just the opposite? What if the information on this phone would exonerate him completely, and I put him at further risk by taking it? I stare down at the phone in frustration.

There's only one way to know for sure.

I swipe the screen. As I expected, there's a passcode required to get any further. But hanging out on tech forums has taught me a few things. Hacking it would be a little tricky, but doable. A half hour's work, and I could get access to Hyde's address book, his messages, his emails, his texts…

The phone shifts in my fingers and I realize my hand is sweating. This shimmering gadget holds the key to all my questions—not just about what happened this morning, but everything that's been going on between Jek and Hyde for months, and everything Jek's been hiding from me. The mystery has been gnawing at me for so long, my mouth is dry at the very idea of seeing it all spelled out for me in glowing pixels.

I raise the phone and tap it against my lips. What I'm thinking of…it would be crossing a major ethical boundary. I've told Jek before that I believe he's entitled to his secrets; hacking into Hyde's phone to read their private messages would be a huge breach of trust. Of course, the murder investigation does change the situation a bit. If Hyde has texts on here that talk about what happened with Danny, that evidence could be vital to the murder investigation. Even if not, there's sure to be a record of Hyde's various other crimes that might interest the police.

But no…no matter how I spin it, the idea is indefensible: the real reason I want to look through the phone is to satisfy my own curiosity. There's no way I can justify that. The only ethical choice is to hand the phone back to the police right now and let them deal with whatever is on there.

CHAPTER

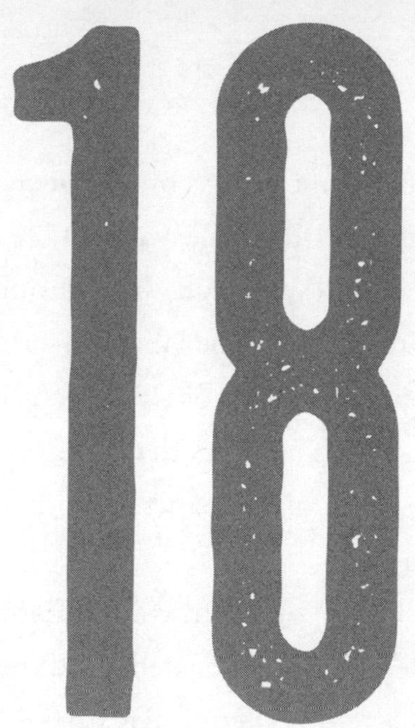

Later that evening, I finally hear from Jek: a brief text thanking me for the tip earlier. That's it.

My relief that he's okay and not in police custody wins out over my anger at him for running off this morning, but I know it's time for us to have a serious talk about everything going on, so I tell him I'm coming over. Jek may still be grounded, but I know Puloma won't bar their door to me.

When I get there, I find Jek looking flustered, his hair in wayward spirals as if he's been clutching and tugging at it, but otherwise all right. He keeps swooping around his room, fiddling with his materials and instruments in an aimless sort of way.

"Watch out," he says sharply as I start to cross toward him.

I freeze and look at him expectantly. "Broken glass," he explains. "Had a little accident."

I look down and, sure enough, shards of clear glass are scattered across the laboratory floor. At first I assume Jek just dropped a beaker or flask in the course of an experiment, but this time it appears that his great glass cabinet was the casualty. One of the panes near the center has been thoroughly smashed.

"Oh," I say. "How did it happen?"

Jek shrugs. "Accident," he repeats. "Haven't had a chance to clean it up yet. Today's been kind of busy."

I look back to him. I'm not at all sure how to broach the conversation we need to have, so I decide to just play it by ear. "The cops," I say, because it seems as good a place to start as any. "How did that go?"

Jek gives up on whatever he's doing and collapses on his couch, so I sit beside him. He rubs a hand over his face. "Okay, I guess," he says. "Considering. They questioned me a long time, but at least they didn't arrest me."

I keep a close watch on his face. "But they do think you had something to do with Danny's murder?"

Jek shrugs uneasily. "Well," he says, "they had their reasons—my name on that trailer, and they figured out that the murder weapon was my bike lock. Then they found my bike abandoned just outside town."

"Guess that didn't look so good."

He glances over at me a little nervously, as if just picking up on my mood. "No," he admits. "But they had a description of the murderer, and I didn't fit."

"No," I agree. "They're looking for Hyde. But they must know that you and he were close."

Jek nods. "They wanted me to tell them everything I knew about him, and my connection to him."

I hold my breath, but Jek doesn't elaborate. "So what did you say?"

Jek shoots me another nervous look, then stands up and returns to sorting his lab equipment. After a moment, he mumbles something I can't make out.

"I'm sorry?"

He sighs and reaches out one hand to stabilize a wobbling beaker. "I told them..." Jek takes a breath. "I told them we were lovers," he says simply, his hand still on the beaker. "Just like you said. That he talked me into setting him up with his own place. But I didn't know much about him, really, and he ran out on me." He looks up and turns a steady gaze on me. "I told them that he played me for a fool."

I nod slowly. "And they bought that?"

Jek shrugs and looks back down at his glassware. "Seemed to."

"But it's not true," I say, my voice quiet but firm. "Is it?"

Jek looks up, startled. I pull the pink-gold phone from my purse and sit there, idly flipping it over and over between my fingers.

"What…?" he tries after a moment. Then his eyes focus on my fingers. "That's Hyde's phone."

"So it is."

Jek swallows. "What are you doing with it?" he says.

I stand and cross the room to lean against the counter. I put the phone down between us, feeling an icy thrill that, for once, I have caught him off guard.

"I took it from his trailer."

Jek stares at me. "With the police standing right there? Why?"

"Because," I say, keeping my voice cool and even. "I thought there might be something incriminating on it."

Jek turns away from me, bristling. "What, so now you're trying to protect Hyde?"

"No, Jek," I say firmly. "I'm trying to protect *you*. If Hyde texted you about drug deals, or some secret he was blackmailing you with…or if he called you after Danny's murder. You could be held as an accessory."

Jek inhales sharply. "That was quick thinking," he says after a moment, returning his attention to his glassware. "Thank you, I guess. But you don't have to worry. There's nothing like that on the phone."

"No," I agree. "There isn't."

Jek's hand slips. A test tube rolls along the counter and shatters on the ground.

"If you ever talk to Hyde again," I continue, keeping my voice as steady as possible, even as my blood is buzzing, "you might give him some advice about tech security. Someone with Hyde's kinds of secrets should really have better protection than the standard lock-screen."

Jek looks up, ignoring the broken glass. "You hacked into Hyde's phone?"

"And I searched his messages. Texts, call logs, browser history, emails. I found records of all kinds of illegal activities. Not to mention some seriously depraved messages…to me, to Camila, to almost everyone we know. Hyde definitely got around, and he earned every bit of his reputation." I lean back a little, resting my hands lightly on the counter. "Funny thing, though," I say. "In all those texts, there's not a single exchange with you. No calls, either. No emails. You guys were supposedly great friends, but you never talked." I look him directly in the eye. "Weird, isn't it?"

Jek doesn't move a muscle. "I can explain," he says at last, his voice slightly hoarse.

"I really wish you would. I'm starting to think I'm going crazy."

Jek turns away and takes a long moment to rub a beaker with his shirt cuff. Then he puts it down and turns back to me. "Hyde was my dealer," he says at last, his voice now clear and confident. "Most of what we talked about was drug related. I made him delete all our conversations as a matter of course."

I watch his face, thinking this over. Hailee told me ages ago that Hyde was dealing Jek's wares for him. I'd seen the evidence myself when I was in Chicago. But as I look at Jek before me, something clicks and I realize that's not what he's saying.

"You don't just mean he dealt your drugs for you," I say. "Hyde was your *supplier.*"

Jek presses his lips together, then nods and lets out a long slow breath.

"God," I say, closing my eyes as the pieces start to fit themselves together in my brain. "This explains so much. I can't believe I didn't think of it earlier. But you've always been the guy other people come to for drugs…it never occurred to me that you would get hooked on someone else's stuff."

I open my eyes and nod for him to go on.

"Hyde had access to something more powerful than anything I made in my experiments," Jek says, leaning back against the sink, his arms crossed over his chest. "I thought I could handle it, because I was experienced in these things. But every time I tried to quit, he kept tempting me back." He looks down, his shoulders tense. "I hardly recognized myself."

My brain is reeling from this new information, and I move back to the couch to sit down. "This morning," I say, half to myself, "when Camila told me about Lane…until then, I'd never thought about drugs as a problem for anyone in our crowd. Even then, I didn't make the connection to what you've been going through."

Jek comes to sit down next to me.

"Lu," he says, fidgeting a little with a ripped seam in the cushion, "I'm sorry. About this morning. Or…last night."

I let out a sour laugh. "Which?"

He looks up, surprised. "Which?" he repeats. "Oh. I guess…this morning. I'm not sorry about last night. That is, if you're not." He leans in a little, his expression tentative. "Are you?"

"Hmm," I say. "Well, I was. I was really fucking sorry when I woke up. Sorry enough to never want to speak to you again."

Jek gives a sharp, guilty nod and looks away. I take a deep breath.

"But you apologizing for this morning," I continue, "helps. Helps me not…regret what came before."

He shifts closer to me on the couch. "Good," he says quietly. He smiles a little and leans toward me, but I stop him with a hand on his chest.

"Wait, Jek…there's just one more thing I have to know." I look deep into his warm, shining eyes. "This morning, when you left, was it because of Hyde?"

"No," he says firmly, not looking away. "I swear, that's not it. I didn't know anything about Carew when I left. I just…" he trails off.

"Panicked?" I fill in.

He nods gratefully. "I'm sorry."

"So you really don't know where he is? Please tell me you haven't been stupid enough to help—"

“All I know is that he’s gone,” says Jek quickly. “Gone for good, this time.”

“And that’s enough for you? You don’t want to see him brought to justice? He’s a murderer, Jek.”

Jek sits back against the couch with a huff. “What’s the point in being vindictive? It won’t bring Carew back.”

“It’s not about retribution,” I say, hardly believing Jek’s reaction. “Hyde is dangerous! What if he does something else like this?”

“He won’t,” Jek says with feeling. “I can swear to it. Hyde will never do anything like this again.”

“Seriously?” I draw away from him in shock. “After all this, you’re still willing to defend him?”

Jek hesitates a moment, chewing on his lower lip. I can tell there’s something else he wants to say, but he won’t let himself.

“Jek,” I say more gently. “I know you were close. That he meant something to you, and it’s hard to forget about that, no matter what he’s done.” I look down, mentally tracing a pattern in the carpet as I collect my thoughts. “I understand,” I tell him at last. “When I saw that phone at Hyde’s place and realized it might implicate you…” I take a deep breath. “I didn’t even care whether you were guilty or not. I hardly gave a second thought before I took it. I just wanted to protect you.”

Jek reaches out and takes my hand. “Hyde meant something to you, too, didn’t he?” he says, and it’s more statement than question. “You liked him.”

I stare down at our hands together. "A part of me, maybe," I admit. "He was…magnetic, in a way. But when I saw what he did to Carew…" I shake my head. "The person who did that was a monster. I don't have any sympathy to spare for him." Jek looks away and nods. I squeeze his hand more tightly. "Jek," I say, "you have to be honest with me. You're not protecting him, are you?"

He shakes his head slowly. "Not this time. Lu, whatever appeal he once had, he's far too dangerous now. You're right."

I let out a sigh of relief. "Well," I say, "he probably won't be back around here. Not with a murder rap on him."

Jek nods his agreement. I relax back onto the couch and feel my muscles melt. I don't think I realized how much tension I've been carrying around, but thanks to finally having an honest explanation for Jek's relationship with Hyde, plus knowing Hyde is almost certainly gone for good, I suddenly feel pounds lighter. Like I can breathe properly for the first time in weeks. I put out a hand and tug Jek toward me.

"What about you?" I ask gently. "Are you going to be okay? I mean…without Hyde's drugs. Is there any kind of withdrawal, or…?"

Jek takes a breath. "Yeah," he says. "There might be some rough patches."

I play with his fingers, thinking about what happened to Lane. "What about rehab? It could help."

Jek shakes his head. "I'd rather not have that on my record. Hyde is gone, and so is my supply, so there's no risk I'll break down and start using again. It's just a question of toughing it out until the chemicals are out of my system."

"Jek, why didn't you just tell me? If you were having a problem, I could have helped. You know I would always want to help you."

"I thought I could handle it," he says roughly. "And…I didn't want help, honestly. I wasn't ready to give it up, I was getting too much from it, and I knew there were downsides, but it seemed worth it. I told myself I was in control, but it was a delusion. Besides, you…" He squeezes my hand, just a little. "You've always believed the best of me. I didn't want to screw up the image you had. I didn't want you to know I was a fuckup."

"Oh, Jek," I say, a dull pain in my chest. I put a hand to his cheek. "It's sweet of you," I tell him, "but you have to understand that I could never think less of you for having a human weakness. Okay?" I look at him seriously. "I promise, you can tell me anything. There's nothing you could say that could make me stop caring about you."

Jek pulls me close and kisses me fiercely, then breaks off and rests his forehead against mine, his eyes closed, his breath coming fast and shallow. "Lu," he says. "Please, don't."

"Don't what?"

"Don't—just…don't tempt me like that."

I smile and nudge gently against his nose.

"Oh, yeah? What if I don't mind this time?"

I move in for another kiss, but he turns his head. I pull back a little.

"You don't want to?" I say softly, a little hurt.

"No," he insists, "I do. But it might..." Jek stops and swallows hard. "I'm not sure if it's a good idea. Maybe we should put this—" he gestures between the two of us "—on hold for a while. Until I'm feeling myself again."

"You mean until you're past the withdrawal symptoms?"

Jek grimaces and nods.

"Is that really necessary? I mean," I say, fiddling with the hem of his shirt, "whatever you're going through...maybe I could distract you."

He catches my hand, kisses it and places it back in my lap. "Please," he says. "Not now. It feels dangerous."

I reach for him again, press my lips to his throat. "So?" I whisper into his skin. "I like a little danger."

"I know," he says, pulling away from me. "That's what I'm afraid of."

CHAPTER

A few weeks pass as the local news has a field day digging up everything they can about Hyde. London is a small, quiet town for the most part, and there hasn't been a murder here in twelve years, which means Danvers Carew's death is on its way to becoming the news story of the year, if not the decade. There's something irresistible in the mystery of it, as the police have hardly turned up a single lead on Hyde: no family members have stepped forward to acknowledge him, no associates from earlier in his life and no one has been able to produce a single photo. And although many people in London claim to know him, they all have so much trouble giving a precise description of his face that the police sketch artist is at a loss. The only thing they all agree on is that there was something strange about it, some mark or abnormality that escaped their conscious notice, but left a deep impression on their imagination.

Without any real progress in the case, all the reporters can do is sift through the town gossip. Every night, there's something else on the news about Hyde's various activities since he arrived in London. Some of the stories I know to be true, because they happened right in front of me. Other reported horrors seem so outlandish that I think they must be invented. But then, who knows? By all accounts, Hyde seems to have been a genius of cruelty and perversity—conscience-free and devoted to torture and depravity the way some people pursue stamp collecting.

Even some of the Chicago TV stations have come by to do stories on the mystery of Hyde's savage crime and subsequent disappearance. Mostly, they describe him as a con artist who probably worked under multiple aliases, manipulating people into paying for things to keep himself untraceable. I worry sometimes about the effect these stories have on Jek. All I want is for both of us to be able to put everything about Hyde behind us, but even with Hyde long gone, somehow he seems to haunt our every move.

It's bad enough that Jek is still struggling with the withdrawal from Hyde's drug, but now some of the reporters are identifying him as one of Hyde's "marks." I expect Jek to be embarrassed when these stories surface, but he tells me he doesn't mind. In fact, the publicity seems to have had an unexpectedly good influence on him: out of the blue last week, he started volunteering as a chemistry tutor at school, and bringing meals and medicine to local farm laborers who have gotten too sick to work. He's even started passing out flyers with those crazy protesters in front of the London Chem buildings. Jek has always been thoughtlessly generous with his possessions, but this is a side of him I've never seen before.

I'm happy that he's found a positive way to deal with the mess Hyde left, but there are times when I wonder if all these good works are born out of true altruism. There's a look I catch in Jek's eyes sometimes, so fleeting I'm not sure if I'm just seeing things. It looks less like goodwill, and more like grim terror. It always disappears in a flash, but for brief moments it's like he's figuring all his actions on some invisible scoreboard, his mind working feverishly to make the reckoning come out in his favor.

Maybe it's just my imagination, but it makes me wonder if I really have the full story from Jek, even now. I knew it was going to take time and work to rebuild the trust we once had, but even though he has explained everything to me, I still feel like there's some invisible wall between us.

It doesn't exactly help that our relationship is still on hiatus—I know I agreed to give him some space until the effects of the drug wore off, but I didn't realize how long it would take. The withdrawal is hitting him harder than either of us expected, and it seems to be getting worse: his face is drawn and shadowed like he hasn't been sleeping well, and he's developed a tremor in his hands. I try to talk to him about rehab or some kind of medical supervision, but he says it's pointless. The drug is unknown to modern medicine, and the world's leading expert on its mechanism and effects is Jek himself.

At least I know that as long as Hyde is gone, Jek can't give in to temptation anymore. Recovery will just take time.

One Saturday, I join Hailee on a trip to Chicago to visit Lane—it's the first time I've seen him since he was picked up by the cops. For the past few weeks, he's been in a locked ward at the hospital, but Hailee says he's improved a lot recently, and that's why he's been transferred to this new facility. It's got a bit more freedom, and it's supposed to be top-ranked for mental health treatments.

From the outside, the building is a dark and imposing tower—a sleek, modern structure of steel and black glass. I shudder at the idea of being locked up in it, but when the elevator doors open onto Lane's floor, the impression couldn't be more different. From the inside, the space is bright and airy, the floor-to-ceiling windows giving gorgeous views out over the lake. The artworks on the walls of the waiting room all conform to the same, soothing color palette, and when a nurse shows us in, the setup is more like a college dorm than an insane asylum.

We find Lane in a large, sunny room, deeply engrossed in a board game with another patient, while a few others watch and toss in suggestions. I feel almost dizzy with relief at the normality of the scene. After hearing Camila's version of what happened, I was worried I'd find Lane crazed or catatonic, but here he is, acting like his old self.

After a moment, he looks up and notices us, and his face breaks open into a wide smile.

"Hailee! Lulu. You guys came."

He jumps up and squeezes us together in a massive hug that almost sweeps me off my feet.

"It's good to see you, Lane," I say.

"Come on," he says. "I'll show you my room."

We follow him into a decent-size room with pale blue walls, two comfy chairs and a big TV—nothing like the padded cell I'd been picturing. Lane sits cross-legged on the bed and nods to us to take the chairs. Hailee asks him what he's been up to, and he laughs about how much reading and TV he's caught up on lately. We talk for a while about a few favorite shows, and it all feels reassuringly normal. Really the only thing that feels weird is the unspoken question hanging over the conversation: What is Lane doing here? He seems fine.

Apparently I'm not the only one wondering, because next time there's a lull in conversation, Hailee asks when he thinks he'll come home.

"Oh," says Lane, fidgeting with his pillow. "I don't know. It depends on…on how things go."

"You know you can leave anytime, right?" she says. "You're here voluntarily."

Lane looks out the window and nods his head.

"Don't you want to be back home?" she prods him, a little desperately. "Go back to school, see all your old friends?"

At this suggestion, a sudden change comes over him, and for the first time since I've been here he looks like someone who is seriously unwell. His expression is flat and emotionless, but his eyes are wide with terror, as if he is watching some gruesome scene visible only to him.

"No," he says, shaking his head vigorously and inching back along the mattress. "No, no, no, no."

"Lane," Hailee says, soft but firm. "What happened that day? Tell us what happened that morning at the grain elevator."

Lane continues backing away from us until he is plastered up against the headboard, saying "no" all the while until it becomes indistinct and turns into a series of inarticulate moans.

"Lane," says Hailee once more, this time sharp and loud, and she rises from her chair. Lane skitters off the bed, crablike, and when he reaches the corner of the room, he crouches down with his arms around his knees and his face toward the wall. He is rocking and babbling quietly to himself, the sounds coming so fast that I can't make sense of them. I can only pick out a word here and there—*drug* is one, and *face*, maybe—but the rest is nonsense.

Watching the change come over him is almost worse than if he had seemed crazy from the beginning. It's like his very humanity has fallen away.

I'm so fixated on him, I hardly notice when a nurse comes in and ushers us out the door.

"You've upset him," he says, shooting us a stern look. "He'll need to be sedated now. You better leave."

On the train home, Hailee and I are mostly silent, lost in our thoughts. It's only when the first houses of London come into view that I find my voice.

"I'm sorry," I tell her sincerely. "I should have done something, said something, but I had no idea how serious things had gotten with Lane's drug use."

Hailee turns to me, her eyes narrowed.

"What are you talking about?"

"That day…the day of Lane's breakdown? Camila told me the police found a syringe at the scene. I had no idea he'd gotten into stuff like that."

Hailee shakes her head. "It wasn't that. Yeah, that's what the cops said at first, because it seemed like the most obvious answer, but they did a tox screen and nothing came up."

I stare at her for a long moment as our train pulls into the station.

"But that doesn't make any sense," I say as she gets to her feet. "If it wasn't drugs, then what could possibly—"

"I don't know," she says sharply. "But it wasn't. Lane was clean."

I can't understand it. I want to talk to Jek, because Jek would know—Jek would be able to figure it out. No one knows more about drugs and drug reactions than he does. And he probably knew Lane better than almost anyone, too. He'd know what chemicals Lane had been ingesting, if any—maybe something the tox screens aren't set up to discover? Or maybe, like Jek, Lane was struggling with the symptoms of withdrawal. That might explain his odd behavior, despite not having any chemicals in his bloodstream. But then, why isn't he getting better? Surely enough time has passed that there should be some improvement.

And if not…what does that say about Jek? I'm not sure if they'd been using the same substance, but it seems likely. And yet, their reactions are very different. Is Jek going to wind up like Lane, babbling madly in a psych ward? Or is the drug affecting him in some other unpredictable way?

I wish I could sort it out, but no matter how much I think about it, I lack Jek's expertise, his brilliance, for seeing the ways chemistry interacts with biology. I mean to ask him about it in school, but he's been out for two days in a row, so I go to find him at his house. I haven't been over since we agreed to take our break, but Puloma nonetheless welcomes me warmly at the door and ushers me down toward Jek's apartment. She explains that he hasn't been feeling well.

"I think it really shook him up when that boy was killed," she says, chatting quietly with me on the stairs. "He started doing all that charity work, plus he was working twice as hard as usual on his experiments. He sometimes locks himself up in there for hours on end. I know he's used to pushing himself, but I don't think he realized how affected he was by such violence, so close to home." She wraps her arms around herself and shivers. "All of us were. I know I don't sleep as well, knowing that monster is still out there." She stares at nothing for a moment, before remembering herself and shaking it off. "Anyway," she continues, "Jayesh wore himself out, and well, school's always been a bit superfluous for him. It seemed silly for him to be exhausting himself for it. Officially, I'm home-schooling him, but..." Puloma shrugs and smiles. She doesn't have to say any more. We both know that Jek is perfectly capable of educating himself, and neither his high school teachers nor his mother have much they can teach him.

Indeed, Jek appears to be hard at work when I go in to see him, his chemical contraptions bubbling merrily away with a variety of multicolored liquids and vapors. Looking around, I notice Jek has fixed up his glass cabinet, clearing away the shards of glass and neatly taping up the missing panel. But while the lab looks as well cared-for as ever, Jek himself is looking even sicker and weaker than before. I can hardly restrain my gasp at his yellowed, papery skin and sunken eyes.

Jek glances up at my entrance, but other than that, he barely acknowledges me. It's a bit of a shock, given what we recently were to each other, but I've learned to take Jek's moods as they come lately. He's under a lot of stress right now, and the best thing I can do for him is just be a friend.

"What are you working on?" I ask, grasping for a neutral topic of conversation to set him at ease.

He gives a half shrug. "Nothing," he mumbles. "Just keeping myself busy."

I notice then that there are boxes stacked haphazardly near his work area, their flaps open, their contents half-disgorged.

"What about these?" I ask, nudging one with my foot. "Are they part of this 'nothing'?"

Jek grimaces. "No," he says. "Those are all useless." He puts down the instrument in his hand and gives me his full attention. "Why are you here?"

His rudeness catches me off guard, but I ignore it.

"It's about Lane, actually," I begin. "I just went up to the city to see him, and it got me wondering—"

"Don't talk to me about him," Jek says sharply, turning back to his experiment.

"What? Why?" I stare at him in confusion. Jek and Lane have always been close. "Jek, did something happen between you?"

"That's none of your business." He puts down a vial he's been filling and sighs. "I was sorry to hear about his...condition," he says, more gently. "He was a good friend. But I don't know anything about what happened to him, and I can't help him."

For a moment, I don't know what to say. I'm amazed at Jek's willingness to simply write off Lane as a lost cause, so much so that he won't even talk about him. It doesn't feel right.

"I don't believe you," I say at last, stepping closer so I can read his face more easily. "You know something...something you're not letting on." I look at Jek from across the lab bench.

"Lane was getting drugs from Hyde, wasn't he? Was Lane on the same drug as you, or was it something else?"

"You don't know half as much as you think you do," says Jek tightly, fiddling with some dials. "I told you I don't want to talk about Lane. If you can't find anything else to say, you might as well leave."

"Fine," I say, grabbing my coat to cover the fact that I'm shaking with anger. "I can see you're not feeling well today. I'll try to come back when you're in a better mood."

I start to move toward the door, but Jek steps around the bench and grabs my arm. Up close, I can see now that his face is shining with sweat. My anger dissipates in favor of renewed worry about his health.

"Lulu," he says, his voice tense. "I'm sorry. But it's better this way. You don't want to be around me when I'm like this."

I don't know what to say to that. A part of me wants to reassure him that I'll stick by him unconditionally, but the truth is, he's right. I don't like him when he's acting this way, and it makes me wonder if I ever really knew him.

After a moment he releases me, and I show myself out.

CHAPTER

I make an effort to visit Jek a few times after that. I feel like I have a duty to sit with a sick friend and try to cheer him up, but every time I go to his door, the memory of that last encounter haunts me, and I feel more dread than pleasure at the idea of seeing him. I'm ashamed to admit I feel a little relieved every time Puloma tells me Jek doesn't want visitors. I'm more comfortable standing on the doorstep chatting with her than descending the stairs to Jek's grim sickroom.

Far from getting better, Jek seems to be slowly cutting himself off from all human interaction, which is what makes it all the more surprising when my cousin Manuel brings him up when we run into each other at the gas station.

"That friend of yours," he says. "The black kid."

"Jek?"

"Yeah. Is he all right?"

I shrug. "He hasn't been feeling well. Why, did you hear something?"

"I saw him today," Manuel says. "He was in the shop asking about some RNAi biopesticide he'd bought from me a couple of months ago. He bought out my whole stock back then, so I ordered more. Last week he came and bought that whole stock, too. I couldn't understand it. I asked what he's doing with enough of this stuff to serve an industrial farm, but he doesn't like to talk about it."

I remember the argument I walked in on between Jek and Manuel at the feed store. It sounds like this is a continuation of that.

"Jek's not a farmer," I tell him. "He uses farm supplies sometimes in science experiments, but I don't know what experiment this stuff is for."

"Whatever it is," says Manuel, "it doesn't seem to be going great. Today he was *pissed.* Told me there was something wrong with the pesticide I sold him, and I needed to go back to the original supplier. I told him this batch came from the same supplier. It was exactly the same as before. But he kept insisting that it was different, that there was something wrong with this batch.

"I kept trying to put him off, interest him in something else, but he was getting really upset. He was making threats, and when that didn't work, he started begging me. Said it was a matter of life-and-death. Finally I called the company, just to prove to him that I know what I'm talking about. Turns out he was right and there *had* been a change. But it wasn't like your friend thought. It wasn't the new batch that was messed up, it was the old one. It was corrupted. There was an unplanned mutation in the RNA, and they wound up recalling it. I didn't notice the alert since I was already out of stock then."

I press Manuel for more information, but that's all he knows. I'm shocked to hear that Jek's been out of the house at all, let alone gathering ingredients for his experiments. I want to believe this means he's feeling better, but I can't shake an ugly feeling that something is very wrong.

I wake up Saturday morning to a text from Jek.

I need to see you. Please come right away.

I stare at the words for at least a minute. Jek hasn't invited me over in ages. I don't dare hope this means he's getting better, but maybe at least he's ready to accept some outside help.

Of course, I text back. I'm on my way.

But before I've even found my keys, my phone buzzes again.

Wait, he texts. I need a favor. Do you still have my blue jacket?

I glance around the room and see it hanging on my closet door as it has been ever since I cleaned up from the night he stayed over. With a twinge, I remember that brief moment of bliss before everything went to hell.

Got it, I text him.

Bring it to me. Please.

I grab the jacket and take it with me, tossing it on the passenger seat of my car. As I drive over to his house under amber-tinted clouds, I try to imagine why Jek is suddenly interested in this jacket, after doing without it for so long. I thought he'd forgotten all about it. Is this some new form of madness, brought on by his withdrawal? But at least he's willing to see me, which is something.

I pull up at Jek's and grab the jacket, but something catches my eye as I'm about the slam the door closed: a flash of neon green disappearing under the passenger seat. I lean over and root around on the floor of the car until my fingers find it. After a moment, I grab it and shove it into my jeans pocket.

I knock at the front door and Puloma opens it almost immediately. Her glum expression brightens when she sees me.

"Lulu," she says. "This is a surprise. But if you're here to see Jayesh..." She offers me an apologetic smile.

"Actually, he texted me," I tell her. "Not too long ago. He asked me to come over."

"Really?" She looks puzzled for a moment before breaking into a relieved laugh. "I'm so glad to hear that! I was starting to worry about him, but if he's having friends over, he must be feeling better. Please, come in."

She steps aside and I follow her into the entryway.

"Has he been…worse, lately?" I ask, fearing the answer despite Puloma's suddenly cheerful demeanor.

"Hard to say, really," she explains. "I've hardly seen him all week."

"You mean he hasn't left his room at all?"

"Oh, he's been coming out at night to grab supplies from the kitchen," Puloma clarifies. "You know Jaycsh and his mole-person routine. He always does this when he's sulking or sick. But it doesn't usually last this long, and a mother can't help worrying." She smiles a little as if to ward off any irrational fears. "He's still getting supplies delivered for his experiments every day," she goes on, indicating a stack of boxes at the foot of the stairs. "So he's still working. I know it's been a tough few weeks for him, and I figure when he wants to talk, he'll let me know. But all the same, I'm glad to hear he got in touch with you." She reaches out and touches my hand, letting concern cloud her eyes. "You'll let me know how he is?" she requests with gentle pressure on my wrist.

"Of course," I tell her in what I hope is a reassuring tone. I don't want to weigh Puloma down with my own concerns, but the truth is, I'm not at all convinced by her optimistic perspective. All I really want is to get down to Jek's room and see what's going on for myself.

Puloma takes me down the stairs to Jek's apartment and

knocks on the door. There's no answer, only a barely audible shuffling sound. Puloma calls out, "Jayesh?"

"Go away," comes a hoarse, muffled voice from inside.

"He doesn't sound good," I say.

"Could be a cold," Puloma agrees in an undertone. "Lulu is here," she calls to him in a bright voice. "She's come to see you."

That muffled voice comes again, closer this time.

"Do you have my jacket?"

"Yes," I tell him, "I have it. Can I come in?"

We hear some more shuffling, then a click as the lock is released. "Yes," comes the voice, even more muffled than before. "Just you."

I exchange a look with Puloma and she squeezes my arm encouragingly.

"I'll be just upstairs," she murmurs. "If there's anything you need, don't hesitate to call me."

I watch her go, then turn back to the door. Taking a deep breath, I turn the knob and push it open.

CHAPTER

I take a step inside, expecting to be greeted by the heavy stench of illness, but instead there is only the usual aroma of burning chemicals, with something faintly sweet underneath. All around, there are signs of furious experimentation, with boxes from various agricultural suppliers piled up all over the living room. Some of them look as if they've been kicked over, and there's a pile of shattered glass near one wall.

I move toward the bedroom, expecting to find Jek groaning under a pile of blankets and used tissues, but the bed is neatly made and Jek is nowhere to be found. The only thing out of place is a small, ornately decorated hand mirror on the floor next to the bed, which looks like it belongs among Puloma's things.

I head back into the main room, but Jek isn't on the couch

or in his lab. The bathroom door, however, is closed. I take a step toward it.

"Jek? Are you in there?"

"Put the jacket on the table and leave," comes the muffled response.

"Come out and talk to me, Jek," I say, trying to keep my voice as steady and calm as possible.

I hear some movement, but the door doesn't open. "Just put it on the table and go," he says. "Please."

"No," I say more forcefully. "I'm not leaving until I've seen you."

There's a long pause. "You don't know what you're asking," he says at last. "You'll regret it."

I don't know what he's talking about, but it's starting to scare me. How sick is he? I resort to the only ammunition I have.

"Come out," I say, "or I'll call your mom right now and tell her something is really wrong." I'm halfway to doing that, anyway. Everything about this situation is ringing my alarm bells.

There's a long moment of silence, followed by some more shuffling. I hold my breath as I wait, but just as I've made my mind up to head back upstairs for Puloma, he answers me.

"Fine," he says, sounding grim. "But I did warn you."

There's the click of the latch, the creak of the hinge and he steps through the doorway. I immediately notice his familiar old pajamas and a ratty T-shirt. I don't see any evidence of sickness… I don't see Jek, either.

I see Hyde.

For a moment, I just stare, my brain fighting to grasp the vision in front of me. It's definitely Hyde, but he looks different—in fact, I realize he looks healthier than I've ever seen him. I remember the sickly yellow cast his complexion had when I first met him, but now his skin is tanned and golden. His features, too, seem inexplicably firmer, more clearly defined. It's almost like he's been growing stronger, feeding off the damage he's inflicted on others.

Horrified at this thought, I open my mouth to yell for help, but he's up against me before I can make a sound, pressing me hard against the wall, his fingers squeezed tight around my jaw.

"Don't scream," he hisses in my ear, his sharp citrus scent filling my nose.

I struggle against him until I manage to get an elbow free and knock him in the ribs. He loosens his grip and I try to wriggle free, but my strength is no match for his. He grasps me harder and wrestles me down onto the couch, where he pins me with the length of his body, his hand still tight against my mouth.

I can feel his hot, panting breath on my neck, feel the hammering of his heart where his chest is pressed to mine. I try to make some noise around his hand, but he presses in tighter with a wild look in his eyes. Just like that, a vision comes to me of Danny Carew stretched out on that slab, beaten almost beyond recognition. I feel the brute strength of Hyde's long, sinuous body all around me, and I know how easy it would be for him to do the same to me.

I force myself to calm down and hold still, though tears of panic and fear leak from my eyes. Gradually Hyde eases off me and turns his attention to the jacket, which has fallen to the floor. He falls to his knees by the couch as he searches the pockets furiously.

I push myself up into a sitting position.

"Where is Jek?" I half sob. "What did you do to him?"

Hyde drops the jacket in a rage and gets to his feet. "It's not here," he roars in my face, pushing my shoulders against the couch. "Where is it? What did you do with it?"

"What have you done to Jek?" I demand again.

Hyde releases me and spins away, scraping his hands through his hair. "I know it was in there. What happened to it?"

I pull the green vial from my pocket.

"Is this what you're looking for?"

Hyde turns and stares at me a moment, his eyes trained almost hungrily on the vial. He makes a move toward me.

"Don't," I say through gritted teeth. "I swear to God, I will snap this in two if you take one more step."

"You wouldn't," he says, but his eyes are wide and he looks panicked.

"Why shouldn't I? I don't even know what it is. It's worthless to me."

He puts out one trembling hand. "Give it to me."

"No," I say, drawing it back. "This is that drug, isn't it? The drug you had Jek hooked on." As I talk, I feel my fear sliding away, replaced by a wave of fury. It's clear that as long as I hold this vial, I have power over Hyde. But that just reminds me of what he and his drugs have done to Jek. I hold the vial up higher before him.

"He told me all about it," I continue. "He's been trying to kick it, and the withdrawal is slowly destroying him. Did you know about that when you started dealing it to him?"

Hyde eyes the vial a moment more. He lunges for it but I'm too quick for him and duck to the other side of the coffee table.

"So was it Jek texting me about his jacket this morning, or was it you? Wouldn't be the first time you've used his phone."

Hyde takes another step toward me, and I continue backing away, holding the vial up.

"How long have you been hiding here?" I ask, though I don't expect an answer. The question is more for myself. Puloma told me she hadn't actually seen Jek in a while. A dull, clammy horror takes me as I try to figure how long it might be since Hyde got rid of Jek and took his place. But why? Why would he want to be locked up here, in Jek's house?

Hyde lunges again, almost catching me off guard this time. "For God's sake, Lulu. Give it to me!" He's breathing hard, veins in his neck rippling as he tries to control himself.

"You're hooked on it, too, aren't you? Is that what brought you back here? Your own supply went dry?"

"Please," he says in a more desperate tone. "Please, I need it."

"I don't give a shit about you. For the last time, where is Jek? What have you done to him?"

He reaches out again. "Give it to me and you'll know soon enough."

"No. Tell me first."

Hyde makes another swipe for it, but I slip out of the way just in time. "Don't test me," I say. "I will smash this right now."

That threat seems to shake him. He lowers his hands, and the tension goes out of his body.

"Lulu," he pleads, his voice cracking. "You don't know what you're doing. That vial…it's not just some drug. It's my masterwork."

I drop my hand and stare at him. "What are you talking about?"

He takes a long, shaky breath. "I tried to tell you before," he continues, "but I knew you wouldn't understand. It's a world-changing discovery, more than any other drug I developed. But the trial is dead. The experiment can't be repeated."

I shake my head, confused. "I don't—"

"That's the last of it. The last of the original batch. There's an ingredient that I'll never be able to track down. I was using a genetically modified biopesticide from your cousin's store, and the reaction produced something beyond all my theorizing. I thought…I thought I had discovered some revolutionary new process. But a couple of weeks ago, I started to run low. I went back to the store and bought more, but this new batch didn't work. It was inert, totally useless. I ordered from every supplier I could find, but it was no good. Finally I went back to Manuel, demanding to know where the original batch had come from. But he told me…" Hyde stops and takes another slow breath. "He told me it was the first batch that had some mutation. And now it's gone."

"No," I say. "That wasn't you. Jek spoke to Manuel."

Hyde keeps talking, his voice so low I can barely catch the words. "My supplies got lower and lower, until I had used the very last of it. That's when I remembered the vial in my jacket. I left it in your room after the night we spent together."

"Stop it," I insist, but a cool pulse of dread thuds inside me. "You're lying—you were never at my house."

He takes a step toward me, slowly this time, not threatening but beseeching. He goes down on his knees and puts his hand out.

"The vial," he says. "Please. Give it to me, and you'll understand everything."

I look into his black eyes and see the torment and desperation there. If I scream now, Hyde will have nothing to lose, and he might attack me. But it won't take long for Puloma to arrive and to get help. It's my best bet for saving myself, and ensuring the capture of a murderer. It's the right choice. But my own curiosity is gnawing at me, too. There's something real to what he's saying—I feel it deep inside me. If either Hyde or I is killed in the next few minutes, I'll never find out what it is, never get the answer to this mystery.

I look down at him trembling before me, and I can't help but feel a twinge of pity for this pathetic creature. Against my better judgment—almost against my own will—some force takes hold of me and I reach out to him. I open my fingers around the vial and press it into his hand.

The relief in his eyes is instantaneous but only momentarily. In a whirl of movement, he twists toward the lab bench and fumbles around until his fingers find a hypodermic syringe. He pops off the protective cap and inserts the needle directly into the vial, emptying it of its strange green liquid. Then he yanks his T-shirt off over his head and throws himself down on the couch, tugging the waist of the pajamas down and feeling for the perfect spot just over his hip bone. He hesitates a moment with the needle poised and takes a few deep, fortifying breaths. Then he gives me one last, burning look before closing his eyes and pushing the needle under his skin.

CHAPTER

The bright green liquid disappears into firm flesh as Hyde applies steady pressure to the plunger. For a moment, he just lies there with his eyes closed, his chest heaving. Then a spasm flickers across his face. It's followed by another one, much more severe, and he bites his lip against a cry. He is shuddering and panting, muscles twitching all through his lean torso. Then his body twists and he curls into a moaning ball in the corner of the couch. The muscles across his back bunch and release under a sheen of sweat. His fingers are knotted up in anguish, his hair plastered to his forehead. He grabs a worn cushion and bites into it, muffling a pathetic whimper.

Another spasm overtakes him, and he rolls over, his back arching, his eyes squeezed shut. The trembling worsens until his whole body is quaking and writhing. He moans and runs his hands over his skin.

It's obvious he is no physical threat to me in his current state, but somehow I'm transfixed by his movements and I can't break the trance long enough to go for help. Whatever my disgust with Hyde, I can't feel anything but pity for him in this condition.

With a choked-back cry, he seizes violently once more and finally I'm spurred into action—not to run away or call Puloma, but to throw myself across his body and pin his arms to his side to keep him from hurting himself. I half expect him to throw me off or turn on me in a snarling rage, but he only shifts restlessly, leaning into the pressure and making whining, fevered noises.

Still leaning heavily on him, I raise one hand to stroke his face and smooth out the restless tension in his muscles. His damp skin has taken on a deep rosy flush. It starts on his chest and throat, then spreads up to his cheeks and down to his belly. I expect it to fade as his body relaxes into exhaustion, but the flush only gets worryingly darker and deeper, tinting the flesh of his torso, his face and then even his arms and hands. When he opens his eyes, the pupils are fully dilated, his lips are swollen from being bitten and chewed, and his hair is so damp with sweat that it looks a shade darker. More than a shade.

I let go of him and move back. Something is *happening* to Hyde.

He looks different. His hair is longer, the loose brown

curls forming darker, more defined ringlets. And when I take a breath, Hyde's bright, citrus blossom smell is fading, or rather shifting into the warm, homey smell of lightly burnt chemicals.

"No," I whisper to myself. "It's impossible."

Hyde's nose is broader and flatter now, and when he opens his eyes again, they are not black but amber brown. And familiar. Eyes I've known since childhood.

"Lu," he says, but it's not Hyde's throaty rasp. He reaches up a hand to touch my cheek. "You stayed."

I look down at him, my eyes searching his face for some explanation of what I've just seen.

"I'm dreaming," I say.

He is utterly spent, his chest heaving but his tightened muscles beginning to relax.

"Jek," I breathe.

He nods.

"Who are you? *What* are you?"

With some effort, he pushes himself into a more upright position. His breath has evened out now, and he's looking at me intently through those familiar eyes. Everything about him, every feature of his face, every line and sinew of his body, I've had memorized for so long. But he feels like a stranger.

"Tell me," I say. "Tell me what the hell just happened."

"I can't," he says, his voice still a little rough. "I mean, I don't completely understand it myself. What you said before, about drugs, about addiction…you weren't far off. Except this isn't an ordinary drug."

I stand up and grab on to the back of a chair, not trusting my knees for support. "You developed it," I say. "*This* was your masterpiece? The one you were working on all summer."

Jek nods. "One drug to affect body and mind. Why not? They aren't as separate as we used to believe. Hormones govern every aspect of your body—your thoughts and emotions, your personality, but also your muscular development, your growth, your shape and size. It's all biochemistry. Why treat them separately?"

"But your skin," I say. "Your hair, your eyes. Hyde doesn't look a thing like you."

Jek smiles weakly. "I spent ages on research, developing theories to explain this effect. But it wasn't until Manuel told me about the mutated pesticide that I realized there was a factor I hadn't taken into account. If I had more time, more supplies, maybe I could eventually isolate the mutation, the catalyst behind this reaction. But I don't have the resources."

"So it was you, then, all along?" I say, my voice trembling. "*You* who raped Natalie and paid her off. *You* who threw those orgy parties. *You* who beat Danny Carew to death with your bike lock."

"No," he says fiercely, his eyes bright. "It wasn't me, I swear. Hyde is…he's more than a disguise. He's someone else completely. Maybe at first, he felt like a part of me I'd always wanted to let loose, but I can't accept that his actions are mine. I can't think back on any of the things he did and see myself in them."

I shake my head. "I know what I just saw, but…none of this makes any sense."

"Then let me explain it," Jek begs. "I don't have much time, but you deserve that much."

I watch him closely, considering my options. I know I should go get Puloma, but something stops me. I've waited so long for the truth. I need to hear it now. I take a deep breath, then motion for him to go on.

"Last summer," he begins. "I was working on some new psychoactive drugs. I came across a paper by Wilhelm Von Hoyrich theorizing that certain chemicals might alter genetics ex post facto to produce a different gene expression. He proposed a mechanism by which a chemical could work through a strand of DNA, reversing the form of chiral molecules to their enantiomers. It was genius. The most exciting theory I'd seen in ages. My mom said the guy was a crank and that it would never work in lab conditions, but I wanted to test it out. I had to work with the materials I had available, and I ran into a lot of dead ends, but by fall I'd had a breakthrough with some compounds I isolated from London Chem's new RNAi biopesticide."

"Jesus," I breathe, sitting down heavily in the chair across from him.

"I tested it on a few plants and the results were… I couldn't believe it, Lu. I watched a monocot flower turn into a dicot before my eyes. It should have been impossible! No matter how many times I worked through the chemical equations, I couldn't make sense of it. Nothing in my research suggested a mechanism for this change."

Across from me, Jek's eyes are wide, and there's something oddly familiar in his expression. He's *excited*. I used to love that look—the raw enthusiasm Jek would radiate as an experiment started to bear fruit. Now it just scares me. As much pain and death as he has caused, Jek still can't help being enthralled by the science.

"You should have stopped there," I tell him. "Jek, you had no idea what you were dealing with. You should have gotten help."

"But it was *working*," he exclaims. He stands and starts pacing, just like the old days when he'd explain to me whatever brilliant new project he was working on. "Don't you see? The science was…the science was *there*, I just couldn't see it yet. And I knew I would, if I just looked harder. If I studied the process more closely."

"So you decided to try it on yourself?" I ask, horrified that Jek would take such a risk.

"I had to see, Lulu! I was up against a brick wall—I needed more data. I didn't want to go public with it until I understood it completely. Besides, the human genome is so much more complex than a plant's. I didn't really believe it would work."

"But it did."

"Better than I could have dreamed," he says, his face lighting up at the memory. "That first time it hurt so much I thought I was dying. I'm pretty sure I passed out for a few minutes. But when I came to and looked in the bathroom mirror, there was a *stranger* looking back at me. This was more than a disguise—there wasn't one feature in my face that I recognized."

I realize then that I'm staring at his face as he talks—at that familiar face—and I have to look away. I feel unmoored, dizzy with all the thoughts crowding my brain as my memories realign themselves with this new information.

"The chemical compound was unstable," Jek continues, "which produced a strange effect. It made Hyde's features slightly indistinct—slippery, almost, as if they hadn't quite fixed themselves in place." I cover my mouth, remembering the uncanny feeling I got whenever I looked at him, and the difficulty everyone had describing him. "No one ever seemed to register it consciously, but it made it harder for people to remember his face. That suited my purposes just fine."

"Your purposes..." I whisper, half to myself. "You started going to the city, putting Hyde to work. You thought you could keep him away from your real life, here in London. But Chicago wasn't far enough. Hyde ran into Hailee there, while he was dealing your drugs, and she recognized them. That's why she told me you were in business together."

Jek isn't pacing anymore. He stands there, watching me warily, the excitement of a few minutes ago sapped away.

"You got braver, then," I continue, my voice growing

stronger. "You started going to parties here. You even told your mom about him. But Hyde got into trouble and you had to use your own money to cover it up."

Jek sits down abruptly and leans toward me, his eyes appealing. "What happened with Natalie Martinez..." Jek lets out a breath. "I woke up feeling sick over it. Worst of all was that he got away with it—I hated him for that. But Hyde never did anything like it again. Not out of altruism or anything, just because he's terrified of the cops. Getting locked up in jail is the worst thing he can imagine."

I stand and walk toward a window. I can't stand to look at Jek right now, while I'm trying to make the boy I thought I knew fit into this strange new story. All I can handle now is facts.

"The trailer," I say. "The new phone. You were trying to give him a separate identity, so the police wouldn't trace him to you."

"Not just the police," says Jek from behind me. "You. From the beginning, you had all these questions about Hyde and how I knew him. No one else really cared. I thought if I could keep him separate from my regular life—moving in different circles, living across town—you'd let it go. I even got him his own bank account."

"But I couldn't let it go," I murmur to myself, and I feel my lips curve into a bitter smile. How much trauma might I have spared myself if I had dropped it? If I had accepted Jek's explanations and left him to his secrets. Would I be better off without this awful knowledge?

I hear Jek's voice again, closer this time.

"I tried to warn you away from him. But the harder I tried, the more curious you got. And Hyde got curious about you. Of course he did—it's his nature. Hyde helps himself to all the things I can't even admit I want."

I turn around at last and face him.

"And did you?" I let myself look into his eyes, still not knowing if I can trust what I see there. "Want me?"

Jek looks at me seriously, his eyes shining.

"Lulu," he says, his voice cracking. "You have no idea. When Hyde started to pursue you, it drove me crazy. I made myself sick, worrying what he might do to you. What he was capable of." He reaches out and I feel his tentative touch on my arm. I can't help but flinch away. Jek swallows and sets his jaw. "I did the only thing I could, under the circumstances. The night we kissed, I got rid of him."

"For a while," I say, my voice hard. "Then you brought him back."

Jek shakes his head. "It's not that simple. Elements of the experiment were...unpredictable. There were variables beyond my control."

"Variables?" I repeat, amazed at his scientific remove.

"Transforming into Hyde had always been painful," he explains carefully, "but in the beginning, changing back to myself was easy. Then slowly, without my really noticing, it started to shift. It got easier and easier to slip into Hyde, until it was about the same going either way. Then it was the transformation back to myself that became difficult. A couple of times, it didn't work at all and I needed to give myself a double dose of the drug. It should have worried me, but I didn't want to think about what it meant."

Jek moves back to his chair and sits down. His hands are clasped in front of his mouth, his forehead creased with thought. When he speaks, his voice is heavy with the ugly memory.

"One day I woke up in my bedroom and felt disoriented for some reason. It was as if the colors were off, and the light was coming from the wrong direction. I reached for my phone to check the time, and that's when I saw it. My hands were Hyde's." He looks up at me, reading my face for understanding. "I had transformed into him while I was sleeping. Without the drug."

I can't help my sharp inhale of breath at the thought. As furious as I am with him, a part of me can only imagine how terrifying it must have been to wake up like that.

"I panicked, of course," says Jek, running one shaking hand through his hair. "What if my mom called me, or one of the kids came looking for me? What would I do? I fixed myself a double dose of the drug and that got me back to normal. And I marked it in my lab notes as a fluke. After that, I started carrying a vial of the drug with me, as insurance, but I didn't dwell on it. Instead, I focused on you and tried to put Hyde behind me. But he kept slipping back in."

Against my will, my mind takes me back through my memories of this time. Jek taking me on dates, holding my hand. Then that day at the butterfly pavilion, when he became so forceful I hardly recognized him. And that night…

"You hit Tom," I say, remembering Puloma's face when she told me. She wasn't just upset, she was baffled. It was so out of character for the Jek we both knew.

Jek looks down at his hands, clenching and unclenching them. "It was just one punch," he says, his voice low and tight, "but I wanted so much more. I could have kept beating him all night." He looks up at me. "I knew I was losing control. Hyde was changing me—making me want things, making me do things I would never have considered before. I had to get away before I did real damage. I transformed myself into Hyde and went to the city to hide out for a while. I thought it would help ease some of the pressure, but I'd kept him caged too long. When he came out, he came out roaring."

I look away, images flashing through my mind. That strange club. Hyde, alone in that room with me… My body is rocked by a horrified shudder at how things might have gone.

"I don't understand," I say weakly. "Hyde had everything he wanted then. Why would he ever change back to you?"

"He was running out of drugs and money," Jek explains. "He'd been running up illegal debts, and the managers of The Glass Horse were threatening him. He knew his only way out of trouble was to disappear for a while. That's why he promised you Jek would be back by the following night."

I close my eyes and try not to think about the next part, but it forces its way into my mind. "That night," I say slowly. "Hyde never told you what I wanted, or what I'd asked for. You knew because you were there. You were *him*."

Jek drops his head a little, as if conceding the point. "When I turned back to myself," he says, "I was furious that you had chosen him over me. But at the same time, I felt like..." He takes my hand in his and I open my eyes. "Like you were the only person who truly understood me. *Us.* It was amazing, given how hard I'd tried to hide everything from you. But somehow you seemed to get it. You promised over and over again that you wouldn't judge me for my secrets, and I never believed I could trust you. But it was true. You weren't afraid of Hyde or disgusted with him, any more than you were with me. You accepted us both. You wanted us both."

He drops my hand and sits down again, a pained expression on his face.

"You have no idea," he says, "how close I came to telling you everything that night. But something held me back. The look in your eyes... I didn't want to lose that. I knew I would tell you eventually, but just for that one night, I wanted us to be Jek and Lulu, like old times, without the baggage of Hyde."

I cross the room and sit down across from him.

"Then it happened again," I fill in, understanding now.

"You woke up in the middle of the night, in my bed, as Hyde."

He nods silently. I can't help it: I put a hand over my mouth, feeling suddenly queasy at the thought of going to bed with one man and waking up with another in my arms. What would I have done if I had woken up like that?

"When I couldn't find my emergency vial, I ran off," says Jek, continuing the story. "I went straight to the trailer and ransacked the whole place looking for another vial, but there was nothing. It was getting light, I couldn't go back to my house. Tom had padlocked the side door, and my family wasn't about to let Hyde in the front. I decided to bike out to the grain elevator to lie low for a while. I thought maybe I could wait out the day there and think of a way to sneak back into my lab after dark. On the way I ran into Danvers Carew."

"Don't." I stop him, holding up one hand. "I can't. I already saw his body. I can't listen to you describe what happened."

Jek nods slightly and hangs his head.

"When it was over, I kept on to the grain elevator. I didn't know what else to do. I was covered in blood, there was a witness… My only hope was to make Hyde disappear. I got the idea to text Lane pretending to be Jek. I asked him to break into my house, into the locked cabinet, and bring me another vial of the drug. I don't know how crazy I must have sounded, but Lane…well, you know Lane. He'd do anything for a friend."

"But what about when he got there with the stuff? He must have seen you."

"I tried to avoid that. I hid in the shadows when he arrived, and texted him to just leave the drug on the floor and go—I was hoping he'd assume I wasn't there yet. But he was suspicious. He started peering around the space inside the grain elevator, calling me to come out and talk to him. I kept silent and eventually he seemed to give up. He put the vial on the floor near the entrance and left.

"By this time I was in such a panic to turn myself into Jek, I dashed forward and grabbed up the vial as soon as he was outside. But Lane hadn't gone very far. He must have seen me from where he was, or heard me and come back. In any case, when he returned, he found me on my knees, a syringe already sunk into my skin.

"He was shocked, of course. Kept asking me where Jek was, why I was using his phone. When I didn't answer, he became more aggressive. He grabbed me, and I grappled with him, trying to get him off me by shoving him up against those rusty old pieces of machinery. In fact—" Jek pauses and looks away guiltily "—as Hyde, I had every intention of killing him. Now that he had seen me, it seemed like the only way to keep my secret.

"Hyde is stronger than I am, but more important is how vicious he is. He never loses a physical fight, just because he is willing to be far more brutal than a normal person. He's completely unrestrained by human morality or decency. Lane fought hard, but soon enough I started to get the better of him. I had him in a choke hold, when suddenly the strength went out of me. The drug was taking effect, and, well, you saw what it does to me. When the change comes, I feel like I'm being ripped apart. I was bent over with pain, and I had to let him go.

"Lane was pretty confused when he saw me crumple to the ground like that. He actually asked if I was all right—me, a guy who had just been trying to kill him. All I could think was that he was going to see my transformation, and my secret would be out. My thoughts in that moment were strange, confused. A part of me was fixated on murdering him to protect my secret as long as possible. But another part felt a sense of relief, almost, at the idea of this double life finally being over. I tried to warn him about what he was about to see, told him to get away, but he was transfixed. The transformation had begun, and I could see on his face that he had no idea how to make sense of what was happening.

"I had watched myself change dozens of times, seen all the effects in a mirror. But I had never seen myself through someone else's eyes before. I watched the horror and revulsion dawn in his expression as he encountered something so far beyond his imagination.

"Then it was over. I looked down at my hands and saw that I was Jek again. I took a step toward Lane, thinking I might somehow explain myself, but it was too late. Even in the body of his old friend, I was nothing but a monster to him. He was pale, drenched in sweat, and his jaw worked but what came out was meaningless babble. Again, I considered finishing him off, but it was clear that he was in no state to share my secret. To be on the safe side, I told him that if he ever told anyone what he'd seen, I'd kill him, just like I killed Carew."

"Jesus Christ, Jek," I say, feeling sickened. "Lane is your best friend."

I can hardly imagine what Lane must have thought, must have felt after seeing the transformation. For me, at least I'd had my suspicions, so when I finally encountered the truth, it was almost a relief to know I wasn't completely crazy. But Lane had no idea there was anything strange about Jek's relationship with Hyde. He would have been completely unprepared. It's no wonder to me that he freaked out.

Jek doesn't bother to defend himself. He just keeps on with his story.

"For a few hours," he says, "I thought I had everything under control. The cops bought my story, and Lane wasn't talking. Then you came by with Hyde's phone."

I nod to myself, seeing it all too clearly now. "I was so confused when I hacked in and didn't find a single message between you. But of course there weren't any. You shared a body. Why would you need to text?"

Jek closes his eyes and represses a shiver. Now that the shock of seeing his transformation has worn off, I realize how sickly he looks. His eyes are glassy, his skin gray and he's growing shiny with sweat. It's almost as if Hyde has been bleeding him of his vitality to boost his own.

"You were so close to the truth," he says quietly, as if it costs him some effort. "Only hours earlier I had promised myself I would tell you everything in the morning, but things were different now. Hyde was a wanted man. Even worse, you'd seen for yourself what he was capable of. Any sympathy you'd had for him was gone."

"You pushed me away with that story of drug addiction. You tried to fix it yourself by doing all those good deeds."

"It didn't work," says Jek dully. "No matter what I tried, the spontaneous transformations kept happening. Anytime I let my mind wander. I had to use more and more of the drug just to return to myself each time."

"Until you ran out," I say, completing the story at last. "The only vial left was the one you'd lost in my room. Your last chance to return to your original body."

Jek looks at me with inflamed, bloodshot eyes. I stare back, my mind a whirl of emotions. I still can't believe it. Every horrible thing he's done, every lie he's lived. But I also see the torment he has endured written so clearly on his face.

"So what happens now?" I ask at last. "If you're out of your supply, what will you do once this dose wears off and Hyde starts to take over again?"

Jek takes a deep breath and lets it out slowly, his eyes staring at nothing. When he looks up at me again, his gaze is steady and determined.

"Hyde wanted that vial today because he thought disguising himself as me was his only chance to get out of this prison," he explains. "He believed that, as Jek, I'd take the risk of leaving here, and then he could transform back to Hyde. He can't imagine that not everyone is as afraid of self-destruction as he is."

I watch his face closely, trying to make sense of his words, but they won't fit together right. "I don't understand," I say at last. "What are you saying?"

Jek doesn't look away. "Hyde is extremely volatile," he says firmly. "His personality is governed by desire, anger and fear. He's terrified of the police, and that fear keeps him in the shadows. But if his desire or anger ever become stronger than his fear, there'd be no stopping him. He'd kill anyone who stood in his way, without hesitation—my mom, my stepbrothers. You. I can't let that happen."

I stare at him, willing his words to rearrange themselves and mean something different, but I can tell that he has been thinking this over for a long time.

"You can't mean it," I say, shaking my head. "I won't let you end your own life to stop him."

Jek closes his eyes. His face is tense and lined like someone much older, and for a moment, I can see the toll that living two lives has taken on him.

"Lu, you don't understand. The Jek you knew is as good as dead now—in a few minutes, I'll turn back to Hyde, and you'll never see me again. If I do this now, though—at least I can take the monster with me when I go."

"Jek, no," I say, forcing my voice steady. "We can buy you some time, there has to be a way. If we can stabilize this, you could continue your research. We could talk to your mom, she could help. With the resources of London Chem, she could perform a genetic analysis. Maybe she could reverse engineer the chemical reaction and recreate the mutated strain from the other batch. Then we could get rid of Hyde for good, and you can go back to just being yourself."

Even though his time is slipping away, Jek doesn't answer me right away. He looks down at me with a softness in his eyes, and touches a hand to my face.

"Lu," he says at last, "there's something you have to understand. Me and Hyde…there's no difference anymore. When I started this experiment, Hyde felt like a completely different person from me, doing things I would never have dreamed of, things that disgusted me. But the longer this has gone on, the more of him there is in me. His violence, his lusts…they've become mine, too. In fact, maybe I was kidding myself all along that we were so different. On some level, everything Hyde wanted, everything he did—those things all started inside of me. That's why Hyde had to have you. He was only acknowledging the feelings I'd been too cowardly to admit."

I try to respond to this, but I can't manage more than a strangled sob.

"There's something evil inside of me," he continues.

"Maybe the experiment created it, or maybe it was always there…but now that it's been unleashed, there's only one way to stop it forever."

"No," I say, half choking. "No, Jek—"

"I feel it coming on," he says, moving away from me. "I don't have much time left. I have to do it now, or I'll have wasted this chance."

Jek stands up and crosses to the glass cabinet. Sweat is beading on his forehead, and his muscles are already straining with the effort of controlling the transformation. He opens the cabinet and pulls out a squat bottle with some kind of white crystalline powder inside.

"What is that?" I say, though a part of me already knows. "What are you doing?"

"Sodium cyanide," he says. "I started keeping it around about a month ago, as a last-ditch solution to my problem."

I rush across the room toward him, but he slips away from me, putting the lab bench between us. "No," I sob, reaching across for the bottle. "Stop, you don't have to do this."

He holds the bottle out of my reach and uncaps it. "Please, Lu," he says, "don't make this worse. I've known this moment was coming for a while now. Ever since I realized I couldn't control the transformations, I've had the idea in the back of my mind. Believe me, I've done nothing but try to think of an alternative for the past month. I tried everything I could think of to avoid this step, and my delay cost Carew his life. If I let Hyde take over again, who knows what evil he might do next?"

I make another lunge for him, but he tips the substance down his throat before I can stop him. For a moment, he's perfectly still, and I can only stare at him, frozen in horror. Then he reaches for the lab bench and leans heavily on it, his breathing fast and shallow. Before my eyes, his face pales even further, and I can almost convince myself that I'm watching him transform again, back into Hyde or maybe some other impossible creature. But I know that's not the case when Jek lurches to the floor and begins scrabbling at his neck, his breathing choked and labored.

I rush over to him and pull his head into my lap.

"No," I say, my voice shaking. "I can tell your mom everything right now. She can fix this. We'll take you to the hospital, pump your stomach."

But Jek shakes his head, his eyes wild and pleading, his breath coming in great gasps. He grabs my hand and squeezes it painfully hard. "Please," he chokes out, his voice thick and constricted. "Just stay with me."

And I do. I sit with him through it all, holding his hand and wiping sweat from his forehead and squeezing him tight through the convulsions.

Once he is gone, I call Puloma and let her see the body. I let her believe the story she has already told herself: that Jek was depressed, had recently turned suicidal, that he'd already taken the cyanide before I came in, and there was nothing I could do to stop it.

She's devastated, of course, but at least she has a story that makes sense. I know I'd never convince her of the truth, in all its insanity. If she had come in and found her son missing and a known murderer dead on his couch, the mystery of it would have been ten times worse.

CHAPTER

Jek was buried about six months ago in the cemetery outside town. Since his death, Lane's mental health has improved steadily, though he still can't stand anyone to mention Jek near him. He has no interest in returning to London, but he's been catching up with his schoolwork while living in the psych ward, and Hailee says he's planning to go away to college next year.

Puloma left Tom about a month after the funeral, and left her job at London Chem, too. She went back east to stay with her parents for a while, and I haven't heard much from her since.

Camila surprised everyone by joining the military after graduation. Some of the family were pretty upset, but I'm happy for her that she figured a way out of this town.

The investigation into Danvers Carew's murder remains

open. Inspector Newcomen and the London police force have long since given up claiming any promising leads, but officially Hyde is still considered dangerous and at large.

As for the rest of London… I want to say that it has changed since Jek died, but I don't think it has much, for most people. For a while all anyone could talk about was Danny's murder and Jek's presumed suicide, and the mysterious drifter everyone agrees was responsible for both.

It kills me that everyone in town thinks Jek's death was a suicide, since as far as I'm concerned, it wasn't that at all. What I witnessed was no act of desperation or despair, but a brave and noble sacrifice to serve a greater good. If nothing else, I wish I could grant Jek the honor of publicly recognizing that. But I'm the only one who knows the real story, and so it's up to me to carry on his memory.

Meanwhile, everything else has pretty much gone back to normal: the scientists at London Chem are still patenting new products and processes, and still ignoring the protesters picketing on their front lawn. The laborers who work every day with the London Chem products are still suffering from the strange sickness that no one wants to talk about. And the kegger circuit still rages while parents look the other way.

It feels different for me, though. Like *I'm* different. For a while after the funeral I felt split in two, like Jek had infected me somehow with his strange condition. Part of me was locked in by mourning, only going through the motions of normal teenage life while immersed in the grief of losing my best friend. Meanwhile, another part observed and analyzed, endlessly replaying the past few months in my head, frantically searching the minutiae of my life for details that would help me make sense of what happened.

So many innocent moments have taken on new meaning in light of the terrible knowledge Jek left me with.

As painful as it all is, there's a certain grim satisfaction that comes with understanding at last. After months of constantly doubting my own mind and perceptions, I finally feel sane again. Ever since I first met Hyde, I'd had the feeling there was something unnatural about him and his relationship to Jek, but Jek kept telling me not to worry about it, that it was nothing. Something in me always knew that wasn't right. I've lost so much in this ordeal, but in discovering the truth, I feel as though I've won a part of myself back.

Lately I've been thinking a lot about what Jek said to me before he died—about how he and Hyde weren't all that different in the end. I didn't want to believe that at first; I couldn't accept it. It was so much easier to preserve Jek in my memory as perfectly good and pure and innocent, but no one is really that simple. The more I think about it, the more I realize how similar Jek and Hyde really were. They were both scientific in their approach to the world. Hyde didn't bother with chemistry, but he was relentless in his curiosity about other people, obsessively cataloging and enacting their most secret desires. He and Jek both craved knowledge, but

Jek lacked the confidence to take his investigations outside the laboratory. Hyde allowed him to do that.

I miss Jek so much…but I find more and more that I miss Hyde, too. For a while, I couldn't think of Hyde as anything but the monster who took Jek from me…but Hyde also recognized something in me I never wanted to admit to—a part of me that's attracted to danger, that craves knowledge and experience, even against my own better judgment. The part that screwed around on my devoted boyfriend when he went missing; the part that hardly hesitated before stealing Hyde's phone and hacking into Jek's secrets. Hyde forced me to acknowledge a darkness I wanted to deny in myself…and in his way, he taught me to appreciate and respect that side of me as much as any other.

Next year I'll be going off to college. Somehow through all this turmoil, I've managed to take my mother's advice and stay focused on my studies and my scholarship applications. Everyone in the family is assuming I'll go into computer science or some sort of tech field. They don't know that I've picked out a couple of chemistry courses for next semester. It was never my best subject, but then, my whole life I was comparing myself to Jek. Now some part of me feels compelled to take it up. To, if I can, carry on his work. With his passion for understanding the universe, it must have tortured him to know that the thing that was destroying him was beyond his comprehension.

I owe it to Jek to seek out the truth he couldn't uncover.

If I can find it—if I can isolate that mysterious compound

that caused Jek's transformations—what doors might that open? Jek's experiment produced results beyond his wildest imagining, but there is still so much left untested. What effects might his drug have on a different subject? On me, for example. Would I split off and produce another Hyde, or someone completely different?

I can't stop wondering what my own shadow-self would be like…

And I can't wait to meet her.

AUTHOR'S NOTE

One of my earliest memories is of watching a cartoon on TV—I think it was Woody Woodpecker, but it might have been Bugs Bunny—in which a character drank a colorful solution from a test tube and physically changed into a dark, looming, threatening beast. It was meant for kids, but even so, the sinister imagery haunted my dreams that night, and I woke up screaming.

That was probably my first encounter with Robert Louis Stevenson's *The Strange Case of Dr. Jekyll and Mr. Hyde*, or one of its many adaptations. It certainly wasn't the last. The story showed up in dozens of different versions—in film, on TV, even in comics. The Incredible Hulk is almost certainly a deliberate homage. *Jekyll and Hyde* beats even *Dracula* for the number of adaptations it has spawned.

What's even more remarkable is how much the character comes up in conversation. A friend talking about a difficult ex-boyfriend, given to mood swings, might describe him as "like Jekyll and Hyde." Sports commentators pull up the comparison, too, any time a player is very good in some games, and very bad in others. "Which will we get today," they ask, "Jekyll or Hyde?"

Thanks to all these casual references, I grew up feeling like I had a pretty good understanding of the story. I never read it, because I didn't think I had to. I already knew the basic idea: mad scientist invents a potion that splits him into a good guy and a bad guy. If I sometimes had trouble remembering whether Jekyll was good and Hyde was bad, or the other way around, that seemed like a small detail.

It wasn't until I was in graduate school that I actually read the original story, when it was assigned by my professor in a course on Gothic Literature. Even then, I resisted it. I already knew the big twist in the story! Wouldn't it be boring?

It wasn't. It didn't matter that I already knew where the story was going, *The Strange Case of Dr. Jekyll and Mr. Hyde* was gripping all the same—maybe even better than it would have been if I'd come to it as an innocent, puzzling out the clues on my own. I was surprised at how chilling I found the hints and rumors of Hyde's terrible deeds, and how suspenseful it was to await Utterson's discovery of the unthinkable truth of Hyde's identity. In Stevenson's telling, the story took on life: this was no banal cautionary tale about the dangers of repressed emotion, but a truly disturbing investigation into the composition of the human psyche.

I'd been misled, I realized, by so many film adaptations that used one actor to play both Jekyll and Hyde. Even with elaborate makeup changes, this approach always leads viewers to feel like it's a story of one man with a mixed-up personality. In the original version, though, Jekyll and Hyde are so physically different that they could not possibly be played by the same actor. I realized, as I read, how crucial that detail is to the horror of the story. Hyde is more than a mask or a disguise—he's an entirely different person.

It was perhaps this angle more than any other that made me want to revisit the story. I wanted to put my own spin on it, but even more, I wanted to remind people exactly what was so weird and creepy about the original. Updating the story to the modern era was an important part of that. The dark, dirty corners of Victorian London felt sinister and menacing to Stevenson's readers, but now they feel foreign and quaint, like something out of a fairy tale. I wanted to honor Stevenson by helping modern readers see his story with fresh eyes, and fully grasp the palpable threat of the original.

Part of doing that was finding modern analogues for various elements of the Victorian story. Handwritten notes became text messages, of course. By the same token, a pivotal handwriting analysis in the original turned into a mobile phone hack in my story. Jekyll's butler Poole became Jek's mother Puloma (which did require a fair bit of rewriting, since moms don't really act like servants). A walking stick became a bicycle lock. One element that couldn't be saved was the last will and testament that Jekyll creates and amends at various points in the original story. I just couldn't conceive of a believable reason for a teenager to have a will or anything like it, so I had to do away with that.

In expanding the story, I also gave a bit more detail about Hyde's activities when he's on the prowl. The original story can be frustratingly coy about what exactly Hyde does that is so terrible. I wanted to give a few more hints, but without venturing into excessive, lurid descriptions. Part of the fun of this story, after all, is leaving the worst bits to the reader's imagination.

Lastly, setting it among high school students felt like a good way to raise the stakes of the story. While most adults these days have a certain amount of privacy and independence in their lives, adolescents are constantly being watched, monitored and judged by parents, teachers and even their peers. Teenagers, I felt, would immediately understand the appeal of becoming someone else for a few hours, and being free from the judgments and responsibilities associated with your primary identity.

For all these changes, though, it was important to me to keep the story grounded in Stevenson's vision. I took it on as a challenge to keep my version as close as possible to his—with characters, plot points, scenes and even patches of dialogue paralleling the original—but with all the force and vitality the story had in Stevenson's day. I hope that reading this version brings more people back to the original, and helps them realize that they don't know that story as well as they think they do.

Q&A

Were you worried about people guessing the ending, based on familiarity with the original story?

I didn't worry about this at all. As a reader, I've never been very concerned about "spoilers"—in fact, I've been known to flip to the back of a book to read the ending before I'm halfway through! To me, the most interesting thing about a story is not the surprise at the end, but the journey you take to get there. Sometimes knowing where a story is headed can help you get more out of it, because you get to watch all the pieces falling into place and see how each decision the characters make builds to the conclusion.

The original story was structured as a kind of mystery—when it first came out, no one knew the ending, so part of the fun was trying to use clues in the story to figure out where it was all going. That's how mysteries work. When I decided to revisit the story, I approached it not as a mystery but as a tragedy. In a tragedy, the reader knows going in that everything will end badly, and the horror comes from watching it happen and being powerless to stop it. (This is also a form of dramatic irony.)

Of course, I was aware that some readers might not have any familiarity with these characters, so I tried to keep that in mind and make the story work for them, too. But even for those readers, I wasn't trying to surprise them with the ending. I didn't want to shock readers so much as give them a creeping sense of dread.

What was the hardest part of writing this story?

Probably the hardest thing about writing a story like this is that the narrator doesn't really know what's going on until the very end. I tried to just sit down and write the story from Lulu's perspective, but I kept getting twisted up, trying to keep track of what she would know when, what other characters knew and what they would unwittingly reveal. In order for the whole story to make sense, I had to sow a lot of details into the plot that Lulu wouldn't understand at the time, but would become important once she found out the truth about Jek.

I needed to know exactly what Jek and Hyde were up to throughout the story, even when Lulu had no idea. I struggled with how to manage this for a while, until eventually I realized the only solution was to write out the whole story from Jek's point of view. Then I went back to writing Lulu's story, but I was able to insert details into the background about what

Jek/Hyde was doing at various key moments. So basically, in order to write this book, I had to write two books—one from Lulu's perspective, and one from Jek's.

The original story is told from the point of view of a man named Utterson. Why did you write this story from a female point of view?

One of the things I've always found interesting about the original story is that almost every single character is a man. Not just Jekyll and Hyde, but all of Jekyll's friends, family members, colleagues and servants. That's not just because it was written a long time ago—even in the nineteenth century, lots of books had major female characters. So I've always wondered why Stevenson made this choice. I still don't have any definite answer.

I thought about keeping this odd detail when I updated the story, but in a modern story it felt too distracting. It was impossible for me to imagine a story in which my Jek wouldn't interact with any women, so as I read through the original story, I looked for characters I could gender-swap to make it feel more realistic. First I thought of making Jek female, but that's been done before, and I felt like it would shift the emphasis of the story and make it about gender, which wasn't what I wanted. Instead, I wound up making almost every other major character female, to balance out the insistent masculinity at the center of the story.

In the book, Jek is biracial, and Hyde's racial identity seems to fluctuate. Why did you make this choice?

When I first started working on the book, I took a lot of time to figure out who Jek was, and how Hyde would contrast with that. I liked the idea that Jek was already this complicated, conflicted person, before Hyde even existed. It's not the fact that Jek is biracial that gives him a "doubled" identity—it's the cultural context he lives in, where everyone around him has expectations of what it means to be Indian and what it means to be Black. Even before his experiment, Jek struggles with the pressures to conform to and resist those incompatible stereotypes.

When it came to creating Hyde as a character, I was interested in the fact that Hyde is a man without a history. I couldn't settle on any one race for Hyde, because he doesn't have parents, or a community, or official documentation, or even a full name. Hyde literally has no background, and that's part of what's fascinating/unsettling about him. This indeterminacy is both part of his mysterious appeal, and also what makes him a little eerie and off-putting—he doesn't fit properly into human culture.

Hyde's racial fluidity is liberating for Jek, but also eye-opening and somctimes horrifying. People around Hyde tend to read him as whatever suits their impressions and prejudices in that moment, allowing him to get away with crimes that would be impossible in Jek's body. In that way, the whole story is an extreme, nightmarish examination of the consequences of racial privilege.

But privilege is anything but simple in this story. There's race privilege examined here, but there are also the privileges (and lack thereof) associated with class, money, education, gender and ability. I wanted to portray the full complexity of that matrix. For example, Jek is in many ways disadvantaged by being dark-skinned, but he is relatively privileged in terms of money, class, family support and gender. Lulu is lacking in some of those vectors of privilege, which she doesn't want to see—she'd like to imagine herself and Jek as more or less equals. But her mom is much more aware of the differences between them, and the ways in which Lulu is held to different standards (thanks mostly to being female, a first generation immigrant and poor/labor class).

Should this story be viewed as a social critique?

When it comes to science fiction and gothic horror, I think social critique is in the DNA of the genres. The Jekyll and Hyde story in all its forms challenges us to reflect on difference, on identity, and the restrictions and expectations placed on us by society according to our identities. These issues are as resonant for us today as they were in Stevenson's day—perhaps even more so.

But while I definitely had those themes in mind as I wrote, I didn't set out to convince the reader of any simple moral lesson. My primary goal was to write a good, gripping story.

A secondary goal was to raise questions and provoke discussion: How do social pressures affect our moral choices? How important is our body to our sense of identity? How do race and gender and sexuality and money and class and illness and education intersect to frame how we see ourselves, and how society sees us? What responsibility do corporations have to their workers, and to their communities? Should ethical restrictions be placed on scientific investigations?

I don't have clear answers to all these questions, and I don't expect the reader to either. I'm not trying to tell anyone what to think, so much as give them interesting and provocative things to think about.

What was your favorite scene to write?

Every scene with Hyde was a lot of fun to write. He's my favorite kind of character: seductive, uninhibited, mysterious and potentially vicious. He can get away with saying and doing all kinds of things ordinary characters won't. I had to stop myself from letting him take over the story—with a character like that, a little goes a long way, and I think he's more powerful in small doses.

Another scene I really enjoyed was the one in the butterfly pavilion. It's such a dramatic setting, it gave me a lot to describe: unusual sights, sounds and smells that helped reflect and intensify the emotions between the characters. I even visited a butterfly pavilion near me to fill my senses with material for the book.

I don't usually play much with symbolism in my novels (not on purpose, anyway), but I couldn't resist the parallel between butterfly metamorphosis and Jek's physical transformations. I thought it added to the drama of the scene that Jek felt as though Lulu was talking about him, even though Lulu didn't know his secret yet.

What was the biggest change from the original story?

I tried to keep the basic meat of the story as close as to the original as possible, given the different setting. That was a fun challenge—especially finding modern parallels for things like telegrams and handwriting and butlers.

One thing I knew I wanted to change, though, was the way the mystery is revealed at the end. In the original story, the truth is finally revealed in two long letters. This is a pretty standard device in stories from the time, but I didn't think it would work in my version. It felt too indirect; it robbed us of the drama of a final confrontation between Jek and Lulu. I wanted Jek to confess his secret to Lulu face-to-face, and I wanted her to see him transform once before he died.

This change wound up being really difficult. A number of plot elements had to be adjusted for it to make sense, and while describing the transformation was fun, conveying the emotions in such an intense scene was a real challenge for me as a writer. I rewrote it many, many times, trying different approaches until I settled on one that satisfied me. I hope all my work paid off for the reader!

Were there any ideas you had for this story that didn't work?

When I first started playing with this concept, I experimented with a lot of different approaches. One thing I originally considered was making the Jekyll/Hyde division more metaphorical. I thought maybe I'd write about a character who seemed like two different people because he was on drugs, or was using a fake identity online, or some more realistic premise like that. But the more I thought about it, the more I realized that approach would sacrifice the essential strangeness that makes this story riveting.

We all know that in real life, sometimes people act different in different situations, to the point where someone familiar can feel like a stranger. Even in Stevenson's day, this wasn't a revolutionary idea. What makes the story compelling is taking this commonplace idea and making it literal. When we say someone has a "split personality" or he "seems like two different people," we're generally being metaphorical. But what if we weren't? What if they really became two entirely different people?

Removing this element from the story would have made it boring and ordinary, when I wanted it to feel weird and unsettling.

DISCUSSION QUESTIONS

1) Jek thinks he's a nice guy. Do you agree?

2) Why do people in the book find Hyde appealing? Do you?

3) Lulu starts out hating Hyde, but gradually her feelings about him become more complicated. What changed her mind?

4) *"It's not my perversions that shock and appall people. It's their own."* What do you think of Hyde's revelation that he only does what other people want? Did it change the way you felt about Hyde? About the other people in town?

5) The story ends with Jek sacrificing himself to get rid of Hyde. Could this ending have been avoided? What would the characters have had to do differently? What different decisions might they have made at various points in the book?

6) At the end, Lulu is thinking about creating her own "Hyde." What do you think that person would be like? What would your "Hyde" be like?

7) What story would you want to update? How would you do it? What would have to change?